STONE KILLER

The white car eased off the pavement and to the top of Jessie Marsh's driveway. The driver took a deep drag of his pipe. Cherry-fragranced smoke filled the car as the man watched the house for a few more minutes. Then, wedging the pipe in his teeth, he pulled out onto the highway.

He drove to the outskirts of Clear Creek, found a phone booth, and dialed the number he'd been given.

"Yes?" A man's voice. Soft, aristocratic, southern accent.

He slipped the pipe from his teeth. "I missed her."

"I'm not paying you to miss her."

"There are easier ways of doing this . . ."

He heard an impatient sigh. "With your hands? That's the way you like to do women, isn't it."

"It's certain."

"And obvious. Just do her the way I told you. And soon."

The man hung up, found a match, relit his pipe, and drew the smoke deep into his lungs. Games, he thought. He's playing his damned games again.

He took another long draw on the pipe and walked back out into the night.

EDGE OF TERROR

MICHAEL HAMMONDS

ZEBRA BOOKS
KENSINGTON PUBLISHING CORP.

ZEBRA BOOKS are published by

Kensington Publishing Corp.
475 Park Avenue South
New York, NY 10016

Zebra and the Z logo are trademarks of Kensington Publishing Corp.

First Printing: July, 1993

Printed in the United States of America

For R. E. Carleton

*With thanks, as always,
to Sharon Jarvis
and Ann LaFarge*

One

"Why would anyone want to kill you, Miss Marsh?"

Pulling her eyes away from the cup of coffee in her trembling hands, Jessie Marsh looked at the deputy again. She forced herself to concentrate on him, trying to gather her senses back into focus. She was in shock, she knew that, but it was all so damn strange. Everything was disconnected, floating. Sitting on the leather sofa in his office, she couldn't remember driving back to Clear Creek in the Blue Ridge Mountains of Virginia, or finding the old courthouse and the Sheriff's Department, but she had.

"Miss Marsh?"

She blinked. "What?"

A smile creased the deputy's lips and tugged the fan of wrinkles around his eyes. "Would you like something stronger in your coffee?"

"Stronger?"

"Bourbon."

She nodded. "Yes," she answered. "Yes, I would."

The deputy walked across the small, spare office to his desk, and she concentrated on him again. He was a tall, lean man in his late forties or early fifties wearing blue jeans, a button-down blue cotton shirt and a well-cut gray tweed jacket. Her eyes concentrated on his face. He had good lines. Strong jaw. Thick mustache and dark hair, both flecked with gray. He opened the drawer and lifted out a pint bottle. Screwing the top off, he walked back and poured some of it into her coffee.

"Thank you," she said, then looked up at him. "I'm sorry, I've forgotten your name."

"Cobb. David Cobb," he replied. "Just take it easy." He pulled a chair to the couch and sat down. "It'll take a little time for your mind to clear. Most of us are not used to violence, especially when it happens to us. Takes a little getting used to. Drink that."

She looked at the coffee, and remembering the bourbon, she nodded and sipped. The liquor spread a sudden warmth through her, and she eased her tall frame back on the couch. At thirty-six, she was small-boned and lean, almost skinny. She was dressed in khaki shorts, a yellow cotton shirt, and running shoes. Her blond-brown, sun-streaked hair was pulled back into a ponytail.

"You said somebody tried to kill you."

She blinked and looked at him. "Yes."

"Tried to run you down."

"Yes. About four miles north of here."

"Up on 16."

"Yes. Well, I guess that's the number. I don't remember numbers of roads, just what they look like. There's a creek there, down a steep bank. And some woods."

He nodded. "I know the spot. And somebody tried to run you down there?"

"Yes."

"Tell me again what happened."

She took another sip. "Not that much, really. I parked about a hundred yards or so away because there was no place to park closer. The shoulder is too narrow. Then I walked back to take some pictures and this man tried to run me down."

"You're sure he tried to run you down?"

"Yes."

"No, I mean, you're sure it was intentional."

"Yes. He stopped, then looked back at me, and tried it again."

"He went by you once, then came back?"

"Yes. He came down the road, then off the shoulder. I fell out of the way, then crawled back up the bank, and he turned around and looked at me, then backed up and tried to hit me again."

"You're sure he saw you?"

"Yes. I know he saw me. He sat there for a moment, turned in his seat, and looked at me."

"Did you see his face?"

"I . . ." she paused. "No. Yes." She smiled. "Sorry."

"It's okay."

"I think the most accurate answer would be *sort of*. I could see the shape of it, but not the details. The windshield and the shadow of the interior of the car blurred it."

"Did he seem familiar?"

She thought about it, then shook her head. "No."

"Was the car familiar?"

"No."

"What kind of car was it?"

She frowned. "Sorry. I'm not good at the kinds of cars. It was white, a sedan. If I saw a picture of it, I might know it."

"License number?"

"Excuse me?"

"Did you get the license number?"

"No. I was a little busy."

9

He smiled. "Right."

She sipped the coffee and it flushed through her. It felt good. She held the cup out. "Could you do that again. I think it's helping."

He poured her another shot and she sipped it.

"You make terrific coffee."

"Old family recipe," he muttered, then went on. "You say he looked at you?"

"Yes."

"You're sure."

"Yes."

Rubbing his chin, Cobb stood up and walked to his desk. He poured two fingers of bourbon into a glass, put the bottle down, picked up the glass, and returned to the chair.

"Why, Miss Marsh?"

"What?"

"Why? Why would someone want to kill you?"

She stared at him. "I have absolutely no idea."

"Are you divorced?"

She nodded. "Yes, but—" she paused. "I see what you're getting at. Yes, I'm divorced, but that's been a year ago. And Bill wouldn't do something like this."

"It was a friendly divorce?"

Her mouth tightened. "I'm not sure any divorce is friendly. But no, it wasn't. It was mean and nasty. But Bill isn't violent. He's more the manipulative type. He would rather hurt me with money, or humiliation."

"He never hit you when you were married?"

"No. Not even when we were getting divorced."

"Why did you get divorced?"

Her eyes narrowed. "This is a little personal, isn't it?"

He nodded. "Yes, it is. But you said somebody tried to kill you. I'm trying to find out why."

She sighed. "You're right. I'm sorry."

"No need to be. Why did you get divorced?"

She smiled, then shrugged. "It was a power thing, really. I'm an artist, a painter, and my art was beginning to do well. I worked as an artist for an advertising firm in D.C., and made very good money at it. I wanted to quit and go out on my own. Bill didn't want me to. He didn't want to give up my salary because it paid the rent, and enabled him to do real estate speculation."

"And he didn't do too well at it?"

"No, not really. His deals were always fast and a little loose. Always within the bounds of legality, but just barely." She sipped the coffee-bourbon. "My wanting to quit was really the last straw. We had been having trouble for most of our marriage. There was always that tension between us. I always felt he was using me, and he felt he was doing what he had a right to do as a husband."

"He was chauvinistic."

"Yes."

"Possessive?"

"Yes."

"Men like that sometimes kill."

Jessie shook her head. "No, not Bill. Not that I think he would try and kill me anyway, but if he were going to do it, he would have done it before the divorce. When he could make some money on it. Now there's no reason at all."

"Life insurance?"

"No. I don't have life insurance."

"Your estate?"

"It goes to my parents."

"Jealousy?"

"No. Everything with Bill had to do with money. Besides, I'm not even seeing anyone." She sipped the

11

laced coffee. "You seem certain it was Bill. Why?"

Cobb shrugged. "Because that's who it usually is. Most people are killed by people they know. And for married people, it's the spouse. First place a cop looks. Most murders and attempted murders are not very mysterious."

"This one is."

He frowned. "I agree."

She settled back on the couch. The leather creaked. "And you have your doubts," she said. "Especially about me."

He looked at her and smiled suddenly.

"What—?"

He tried to push the smile away. "Sorry. I just flashed on Peter Sellers doing Inspector Clouseau. 'I suspect everyone. I suspect no one.' Then he falls backwards off a couch. Or something like that."

She smiled, too.

"What I'm trying to say is, yes, I doubt your story. But it's also my job to believe you up to a point."

"All right, what do *you* think happened?"

The smile faded. "Are you able to take honesty?"

"I hope so."

He sighed. "I think you were on the side of the road. It was coming on twilight. Someone came down the hill fast, didn't see you. Almost hit you. Stopped when they realized what happened. Backed up. Then got the hell out of there when they saw you were all right." He sipped the bourbon. "On the other hand . . ."

"On the other hand, what?"

"On the other hand, you have on a yellow shirt. Light colored. Easily seen. And you're tall. Also easily seen." He sipped the bourbon. "Have you made anybody angry lately? Especially in the last twenty-four hours."

12

"No. I haven't seen anybody in the last twenty-four hours. Why?"

"The reasons for most murders occur within the twenty-four hours before the act. A husband and wife argue. Two guys want the same girl in a bar. One drug dealer cheats another. The impulse explodes and — *pow*."

She shook her head. "I've been at home for the past five days. It was raining, so I got a lot of work done in my studio."

"No one visited you?"

"No."

"And you didn't go out?"

"Yesterday? No."

"You didn't go to the grocery, drug store, liquor store —"

"No. Once I start working like that, especially when I'm getting ready for a show, I tend to do nothing but that. I work, and read, and sleep."

"In the whole five days, you didn't go out, and no one came to see you?"

"No. I know it sounds odd, but that's the way I work . . ." she paused. "Oh, well, there was one thing."

"What?"

"I had to buy a new tire. I had a flat last week, and the man from the garage came out and picked the car up. Took it into Clear Creek, put a new tire on it, then came back out. He gave me the keys and I paid him."

"And that's it?"

"I'm afraid so."

Cobb sighed. "I don't think anyone would kill you over a new tire."

"No, I don't either. And I know Jack, the mechanic. He's been working on my car since I've been

13

in Clear Creek. The flat is the only bad thing that's happened to me in a while."

"Tell me about the day before the five days of work."

She shrugged. "I drove over to the Neck, where the Rappahannock runs into the Chesapeake. I was looking for pictures . . ."

"Pictures?"

"I take pictures, photos of things, well, like the creek today. I use them as references for my work."

"You mean you use them for your paintings?"

"Yes."

"I thought artists went out and drew them, you know, with a pad or easel or something."

"Sometimes I do. But the weather doesn't always allow that. Or the light changes. So I use photos."

"So you took photos along the shore?"

"No, not really. I had only been there for an hour or so when I had the flat. I called Triple A and they came out and fixed it, and by that time the day was shot, so I went home."

"And that's it?"

"That's it. No. I ate in a small seafood place. Soft-shell crabs. Then I went home."

He eased back in the chair and sipped the last of the bourbon. "Shit," he sighed, then looked at Jessie. "Sorry."

"That's all right. I was thinking the same thing." She sipped her coffee. "And I'm beginning to see what you mean. It doesn't make any sense, does it?"

"No."

She stood up and walked to the desk and poured herself more bourbon. "I could almost accept what you said about it being an accident, except for one thing."

"What's that?"

14

She shrugged. "I'm not sure how to say it. When he came at me, both times, there was a . . . purpose . . . an intent . . . it wasn't an accident. Both times, the car turned, angled for me."

"All right," he said. "But we come back to that same question again. Why? Why would someone want to kill you?"

She walked back to the couch. The leather creaked as she sat down. "Same question. Same answer: I have absolutely no idea."

Two

They went over it two more times, then gave up, and it was after dark when Cobb walked Jessie to her car, an old '65 Mercedes SL parked in front of the courthouse. Around them, the small town was quiet, no traffic on the streets. A cool May breeze brushed the dogwoods and oaks. Shivering slightly, Jessie reached inside the car, pulled out a blue cotton sweater, tugged it on, and turned to Cobb.

Cobb looked the old Mercedes over. "Nice car."

"Thanks."

"You must do pretty well with your painting."

She smiled. "I do, Mr. Cobb. But I told you that."

He grinned. "Yeah, you did."

"You're still doing the Inspector Clouseau thing—"

"A little—"

"Testing me. That's why we went over the story three times, isn't it?"

"As a matter of fact, yes."

"How did I do?"

He laughed. "You're very direct, Miss Marsh."

"Bullshit takes time, Mr. Cobb. It's one of the reasons I got out of the business world. And you didn't answer my question."

"No, I didn't. Your answers are consistent."

"That's why you had me go over it several times, to see if I would tell it differently or get the details wrong."

"That's right."

"To determine if I'm a nut."

He didn't hesitate. "That's right."

"Do you get a lot of them?"

"No. Not a lot, but some." He leaned against the car. "Does that make you angry—that I doubt you?"

She paused. "Maybe a little. I was there, remember? Diving down that bank wasn't the most fun I've ever had." She smiled. "The first time, maybe, but after that it got a little old."

He nodded. "I know the feeling. Do you want protection?"

"You mean somebody staying with me?"

"Yeah."

"No. Definitely not."

"Why?"

"I'm a private person, Mr. Cobb. Probably a little bit of a loner. Especially since I've been divorced."

"You don't get lonely?"

Her eyes narrowed, and a slow smile pushed through her lips. "Interesting."

"Interesting?"

"I can't tell if you're working or not."

He blushed slightly. "I was."

"Do you?" she asked.

"What?"

"Get lonely?"

He cleared his throat uncomfortably. "We were talking about you."

"Right. We were talking about me. Okay. Do I get lonely? Sometimes. But I don't want anybody around. I can take care of myself—"

"I'll bet you can."

17

"I like taking care of myself. I've gotten used to it. And with just myself, it makes my world easier to manage. I like being in control of my life."

"Don't we all."

"And," she added, "I have a gun at the house."

"Nothing like a gun for control. Do you know how to use it?"

"Now it wouldn't do me much good if I didn't, would it?"

He shook his head. "No," he answered. "Why is it, all of a sudden I feel like I'm on the defensive?"

She stared at him for a moment, then her eyes softened slightly. "Somebody tried to kill me, Mr. Cobb. It scares me and pisses me off. Everything else seems a little superfluous. Especially pointless questions. How would you feel?"

"Probably the same."

"At least we agree on that. So, am I a nut or not?"

"No, I don't think you're a nut. But I think you might have misread the situation. I'll go out to Miller's Creek tomorrow and take a look around, but I don't like my chances of finding anything."

"So that's it?"

"Without more to go on, there's not a lot I can do."

She shook her head. "I suppose not."

"I'll be in touch, Miss Marsh. One way or another, I'll let you know what I find."

She nodded. "I appreciate that."

Cobb watched as she got into the old SL and drove away, then he walked back into the old courthouse and down the musty hallway to the Sheriff's Department.

The dispatcher, Ned Foreman, looked up from the switchboard. He was younger than Cobb, forty-seven, but looked sixty. He was a little like Walter

18

Brennan; he had looked old even when he was young. Colorless, thin hair, weathered skin, but in contrast, incredibly bright, curious blue eyes. And he was a natural gossip.

"Pretty woman, Lou," he remarked, using the diminutive of *lieutenant*.

Cobb leaned on the counter. "This is Clear Creek, Virginia, Ned, not Philadelphia. Don't call me Lou. I hated it in Philly and I hate it here."

"Okay, Bubba."

Cobb's mouth soured. "That's worse. Bubba. Do I look like a Bubba?"

"A little, yeah."

Cobb sighed. "Okay." Then nodded. "But to answer your question: That she is."

"What?"

"A pretty woman."

"And a nut."

Cobb's eyes settled on him. "You think so?"

"Hell, don't you? Story like that."

Cobb rubbed his chin. "No, I really don't, Ned."

The dispatcher smiled. "You're listening to her legs and ass, Dave. That's a nut story. Another paranoid wanting attention. Bet she asked for protection. Bet she wanted somebody to stay with her around the clock."

Cobb shook his head. "No, she didn't. I asked her and she emphatically didn't want protection. Oh, she's paranoid all right. Anybody who's nearly been killed would be, but she doesn't fit the rest of the profile."

"Sure . . ."

"She doesn't. For one thing, she's got a sense of humor about it. You ever see a nut that had a sense of humor about it?"

"Well—"

"And she's not a victim. Victims have always been victims. The *Everything-Happens-to-Me* personality. Emphasis on the *Me*. Capital M. This woman wasn't like that. She was amazed at what happened to her. And angry. That doesn't fit the Capital M."

Foreman smirked. "She's a nut, Dave."

He shrugged. "Maybe. But there's something else, too . . ."

"What?"

He shook his head. "That's just it, I'm not sure. I've got a tune going for me."

"A tune?"

"A hunch. Something you can't quite put your finger on, like a tune you can't remember."

Ned's eyes settled on him and narrowed. "Or a name?"

Cobb looked at him questioningly. "Name . . ." he began. Then he blinked, and his stomach suddenly chilled. "Oh," he said. "No. Lydia Paulson was different."

"Not *that* different."

His jaw tightened. "No. Not that different," he admitted.

"And it wasn't your fault, Dave. Everybody said that."

Cobb smiled grimly. "Yeah, everybody said that. But she's still dead." He pushed away from the counter. "I'll be in my office."

He walked into his desk, sat down, and started through the budgets again. There were some days he wished he hadn't let Sheriff Seth Hardesty talk him into taking the job as Chief of Detectives. Usually when he had the budgets on his desk. He could still remember Seth's pitch as they sat there at the sidewalk restaurant in Society Hill in Philadelphia drinking ale and watching girls go by.

20

"You've got nothing to keep you here," Seth had insisted. "Hell, you can take early retirement, come up to the Blue Ridge, and show us hillbillies how it's done. Go fishing every day."

"I hate fishing."

He ordered two more beers. "Hunting then, I know you like hunting. And you love the area. You've always said you do. You can just sit back and . . ."

"Seth —"

"What?"

"What do you want?"

He tried to assume an innocent look. It was difficult for a politician. "Why, I want you to come to work for me."

"Then what are you leaving out?"

"Why, nothin', Dave boy, nothin'. Why would you —"

"Because you're doing this country boy act. Hillbillies. Jesus, Seth, you have one of the best departments in the state. I'm always amazed at how sophisticated rural departments are."

Hardesty's handsome face darkened. "We have to be, Dave." He shook his head. "It used to be like Andy Griffith in Mayberry. Nice, gentle places. People didn't even lock their doors. Do you know that the whole time I was growing up, we didn't even have a lock on the door . . ." He sipped the beer. "But the city has spilled over . . . we've got it all out there. Drugs mostly, and that brings everything else." He leaned on the table. "No, the truth is, I need somebody as Chief of Detectives —"

"Oh, shit, Seth, administration?"

"And investigation. Both. It's still a small department. I had a couple of boys comin' along real fine, then they got wind of the city and what kind of

21

money they could make. No, I've got good people, but none with the experience that's needed."

And he'd let Seth talk him into it. The truth was, there really was nothing for him here. Not anymore. Not since his partner, Danny, had been forced to take retirement. And Mandy had divorced him.

He'd come to Clear Creek three years ago—things had been more relaxed here. He worked hard dividing his time between administration and field work. And only occasionally did a bad one come along.

Like Lydia Paulson. He remembered her sitting across the desk from him. Small and delicate. Pretty. Nervous as she lit a cigarette, her hands trembling.

"This guy is crazy," she'd said. "I mean really crazy. I went out with him a few times and now he thinks he owns me. Says I'm his, that we belong together. I need protection, Sheriff. Maybe a deputy or something to stay out at my place . . ."

A capital M, Cobb had thought. A born victim.

He had done what he could. Did what the book said to do.

He had talked to the guy. James Alfred Hodges. Nice guy. Rational. Smiling. Said Lydia Paulson was the crazy one, that she was imagining things.

Paulson came in again, asked for protection again. The only thing Cobb could do was recommend an injunction. Judge Cannon granted it.

Cobb sighed and walked to the coffee maker.

He had done what he could do, what the law said to do.

Then one day Hodges broke into Paulson's house. He shot her six times with a 9mm. Then he turned the gun on himself.

Cobb poured himself a cup of coffee and walked to the window and looked out at the town and the night.

"It wasn't your fault," Ned had said. *"Everybody said that."* He smiled grimly. Not everybody, Ned. Not me.

He frowned and tried to push Lydia Paulson from his mind.

There were similarities in the two cases, but that's all they were. Similarities. The two women were nothing alike. And the cases were really nothing alike.

The frown deepened. "Yeah, Dave boy, keep telling yourself that."

Hell, maybe Ned was right. Maybe this was just guilt working on him. He tried that. Tried making it fit.

But the nagging was still there. Something else. Something other than the two women. Something that was just beyond his reach. Something that made him uneasy. Something . . .

"Shit," he grumbled. The harder he tried, the more it eluded him. Shaking his head, he forced his eyes back to his desk. And the budgets.

Pouring himself more coffee, he walked back to the desk and went to work.

Three

Jessie drove through Clear Creek, through the pre-Civil War downtown area with its colonial and federalist facades, then the campus of Evergreen College. It was a bright, moonlit night and beyond the town, the Blue Ridge shouldered the sky in the distance. She tried to let the driving relax her. It usually did, but not tonight. The scene on the road played and replayed itself, and Cobb's bourbon and coffee had become only a memory.

She stopped at a convenience store on the edge of town, washed her face with cold water in the tiny restroom, bought a cup of coffee, returned to her car, and pushed into the countryside.

The road and the coffee seemed to help. Her mind cleared a little, but when it did, she wasn't sure she liked it. Cobb's point began to make more and more sense. *Who would want to kill her?*

She had no enemies. Well, other than Bill. And as much of a bastard as he was, she really didn't believe he would do anything to harm her physically. Mentally, yes. Mind-fuck, yes. But really try to kill her? No.

So who did that leave?

No one.

She smiled grimly. Here I am, she mused, trying to think of enemies, of someone who might want to harm me, and I'm disappointed that I can't. What a bummer.

She concentrated. Anyone at the Haug Gallery? No, everyone there was for her. The better she did, the better they did. She probed back to The Light Show, the agency she'd worked for. She had stepped on no toes there. More than a few people wanted her job, but not enough to kill for it. Especially not now that she was gone.

She sighed with frustration.

Maybe Cobb was right. Maybe it was an accident, she thought, then the image of the man in the white car was there. Sitting there. Watching. Staring.

Her hand gripped the steering wheel. He had *known* she was there.

"Damn . . ." she sighed, and sipping the coffee, she looked around. She had been so deep in thought, she wasn't paying attention to where she was. She glanced up and around. Night. The road. The mountains in the distance.

Then she glanced in the rearview mirror. A flash of white gleamed through the glass, then was gone.

Her hands tightened on the steering wheel and she looked at the mirror again.

There was nothing there.

Her heart pounded in her chest like a trip-hammer. She slowed the SL a little and looked again, eyes searching the darkness.

Still nothing.

Her jaw tightened. Now I *am* being paranoid, she thought.

Easing down on the gas pedal, she drove on, but her eyes kept going to the rearview mirror.

25

It took her about thirty minutes to drive the fifteen miles to her house. A three-level modern, all angles and glass, it was set deep in a stand of pine and oak between two steep hills.

She waited until she was in front of her garage door, then opened it with the remote and drove in. She hit the remote again, then waited until the huge door had rumbled shut before she climbed out.

Unlocking the door to the kitchen, she went in and turned on the lights. Making sure the bolt and lock were set again, she walked through the kitchen and into the living room which was bordered on one side by a solarium. Turning on the floodlights, she could see the wide deck beyond the solarium. Nothing there.

Her breathing eased a little. The house was a secure one, at least there was that. Because it was partially heated by solar, the windows were sealed. Other than the front door and the one into the garage, there were two sliding glass doors — one in her bedroom, the other in the guest room. Both opened onto high balconies, and both were locked with lengths of board in the runners. They couldn't open. Still, she thought, I'll check them.

She walked through her studio and then on up to the third level. She checked the doors. They were locked and the wood lengths were in place.

She went back to the stairs, then paused, remembering the gun in the nightstand beside her bed. Walking back into her bedroom, she opened the top drawer. An old issue of *American Artist*. She looked under it. No pistol. She opened the next drawer. It was there. A dark shape, gleaming dully. A 9mm her father had bought for her when she moved in. She smiled, remembering his insistence. "If you're gonna live in the woods like a hermit," he said, "you've gotta have some protection." There had been no discussion about it. He put the pistol and the ammunition in the drawer. It had been there ever since. She reached down for it, then hesitated and frowned. It wasn't that she was afraid of it, or disliked guns. She disliked the idea of needing one.

"Oh, hell," she sighed. This was no time for a one-sided philosophical discussion.

Picking up the pistol, a Browning, she released the clip. It was full. Then she pulled the action back. There was a round in the chamber. She eased the action back into place, then pushed the clip into the handle, made sure the hammer was down, then carried it back down to the living room.

She crossed to the bar and poured herself two fingers of Benedictine and Brandy. She carried the B and B and the pistol to the Henredon sofa and curled into the off-white cushions. Pushing back into the soft down, she looked out at the deck, sipped the B and B, and tried to relax.

It didn't work.

The tension stayed with her like a memory of steel. She looked at the pistol. And thought of the deputy, Cobb. She found herself smiling a little. She had given him a hard time. But then, he'd given her a hard time. The smile faded. No, he hadn't. He was doing his job, and he was probably right. It was probably just an accident.

And again, the image of the man in the white car was there. *Turning. Watching her.*

Touching the pistol, she sipped the B and B and looked out at the night.

The white car eased off the pavement and to the

27

top of Jessie Marsh's driveway. The driver took the pipe out of his mouth and his tobacco pouch from his pocket. Staring through the woods at the lights of the house, he went through the ritual of packing the bowl, then lighting the pipe.

Cherry-fragranced smoke filled the car and the man watched the house for a few more minutes; then, wedging the pipe in his teeth, he pulled out onto the highway.

He drove to the outskirts of Clear Creek to a small diner. Inside, the air was heavy with the smell of onions and hamburger grease. He saw the pay phone on the wall in the hallway leading to the bathrooms.

Using his credit card, he dialed the number he'd been given.

"Yes?" A man's voice. Soft, aristocratic, southern accent.

He slipped the pipe from his teeth. "I missed her."

"I'm not paying you to miss her."

"There are easier ways of doing this—"

He heard an impatient sigh. "With your hands?" he snapped, the aristocratic accent forgotten. "That's the way you like to do women, isn't it?"

"It's certain."

"And obvious. Just do what I told you."

The muscles in his jaw quivered. "All right," he said, and hung up.

He paused for a moment, found a match, relit his pipe, and drew the smoke deep into his lungs. Games, he thought. He's playing his goddamn games again.

He took another long draw on the pipe and walked back into the night.

David Cobb pushed the budgets away and walked to the coffeepot, picked it up, then shook his head.

28

No more coffee tonight. He looked at his watch. Ten-thirty. Go home, he told himself.

Switching off the lights, he walked down the hall, said good night to Ned, and walked out into the cool night to his Bronco and started home.

At the stoplight in front of the college, he tugged his signal down for a left-hand turn.

He peered down the road that led out of town and thought about Jessie Marsh. She lived out that way.

The light turned green. Pulling his turn signal off, he went straight, driving away from town and toward Jessie Marsh's address. It would be about fifteen miles out if he remembered right. It was a nice night for a drive. At least, that was what he told himself for the first couple of minutes.

A sudden uneasiness pressed through him. Like a cold razor.

He pushed down on the gas, and the Bronco bolted through the night. He didn't know if it was the tune, or something else, but the feeling that something was wrong intensified.

The parallel was what his old partner Danny Herbert had called it. For parallel universe. A region with a different set of rules and logic. "And we glimpse it occasionally through the bad guys," he said once, probably when he was drinking. "A place of chaos . . ."

Even though he thought Danny was full of shit, Cobb had that feeling now. That things were slowly coming unraveled. Out of control.

Driving, deep in thought, he only half-saw the white car flash by him.

Blinking, he looked up and watched the white car sink into the darkness of the rearview mirror.

Great, he thought grimly. You're getting as paranoid as Jessie Marsh.

29

He shook his head and thought about turning around, but decided to go on. It was only a mile or two now.

He found her driveway and pulled off into it. The lights of her house were on.

Everything seemed to be all right.

Climbing out of the Bronco, he walked along the road until he could see the other side of the house. Clear. Floodlights illuminated the area well.

He walked back to the Bronco, got in, and sat there for a moment. He looked at the house. The lights were on.

"What the hell," he grumbled, and turned down the drive.

He parked in front of the garage, went to the door and knocked.

No answer.

He knocked again.

The door rattled and opened and Jessie Marsh stood there blinking at him with sleepy eyes. And a 9mm.

"Hi," she said. "What are you doing here?"

"Just thought I'd see if you were okay—" he nodded toward the pistol. "That's not the best way to greet a police officer."

She looked down at the gun and lowered it. "Sorry. I fell asleep on the sofa. Would you like to come in?"

"No. I'm sorry I woke you—"

"It's okay, really. I appreciate it."

"Unless you'd like me to check the house."

"I did it. It's hermetically sealed. A little paranoia can go a long way."

He smiled. "All right. Good night, Miss Marsh."

"Good night."

"Like I said, I'll be in touch."

He started to turn. "Hey—" she said.

He paused.

"Really," she said. "Thanks."

"No charge," he said and as he walked to the Bronco, he heard the door close and lock.

Driving back toward town, he told himself everything was all right. She was fine. Had a gun for protection. And besides all that, it was probably just an accident.

That's what he told himself.

But the uneasiness was still there.

Four

David Cobb drove through the chilly first light of morning. Warm in the cab of the Bronco, he sipped his morning coffee from a thermos cup and watched as the Blue Ridge began to gain shape from the darkness of the western sky. Most mornings he would have enjoyed it. This was one of his favorite things to do. Cruise the back roads, drink coffee, and watch the morning come. But not this morning.

The uneasiness was still with him.

He had stayed awake most of the night thinking about Jessie Marsh and her story. And the more he thought about them, the more the uneasiness grew, and the more the association with Lydia Paulson's case seemed to fade. His hand tightened on the steering wheel. The association, not the guilt. That would probably always be there. He accepted that now. Maybe it did push him, but there was something else there, he was certain of that. Something Jessie Marsh said. He frowned. It was there, yet stayed just beyond his reach.

He topped a hill, then descending it, he saw Miller's Creek, the place Jessie Marsh said she'd nearly been hit.

Angling across the highway and onto the narrow shoulder on the left side of the road, he stopped, two wheels still on the right of way, and turned on his emergency flashers. Leaving the engine on and carrying the cup of coffee, he opened the door and stepped into the morning. He shivered against the briskness, and with one hand he pulled his corduroy jacket a little tighter around his blue crew neck sweater, then took a sip of coffee. He walked along the shoulder, his eyes scanning the ground.

The new light made deep shadows, and the grass was thick.

He frowned.

Too thick.

Kneeling down, he was able to see that the grass had been mashed down, but now was beginning to spring back up. Somebody had been on the shoulder, but there would be no tire tracks because of the grass.

Standing up, he walked on down to the creek, his eyes staying on the shoulder. The grass was still too thick.

As he came even with the creek, he paused and looked down the slope, then back to the shoulder. There was only about two to three feet of shoulder here. Very narrow. He looked at the slope. It fell away sharply. He looked back to the shoulder, which narrowed as it came closer to the creek. He frowned. The feeling nagged at the back of his mind again.

"Shit." He sighed and looked back down the slope, and his eye caught a glint of light about halfway down. Putting the cup down, he sidewalked down the bank until he came to it. Leaning over, he picked it up. A camera lens. 50mm. Broken.

Up the hill, his radio crackled through the brisk air.

33

"Central to one. Central to one. Over." It was Ben Mitchell, the day dispatcher.

Slipping the lens into his pocket, he made his way back up the steep hill, picked up his cup, and walked to the Bronco. Reaching inside, he grabbed his mike.

"Central, this is one. What is it, Ben?"

"Just got a call, Dave. Somebody's spotted a body off the road down at Moon Creek."

"Dead or alive?"

"Didn't say."

"You mean they didn't check?"

"Didn't say."

"What the hell did he say?"

"Not much. Just this call. Fella said he was driving along the bridge over Moon Creek and saw a body to one side of the road. Over."

"The caller leave a name?"

"Just told me about the body and hung up."

Cobb frowned. "Terrific," he grumbled to himself. Moon Creek was at the far end of the county in a remote part of the mountains. Into the mike, he said, "All right, Ben, I'm on my way."

The ringing of the telephone bolted Jessie awake. On the sofa, she jerked upright and the 9mm tumbled from her lap and thumped to the floor. She sat up. The room was full of gray morning light. The ringing came again, and she pushed the comforter off and looked down at herself. She was fully clothed. She ran her fingers through her hair. She remembered sitting there, sipping B and B and staring out at the night until she'd just passed out from inertia. Then the deputy, Cobb, had come by, and she must have come back to the sofa instead of going up to bed.

The ringing came again. Standing up, she hurried into the kitchen and snatched the receiver from the wall unit as it was ringing again.

"What . . . hello," she said.

"Miss Marsh?" It was a man's voice, polite, slightly accented.

"Yes."

"Miss Marsh, this is Deputy Spainhauer over at Clear Creek. Lieutenant Cobb asked me to call you. Sorry if I woke you up."

"It's all right. What does he want?"

"They found a car up near Walton. A white Sable. Sheriff Cobb thinks it fits the description of the one that nearly hit you. He wonders if you could come up and take a look at it."

"All right. Where's Walton?"

"About twenty miles north of you, up in the mountains on 25."

"Where does he want me to meet him?"

"Just head for Walton. It's about a mile this side on 25."

"I'll be there in about an hour," she said and hung up.

She walked to the sink, ran two cups of water in the kettle, then put it on the stove. She hurried into the bathroom off the kitchen, and by the time she had washed her face and brushed out her hair, the kettle was whistling. She walked back into the kitchen, ground some French roast, and poured the water through the drip coffeepot. The smell of coffee filled the room as she took two blueberry muffins from the bread drawer. She didn't toast them, just tore a piece from one and, chewing it, looked down at herself again and frowned. Well, this would have to do. She didn't have time to change. The coffee ran through and she poured herself a steaming mug, then walked back to the sofa and

35

picked up her purse, then the 9mm from the floor. She paused, staring at it, then pushed it into her purse and carried it back to the kitchen where she gathered up the coffee and the muffins and hurried out to the SL.

The morning was gray and cloudy, a few wisps of fog in the pine and oak, and dogwood. The coffee helped wake her up. They found it, she thought. They found the damn car.

The hills deepened, and the road became narrower with dangerous hairpin curves. She sipped the coffee, remembering the road. It was probably the most treacherous stretch in the area.

She braked as she went into a long curve, then started down a hill. She passed a side road, and something in the rearview mirror caught her eye. Glancing up, she saw the white car float into the mirror.

Fear exploded through her in a white-hot rush.

At first she thought she'd imagined it. She looked again. The white car filled the mirror. Following her.

Her breath thickened in her chest, and, for a moment, she couldn't breathe. Her hands gripped the steering wheel, and she pulled air into her lungs slowly. She suddenly remembered sailing with her father on the Chesapeake off Kilmernock. The wind had taken the sail, almost tipping the boat over. She'd panicked then, and her father took over for her, righting the boat. "Disasters happen," he said later. "Sometimes on their own. And sometimes you help them along. Back away from the situation. Breathe a kind of coldness through your mind, and do what you can do. Sometimes it's not enough. Sometimes it is." Then he'd taken her back out into the bay, and put the boat in exactly the same position they'd been in. This time, she righted the boat.

Later, it had become a part of her work method.

Instead of thinking, she moved, and found her solution in movement. Instead of thinking about painting, she painted. Focused.

She breathed deeply. This was a lot different from painting or sailing. But she focused, settling a coldness through her mind. Concentrated. Paint, she told herself. Focus. She was still afraid, but doing something.

She looked up at the mirror. The car hovered there. All right, she thought. No more surprises. I know you're there.

She looked around. No farmhouses. No convenience stores. Just the road. And the mountains.

Okay, she thought, and put the mug of coffee down on the floorboard on the passenger side.

She looked at the mirror.

He was still there.

Then, suddenly, the car bolted forward, rushing even closer into the mirror.

Without looking back, she slammed the gas pedal and the old SL responded beautifully. The engine roared and the car lurched forward, speeding away from the white sedan.

She dipped down a small hill, rounded a curve, then started up a long incline. She kept the gas pedal to the floorboard and the SL never hesitated. It took the hill easily.

She glanced at the mirror. The white sedan was still with her, right on her bumper. They crested the hill, then dropped into a steep switchback. Jessie let off the gas and hurled into the turn. The old SL banked it like it had claws.

Behind her, she saw the white car swerve slightly, then heard the squeal of brakes. She smiled. The SL was built as a racing car. The sedan wasn't. It was too top-heavy. Another curve angled into the darkness. She pressed the gas down, gaining speed, then coming into the curve, she let up, and cut through it, cutting off the worst end. The road straightened and she hit the gas again.

She looked down at the speedometer. Seventy-three. Seventy-four. They blasted down the road. The white car bolted forward into the left lane and raced up beside her.

She glanced up. She could almost see the man's face as he looked at her; then the white car lurched into her lane, slicing into her hood.

She pressed down on the brake, suddenly slowing. He rushed past her into her lane, almost off the highway, then fishtailing slowly, he regained the road.

She slowed, too, staying behind him.

In front of her, silhouetted, she saw him look up at his rearview mirror.

They rushed down the hill and into an intersection, and she made her decision in reflex. Braking, she hurled through a right turn.

She skidded across the left lane onto the shoulder. Holding the wheel, she guided the SL back onto the road, hit the gas, and sped away. She looked up at the rearview.

No white car.

She pushed the gas pedal to the floor. The speedometer inched up. Sixty-five. Seventy. Seventy-five. She looked up again—nothing. She rushed down a hill and through a curve. A sign for a county road blurred toward her. She looked up. Still nothing.

In front of her, she saw the opening for the county road and hit the brakes. She skidded, fishtailing, then nosed into it.

She drove about a hundred yards, then stopped, turned around, and parked. Reaching into her purse,

38

she found the pistol and pulled it free. Holding it, she looked toward the road, waiting.

Her finger tightened on the trigger.

No one came.

After a long time, she settled back into her seat. Then the realization hit her like a blow.

He had been waiting for her.

Five

Turning the Bronco around, Cobb drove over the length of highway above Moon Creek a third time, his eyes squinting into the light rain and brush.

He frowned and shook his head and eased over to the side of the road.

Leaving the engine running, he climbed out of the car and walked back along the shoulder. The light misty rain pattered down on him, but he walked slowly; tugging his collar up, he kept his eyes to the side of the road and the brush. Mostly sumac, ivy. A downed log. He paused, examining it carefully. It was a log. He walked on. A tire. A shoe. Why was it always one shoe? Where the hell was the other one? He walked a hundred yards, then turned and came back. Nothing.

"Shit," he grumbled as he climbed back into the Bronco.

He drove up a mile, then turned around and started back slowly.

He picked up the mike.

"One to central."

"Central here."

"There's nothing here, Ben. Are you sure he said Moon Creek?"

"Yeah. Wrote it down right here. Moon Creek."

Cobb's jaw tightened. "Somebody playing games with us?"

"Most likely."

"I'm coming back," he growled. "One out."

"Central out."

Wheeling around, he gunned it for home.

It was a long time before Jessie stopped shaking, but the fear was still there, staining her thoughts and movements with a strange, slow thickness.

She breathed deeply and looked out at the road, the fog, and the mountains. The pale sun struggled through the thick gray, finding shapes and shadows. There was a barn across the road, all weathered planks and holes. The gray ebbing light caught it in its slow, immutable process of unbuilding itself.

There was a time she would have found beauty in that.

Not now.

Someone was trying to kill her.

There had been room for doubt before. There had been the possibility of what happened yesterday afternoon being an accident. Or at the least, someone had been angry or a little crazy momentarily.

No more.

He had been waiting for her. The call had been to get her out here. Alone. Her hands tightened on the steering wheel. Somebody wanted her dead. Had tried twice.

And would keep trying.

The misty rain ebbed away and Cobb turned off his wipers.

"Central to one."

He picked up the mike.

"One here."

"Got an accident at Tyler's Curve, Dave. You close?"

"Yeah."

"You mind handling it? No injuries, but a lot of rubberneckers. Need traffic control."

Cobb's jaw tightened. Since they had improved 54 because of the commuter traffic from D.C., there had been more and more accidents on that curve. Before the improvement, the road had been so potholed you couldn't get enough momentum to take the curve with any speed. "All right," he said. "I can be there in fifteen minutes. And call the state again and tell them we need a goddamn hazard sign out there. Again."

"I did that the last time. They've got it on their list."

"Well, call them again."

"All right. But it's gonna be like Miller's Creek. Hell, how long did it take to get that sign out there?"

"I don't know. About a—"

The nagging that had been in the back of his mind suddenly stirred, making the connection he had been trying to make since last night.

"I'll be damned," he whispered.

"Didn't hear the last part of that, Dave."

"Get hold of Jimmy. Let him handle it, then find a phone number for Jessie Marsh and call her, then patch me through."

"But—"

"Just do it. I'm headed for Clear Creek now."

She sat for a long time trying to sort through her options. There didn't seem to be any.

First go home, she thought. Then—

She swallowed. No. She knew she couldn't do that. He would know to find her there.

She ran her fingers through her hair. Then what the hell do I do, she wondered. Sit here on this goddamn country road until he comes? Until he kills me?

The anger flushed through her then.

No. She wouldn't do that. And she wasn't going to give in to panic. She wouldn't give the sonofabitch that.

She closed her eyes and drew in deep breaths. Think, Jess, she whispered to herself. Think.

She couldn't go home.

All right, what do I do? Find someplace safe. Get out of sight. That was first.

Starting the motor, she pulled back to the main road, then paused and turned away from the direction she'd come. She drove at fifty-five and kept an eye on the rearview mirror. After fifteen minutes, she came to a small town. Gas station. Houses. Motel. Farm supply store. Cafe. She pulled into a convenience store and considered the motel for a moment. Typical small-town place. Brick. One story.

Start thinking, Jess. *Start thinking*.

This was the first place after the turn back there.

The first place he would look.

So this was out. Where then? She paused. A place with more motels, she thought, and drove back into the street, passed the motel, and kept going.

"Central to One."

"One."

"Still no answer on that call to Jessie Marsh, Dave."

43

"You can stop. I'm there," he said as he turned off the highway and into Jessie Marsh's drive. Through the pine and oak, the house slowly slipped into view. His heart pounded. He remembered driving up to another house three years ago. Lydia Paulson's house. That time he had been too late.

Not this time, he thought. Please. Not this time.

Parking in front of the garage, he walked around it toward the front door. There was a window in the garage and he peered through it, then let out an audible sigh.

No car.

Good, he nodded. At least he hoped it was good. He walked to the front door anyway. Rang the bell anyway.

No answer.

He paused, considering it for a minute. Then he slipped his pistol from its holster and tried the knob. Locked. He stepped back and kicked the door once. Then again. It was a good door. He kicked it once more. The wood around the door split. After two more kicks it was free. He stepped into the house. Keeping the .45 up in a firing position, he went into the living room. Kitchen. Then upstairs. He checked each room, making sure there was nothing there.

Nothing, he breathed thankfully. He went back to the front door, pulled it shut, and holstering his .45, he ran back to the Bronco and picked up the mike.

"One to Central."

"Central."

"Ben, put out an APB for Jessie Marsh's car," he ordered.

"Will do. What's this all about?"

"I wish I knew," Cobb replied, then starting the engine, he drove back up the drive.

Six

Jessie wound through the country roads until she came to Route 29. She turned north and drove until 29 joined with Interstate 66, then got off at Manassas. She drove through the town, passing all the motels on the main strip. On the outskirts of town she found another motel, got a room off the street, and checked in. The room was the usual characterless, whitebread chain motel room. Small and clean, with a bed, a TV, and a shower and tub.

She double-locked the door, checked the windows, pulled the pistol from her purse, then sat down at the small writing desk. Placing the gun to one side, she found paper in the drawer and a pencil in her purse and began considering her options.

The pencil hovered over the blank page.

Options.

The blankness of the paper seemed to spread to her mind. She couldn't think of anything.

Nothing.

Sit in a motel room for the rest of your life, she thought bitterly, and put the pencil down. Usually she was good at problem solving.

This time there was a catch.

She was out of her element. This wasn't her kind of problem. Her hand gathered into a fist. All right, Jess, she thought, whose kind of problem is it?

The police. And she remembered David Cobb.

She reached for the telephone, then hesitated. *"I think you've misread it,"* he'd said. And she had no more proof than she'd had before.

But he'd come by. Checked on her. And she had to talk to somebody. She had to try.

Picking up the telephone, she dialed an outside line, and after getting the number from information, she called the Sheriff's office in Clear Creek.

The dispatcher answered and put her through to Cobb. He sounded relieved.

"I'm glad you called," he said. "Where are you?"

"Manassas."

"Manassas? Why?"

She frowned. "If you didn't think I was crazy before, you will now. It happened again."

"Happened again? What happened again?"

"He tried to kill me again." She shook her head. "God, it even sounds crazy to me and I was there."

"No, it's not crazy. I believe you."

She was stunned. "You do?"

"Yes, I do."

"Why? I wouldn't believe me if I were you."

"Just tell me what happened. Take it from the beginning."

She related the story exactly as it had happened.

"You're sure it was the same car?"

"Yes."

"And the man who called you said his name was Spainhauer?"

"Yes. And I've got a feeling that nobody named Spainhauer works for you."

"No. You're right, the call was a set-up. That's

46

one of the reasons I believe you. I was set up, too. I got a call about seven-thirty this morning—they pulled me away to the far end of the county. Very carefully orchestrated."

"Why?"

"I have no idea." He paused. "I'm going to ask what may seem like an odd question."

"All right."

"Well," he began, clearing his throat. "When you were in D.C., did you know anybody in organized crime? Or the espionage community?"

She seemed startled. "Excuse me?"

"Sorry. That was a little out of left field—"

"A little? Organized crime? Espionage? You mean like guys who get killed in barber shops, or meet in parks and exchange newspapers. Like that?"

"Yeah, something like that."

"That's a little further than left field."

"Maybe, maybe not. Let me back up a little. I went out to Miller's Creek. There were no tire tracks because of the grass. But there was something else, something intangible."

"Intangible?"

"The shoulder itself. I didn't remember it until later, but over the years a couple of people have had wrecks out there."

She shook her head. "I must have missed something somewhere."

"Those that had the wrecks came over the same hill too fast, weaved over onto the shoulder, and because the shoulder is so narrow, they lost it and went down the bank. The last one was about a year ago."

"I'm still not following."

"The shoulder is narrow. So narrow that the usual thing that happens is that people who get off on it, end up going over. Your man came onto the edge on purpose, yet was able to stay on the shoulder, like threading a needle. You picked the place at random, so he did this without driving it beforehand, or knowing that he was going to do it. In other words, he did it cold. And he did it perfectly the first time, then did it again when he backed up. What we have is one damn fine driver. A professional."

"I think I see what you're getting at. Only someone who was used to doing things like that could have done it without going over the bank."

"That's right. And there are the phone calls, the way they were done. Neatly. Carefully. The way a professional would do things. So, if he was a professional, who would hire him? If we eliminate your husband and take in the fact that you lived in D.C., then we come up with the two most obvious possibilities."

"Organized crime and spies."

"Right."

She paused. "That's an incredible leap from a narrow shoulder to the Mafia and the CIA."

"No, not just that. Two attempts, both supposed to look like accidents, the second very carefully set up. Working from what we have, we come up with what fits."

"It may fit, but it doesn't make any sense."

"Humor me."

She frowned. "OK," she said. "Do I know anybody in the Mafia? Or the CIA?" She shook her head again, then smiled grimly. "That wonderful qualifying answer comes to mind—*Not to my knowledge*. In other words, no. I don't even know anybody who's been arrested. Well, other than speeding tickets."

"Wise guys and spies don't get speeding tickets. How about politics? Senators, congressmen. Movers

48

and shakers. Surely you met people like that through your art, or when you worked in D.C."

"Well, yes . . . at parties, receptions . . ."

"Anybody in particular? Anybody stand out? Anything unusual happen?"

"No. Not that I can remember." She shook her head. "This really is crazy. The more I know, the crazier it gets. None of that is real. I mean the Mafia, the CIA, hired killers . . ."

"Oh, they're real, Miss Marsh. It's just that most people never cross their paths. So for them, they don't exist. But they do, believe me, they do."

She sighed. "I know. I guess the question now is what do I do?"

"Two things. First, start writing. Write down everyone you can think of who might be a lead. All the parties you went to, all the business dealings you had, all the men you went out with. And what you did the week you painted. And the twenty-four hours before. Be as specific as you can. Second, I'm going to bring you in."

"Bring me in?"

"Come after you and take you to a safer place."

"When?"

"Sometime this afternoon. I'll call you back at one o'clock and we'll go from there."

"And if there's nothing there? If we can't find it?"

She heard him sigh. "How long can you hide, Miss Marsh?"

"What—?"

"How long can you live like you have for the past few hours?"

She swallowed. "I get your point," she said. "I'll start writing."

Seven

After hanging up, Cobb walked out to his Bronco and paused for a moment, his eyes easing over the courthouse lawn, the storefronts. And the cars.

No white sedans.

But then, he wouldn't be fool enough to keep on driving it.

Climbing into the car, he drove out of town. On the highway, he put the Bronco on fifty miles an hour and watched the rearview mirror.

Cars, pickups, and vans came and went. Everybody passed him.

Nobody hung back.

He smiled to himself, almost with relief. Whoever was there *was* a pro.

It wasn't until he was past the county line that he spotted him.

Cobb had passed a convenience store, and about two miles down the road, as he was topping a hill, he saw the green Honda crest the hill behind him. The Honda had passed him twice and was parked in the store lot as he'd gone by. Cobb nodded. He was pretty good. No parking beside the road, only in places he wouldn't be noticed.

Cobb drove on, mulling it.

First choice: he could pull over and wait for him and get the plate as he passed. But the car would be rented. The license he'd used and the credit card would be under a cover name. Second choice: pull him over and get a look at him. He frowned. That would let them know he was on to them, and they would just change men. Third choice: he could pull him over and take him in and question him. The problem was, he had no cause. At least none that would stand up in court. The guy would be out in an hour, and they would change men. And he was out of his jurisdiction. In order to do any of those things, he would have to set up something through the local authorities. Time. And paper work.

Last choice: Get a look at him without him realizing, then somehow turn the tables on him. Follow him.

Cobb drove into Culpeper. Once it had been a lovely small town. Now it was a pretty medium-sized town, but growing. It was fast becoming a suburb of D.C.

Cobb laced through the streets until he came to the business area. He parked on a side street and walked around the corner to a small diner that served breakfast all day. It was only about half full, and he made his way through the tables to a table facing the door. The smell of grease and eggs and sausage and coffee was heavy. A plump waitress took his order and brought him coffee. He sipped it and started watching the door.

Customers wandered in and out and Cobb began his guessing game.

A young father and his five-year-old son. He smiled. Now that would be a great cover. Carry a five-year-old around with you.

A young guy in sweats.

Another one in fashionably-old clothes. Yuppie.

A man in his forties. Graying hair. Dressed like an off-work business man—windbreaker, jeans, running shoes. Smoking a pipe. Cobb caught a whiff of the tobacco as the man sat down. Cherry-fragranced.

The waitress brought Cobb his breakfast of eggs, sausage, fried potatoes, biscuits, and gravy. He ate it slowly.

A few people left, a few more came in. Big guy in a baseball cap, jeans, flannel shirt with another man dressed almost the same way. Different colored flannel shirt. They talked about hunting.

Two college girls, giggling, eyes roaming. Out for atmosphere.

Cobb watched them. The young guy in sweats drank a cup of coffee and left. The Yuppie had milk and a sweet roll. Pipe smoker worked on a full breakfast.

The man in sweats left.

Halfway through his eggs, Cobb glanced at his watch and frowned, acting as if he'd just realized he was late. He wolfed down a couple more bites, gulped coffee, then picking up his ticket, he paid his bill and hurried out.

He looked back. No one following.

He walked on, around the corner. His eyes quickly took in the street.

No green Honda.

He walked toward the Bronco, glancing back. No one.

Shit. He was really good.

Cobb climbed in and eased out into the street. No one following.

He drove to the cross street, turned and drove out of town. A few cars fell in behind him, none of them a green Honda. He'd changed cars, or there were two of them.

The traffic behind him thickened as they approached 29 North. His hand gripped the steering wheel. He'd lost him.

But Cobb knew he was still there.

Eight

At first Jessie could think of nothing to write. She sat at the desk and stared at the blank page. Then she thought back to her opening at the Gallery, and began by writing down when she arrived; then she tried to put down everyone's name that she met.

She came up with four people, eased back in the chair, and frowned. Four out of about fifty people.

A senator. A congressman. She remembered their names. A woman who worked for the DEA. A congressional aide. She didn't remember their names, only what they did. They had talked a lot about themselves and their high-profile jobs. They were in the big time and wanted everybody to know it.

She tried it again.

This time she closed her eyes and walked herself back through the opening.

She parked her car, and went inside. The owner, Kay Haug, met her at the glass doors of the modern building. An attractive woman in her late forties, trim and graceful, she moved and looked a little like Angie Dickenson. She hugged Jessie and they went inside.

She tried to reimagine the whole reception. When she was finished, she looked at the page.

Two more. Faces, occupations. Not names.

A colonel in the marines, and a man who said he worked at the White House. A little vague. No, very vague.

Great.

She put the pencil down, then paused and looked at the telephone.

"Why not do this the easy way," she muttered and, picking it up, dialed the gallery.

The receptionist, Trish Wells, answered. "Oh, hi," she said in her cheery-blonde voice. "She's on with somebody right now. Can she call you back."

"No, I'll wait. Any sales?"

"Ahh, I think so. The daylilies and the English street scene. You want me to look?"

"No, that's all right."

"How have you been?"

Jessie smiled. *Oh, somebody's tried to kill me twice, and I'm holed up in a small, cheap motel room.* "Fine," she replied.

"Here she is," Trish said.

"Hi, Jess."

"Hi."

"I'm glad you called. We sold the daylilies, the street scene, and the rooftops. Do you have something new for me?"

"Some florals and a seascape."

"Good. Florals and seascapes do really well. A woman in Arlington is decorating a new house and she—"

"Kay, I'm sorry, but I didn't call about business. Something has come up, and I need to ask you about the opening."

Kay paused. "Are you all right? You sound funny."

"I don't feel funny, believe me."

"What's wrong? Is it Bill? Has that bastard—"

55

"No, Kay, it's not Bill. It's something else."

"What?"

Jessie sighed. "Something serious. I'm sorry, Kay, but I really can't go into it right now. I need to talk to you about the opening."

"You're in trouble, aren't you?"

"Yes. Kay, the opening—"

"What about it?"

"I'm trying to put some names to some faces."

"Who?"

"Well, the first was a woman from the DEA. Do you remember her?"

"Yes . . . ah, Annabella Peck."

"Then a marine colonel, a kind of macho type."

"Phillip Cotten."

"God, you're really good at this."

"Names are my profession. Who else?"

"A congressional aide."

"Hmm, there were a couple of those. What did he look like?"

"Curly brown hair, good looking . . ."

"John Campanella. Works for Senator . . ." she sighed. "I'll have to look that one up."

"The last one is the hardest. He said he worked at the White House, but never really said what he did. He just told lots of inside stuff, you know, what the President had for breakfast, that kind of thing."

She paused. "Sorry, that one doesn't ring a bell. I'll look him up."

"That's right. You keep lists, don't you?"

"Lists, files. Everybody that comes into the gallery."

"Phone numbers, addresses . . ."

"Absolutely."

"Make a copy of it, will you, and I'll come by and pick it up."

56

"All right, but—"

"The people who were there, do you know all of them?"

"Well, most of them. Some were suggestions."

"Kay, were any of them . . ." she paused. "Damn," she sighed. "How do I ask this . . . were any of them in the intelligence community or did any of them have Mafia connections—"

She could almost hear Kay's mouth fall open. Then she said what Jessie had said. "Excuse me?"

"I know, I know. It sounds crazy, but I need to know."

"Jess, what's happened?"

"Kay—"

"I mean, it's not every day somebody calls me and asks about the CIA and the Mafia. You really must be in some deep shit."

"I'll explain later. Was there anybody like that at the opening?"

She sighed. "All right." She thought for a moment. "Not really. There was a guy there from State. One from Justice. Come to think of it, about half of them work for the government. Hell, Jess, this is a company town. And if they don't work for the government, they're connected some way. Think-tanks. Consultants. Jesus, there are more consultants here than anything else. They must consult each other. And lawyers—"

"Kay."

"What?"

"Back on the subject."

"Oh. Right. Mafia and CIA. Shady types." Jessie could hear her tapping something—a pen or pencil. "I'm sorry, Jess. No one comes to mind."

"Thanks, Kay. I'll be by later to pick up the list."

"Jess, I want to know what's going on. Let me

help."

"You have helped. I'll talk to you later."

After hanging up, she looked back to the sheet of paper. Wadding it up, she threw it away and slipped another one from the drawer. All right, that covered the opening. How about other people she'd met at the gallery? And work. Or just in passing.

She put the pen down and closed her eyes. This was hopeless, she thought. I can't remember everybody I've met.

Then she thought about what Cobb had said, about leaving everything behind. Frustration and anger boiled through her. Her fingers curled around the pen. No, dammit, she wasn't going to give in.

Picking up the pen, she started writing.

Nine

Cobb drove up Route 29 to 66 and the freeway. The traffic and the rush started immediately. He drove past Manassas and on to Vienna. As the Metro station came up between the lanes, he turned off the freeway, parked in the lot, and walked into the windy passageway over the highway that led to the tracks.

As he reached the turn to the ticket machines, he stopped, turned, and walked back out into the passageway. Then he paused, and taking an old envelope out of his coat pocket, he pretended to look at it and faced the way he'd come. A few people hurried by him. None of them had been in the restaurant in Culpeper.

Slipping the envelope back into his pocket, he walked back out to the Bronco, got in, and drove out to Nutley Street and turned toward downtown Vienna. He stopped at the first motel he came to and went inside. The telephones were in the hallway to the bathroom. He could see clearly into the check-in area.

He dialed Jessie Marsh's motel room.

"Yes?"

"Cobb," he said.

He heard a sigh of relief. "You don't know how good it is to hear from you."

He frowned. "Maybe not."

She paused. "Why?"

"Because I'm being followed. And they're good."

"They?"

"Yeah. It has to be." He told her about being followed out of Clear Creek, then the restaurant, and the Honda being gone when he came out. "In order to do that," he said, "there has to be more than one. One to change the car, and one to stay on me."

He heard her sigh. "I . . ." she paused. "I keep wanting to ask why, but that's pointless, isn't it?"

"Yeah. I'm going to come pick you up, but first, get rid of your car. Drive it across the street . . . but get it out of sight. Then go back to your room."

"All right."

"What's the layout of your motel?"

"Layout?"

"You're on the backside, you said that. Is there more than one floor?"

"Yes. Three."

"And you're on the ground floor?"

"Yes."

"Where? End, middle . . ."

"Almost at the end."

"How near the office?"

"At the opposite end."

"I'll call you back in fifteen or twenty minutes."

"Mr. Cobb, what are . . ."

"Fifteen minutes," he said and hung up.

He walked back through the lobby and out to the Bronco. As he reached for the door, a warning bell went off in the back of his mind.

He paused.

Something was wrong, he thought. Something . . . Then he smelled it again.

A cherry fragrance.

Pipe tobacco.

Then he remembered the man in the restaurant in

60

Culpeper. Big man. About fifty. Windbreaker and jeans. Smoking a pipe. Cherry-fragranced tobacco.

Cobb smiled. You finally made a mistake, you sonofabitch.

Climbing into the Bronco, he drove from Vienna to Tyson's Corners and to another motel. He parked and went inside. The pay telephone was between the bar and the dining room, and he didn't have a clear view of them. It would be easy for someone to get close to him.

He walked back outside and started the Bronco, threading his way through Tyson's Corners back into Vienna. He didn't look in his rearview mirror.

He knew they weren't back there. Not that close.

He drove to a residential side street, a dead end. He parked and got out of the Bronco. No car moved on the street. Oak and hickory leaves fluttered in the wind.

A small boy rode a tricycle up and down the driveway, his mother watching from a lawnchair.

Keeping his eyes on the street, Cobb began to check over the Bronco. First the wheel wells, then the bumpers. He found it on the back side of the rear bumper. Just a small lump, but there. A transmitter.

Terrific, he thought. Leaving it there, he climbed back behind the wheel.

He drove to another motel and went inside. The telephones were in a room off the lobby. He dialed Jessie Marsh again.

"Yes."

"Schedule change. I'll be there in about half an hour. I'll stop in front of your room. Just come out and get in the back seat and lie down."

"Right to my door?"

"They've put a bumper beeper on the Bronco," he said, "and following about a mile back. When I stop for any length of time, they'll come in. Anyway, just

61

come out and get in. Clear?"

"Yes."

He hung up and went back out to the car, got in, and drove.

He stopped at two motels, then drove out to the freeway and back toward Manassas.

He got off the freeway, stopping at the Ramada, Days Inn, and Red Roof. Then he drove across town to Jessie's motel. He found her room number and stopped in front of it. As she came out, he opened his door and pushed the seat forward. She got in wordlessly and he walked to the back of the Bronco. Reaching behind the bumper, he tugged the transmitter free, turned, and put it on the bumper of a Shadow parked in front of another room. Then he rushed back to the Bronco, got in, and drove out of the parking lot. Lying in the back seat, Jessie looked up at him.

"Now what?"

"Now we try to get clear."

Ten

They drove to Warrenton, then angled away from 66 and the town into the soft, rolling foothills of the Blue Ridge.

Lying down in the back seat, all Jessie could see were occasional houses, treetops, sometimes the mountains.

"Is it all right for me to get up now?"

"No."

"No?"

"No. Just stay there."

She frowned. "I'm not really comfortable."

"You're alive."

She eased back down.

"Where are we going?"

"West Virginia."

They rode for a minute.

"Okay," she asked. "Why West Virginia?"

"A friend of mine has a cabin there. The only time we use it is during hunting season. The fall. It'll be empty now. It's also very remote. No people around."

"Then what?"

"Start going over what you've got. Try to put some of this together."

"I'll ask this time. What do you think is going on?"

"I don't know. But whoever is doing this has put together quite a team. A good one." He glanced back at her. "How are you coming on your notes?"

She shook her head. "Nothing that leaps out at you. Nobody who looks like Marlon Brando or Sean Connery. I wrote down everyone I could think of that I met at openings or parties. I came up with a few names. A marine colonel, a DEA employee—"

"An agent?"

"No, she was an administrator of some kind."

"Who else?"

"A man who works at the White House, a senator, congressman, an aide. I called Kay Haug, the woman who runs the gallery I use, and she has a list of the people who were at the opening. Phone numbers, addresses, all that kind of thing—"

"That'll save a lot of work. We'll call her from West Virginia and have her send it to the office."

"I've got to tell you, though, I don't think it's any of them. None of them stand out. Nothing happened. Nobody made me an offer I couldn't refuse. Nobody wanted his martini shaken, not stirred."

He smiled. "Too bad it's not that easy."

She shook her head. "I don't think there's anything there. We stood, sipped wine, ate cheese, had superficial conversations about art for five or ten minutes and that was it."

"You never met any of them afterwards?"

"No."

"Did you see any of them afterwards? In passing someplace? A store, or movie, or on the street?"

"I don't think so . . . no."

"Did any of them buy anything?"

"Not that I know of . . . oh, yes. The congressional aide did. A landscape, I think."

"How about since?"

"I don't know. Maybe."

"Have any of them called or written you?"

"No."

He sighed. "You're right, there's not much there, but we have to start somewhere."

They rode on, the tires humming, the seat vibrating under her. Her eyes rested on Cobb. A handsome man, she thought. This is no time to be looking for a date, she thought, but her eyes stayed on him. He had good, strong lines in his face. Strong, square jaw. Muscular arms beneath the corduroy jacket. The mustache was trimmed, and his longish salt and pepper hair feathered over his ears and collar. He must have felt her staring at him because he glanced back, his eyes narrowing. "What . . . ?"

She smiled. "Nothing. Sorry."

"Sure, it was something. What?"

She shrugged. "Oh. You just wonder about people. You don't seem like a . . ."

"Cop?"

"No. You seem out of place somehow."

He smiled. "Isn't everybody?"

"I mean, you're very good at all this. That's not something I would expect from a small-town policeman."

"Small-town policemen get a bad rap."

"I'm sorry, I think that came out wrong."

He smiled. "It's all right, I know what you mean. I wasn't always a small-town cop . . ." His eyes went to the rearview mirror, and he frowned. "Shit . . ." he whispered and there was a tinge of warning in his voice.

"What?"

"A blue Ford has been back there a while. I've caught sight of it a couple of times. Just stay down."

In the front seat, Cobb looked up again and his jaw tightened. She looked at the rearview and saw the Ford in the glass.

Cobb speeded up, and the Ford speeded up.

He sighed.

"We're in trouble," he warned.

She eased up and looked out the back window.

"Stay down," he growled.

She started to crawl into the front seat.

"I said—"

She paused and looked at him. "I heard what you said. I don't like not knowing what's going on. Besides, it's pointless now."

She sat in the passenger seat and buckled her belt.

"You're placing yourself in danger—"

"No more than you."

"I'm paid for it."

"I'm not going to lie back there blind," she countered. "It's *my* ass."

He glanced at her, then smiled. "Yeah," he nodded. "It is." His hands gripped the wheel and he moved forward. "Hold on," he ordered. "This is about to get interesting."

He pressed down on the gas pedal and the Bronco lurched forward, bolting down a long hill and starting up another.

Cobb's eyes scanned the sides of the road and he shook his head.

Jessie watched him. "What—?"

"No side roads," he answered. "They've picked a good spot, if—"

He looked ahead.

"Don't do that. Finish your sentences," she pleaded.

"If there's somebody ahead, and they're trying to pin us in." He eased off on the gas. "Find me a place to go off—"

"Go off?"

"This is a four-wheel drive. Find me a place to go off—"

"Damn," she whispered and looked to the side of the road. The narrow shoulders fell sharply away. Too steep to get down.

They blasted up and over a hill.

In the distance, he saw another car coming. The green Honda.

It veered over into their lane and speeded up.

"Oh, shit," Jessie whispered.

Cobb gripped the wheel, keeping the Bronco in the lane. They were about a mile apart and closing fast.

Jessie looked at him.

"What the hell are you doing?"

"They're bluffing."

"How can you tell?"

"They're bluffing."

"What if they think you're bluffing?"

"Then we're all dead."

The Honda raced toward them, staying in their lane.

Jessie pressed back in her seat, and her feet came up in reflex, bracing against the dash. The Honda bore in on them. A hundred yards. Jessie began to moan. Then scream. The Honda held its ground. So did Cobb. "Ohhh . . . shit . . ." she shouted, and so did Cobb. She was almost standing against the dash now, and Cobb's arms were stretched out straight, hands like steel on the wheel, the muscles corded along the bones. She looked back to the road, and for a moment, there was nothing in the world except the road and the green Honda and the motion that bound them. No thought, no past, no future. Only the motion.

Then the Honda was so close, she could see the outline of the man behind the wheel.

Ten yards.

Then it veered, swinging into the other lane and the car came into them. She felt a thump, then the scream of metal as the Honda raked along the side of the Bronco.

The Bronco wobbled, skidding across the pavement and onto the narrow shoulder above a steep embankment. The back tires caught the soft earth and the rear end swung around and dropped down the embankment.

The Honda fishtailed and spun around then stopped, facing them. Behind the Honda, the Ford dipped into the road, careened around sidewise, and vaulted down the embankment.

The Honda rolled forward and gained speed.

Cobb kicked the door of the Bronco open. Then, reaching over, he gripped Jessie's shirt and pulled her across the seat and out the door after him.

They tumbled to the ground. Then Cobb scrambled to his feet, pushing along the side of the Bronco toward the front and the roadway.

Pulling his 9mm from its holster, he swung around the hood and leveled his pistol at the oncoming car.

It rushed toward Cobb. He fired three times, punching a triangle into the windshield of the oncoming car.

The Honda turned sharply, trying to make an impossible ninety-degree angle. It didn't make it. Instead, it hurled up onto its side, hovering for a moment; then, still moving, it slammed down into the pavement. Metal screamed as it plowed into the asphalt and a sudden wash of glass and shrapnel exploded toward Cobb.

Turning, he tumbled to the pavement.

The Honda continued to scream, then the sound ebbed away as it came to rest a few feet away.

Cobb raised his head and glanced over his shoulder at the ruined car.

"Jesus," he whispered, and pulled his feet up under him to get up. He put his weight on his legs — and went down.

His eyes went to his legs. His lower left pant leg was dark with blood. Pushing up on his good leg and using his hands, he stood up and hobbled toward the wrecked Honda.

Coming around the side of the Bronco, Jessie saw him. And the blood.

"Mr. Cobb—"

"Can you drive a four-wheel?"

"Yes—"

"Turn the hubs, and get it out of there," he said, then turned toward the other car.

As he made his way to the Honda, Jessie turned to the Bronco. She quickly rotated the hubs on the front tires, then climbed in. She twisted the key and the engine roared to life as she pulled it into four-wheel.

This time the front wheels caught and the Bronco leaped over the edge of the shoulder and back up onto the pavement.

She drove toward Cobb and the Honda. The windshield of the Honda was gone, and the driver was slumped through it. Cobb bent over the man, his hands going through his pockets.

Then he stood up, staring at something. He turned and looked at the Ford in the ditch. The other man was leaning against the car with something in his hand. It was a radio microphone.

Jessie drove to Cobb and stopped with the passenger door toward him.

The door jerked open and Cobb dragged himself into the seat.

"Go," he shouted. "Go!"

Jessie hit the gas and they barreled down the road.

"We're in deep kim-chee," Cobb said and held his hand out to her. There was a wallet in it. And in the wallet was a badge.

She stared at it in disbelief.

"Watch the road," Cobb urged, and she pulled her eyes back to the highway.

She shook her head. "I don't understand."

"He was a cop," Cobb said. "And his partner just called us in."

Eleven

At the first crossroad, Cobb motioned for Jessie to turn. She swerved off the main highway and stopped. She slipped the Bronco back into two-wheel drive, jumped out, turned the hubs, then got back in and sped away.

"Nicely done," Cobb said. "Here and back there."

"Thanks," she replied, looking at his leg. There was blood on the floor mats.

"We need to—"

"We need to get the hell out of here," he finished, pointing to another small county road.

She turned down it, speeding past manicured horse farms and barns; then at the next road, she turned again.

Cobb nodded. "That's the idea. Now stop again."

She looked at him. "Now?"

"Now."

She stopped, and he reached for the door handle, then swallowed hard, his hand trembling. "You'll have to do it."

"What?"

"A bug," he explained. "I found one earlier, but they played it safe and put two on us. That's how they found us. It'll be small, about the size of a quarter. The first one was on the back, so go to the front, feel the bumper and the wheel wells."

Nodding, she got out. It took her ten minutes, but she found it the second time she searched the passenger side, just under the door. She threw it into a field, then continued driving.

"Now get us damn good and lost," Cobb ordered.

"I'm already lost."

She turned again, this time down a dirt road. Thick woods began to close around them. They rolled down a hill and crossed through a creek, then Cobb nodded. "Here," he said. "Park here."

She rolled the Bronco in parallel to the rushing water, turned off the engine, and looked at his leg. "We need to do something about that."

The muscles in his jaw tightened. "I'm all right, I'll just . . ."

She sighed and shook her head. "Quit being so goddamn noble and let me do something about that."

His eyes met hers, and he nodded.

"You're right," he said. "There's a first aid kit in the console." He opened it and rummaged through papers, ammunition, a pistol, and clips. "Here," he said and tugged the kit out and handed it to her.

She got out, walked around to his side, and opened the door.

Taking the kit from him, she opened it and found a pair of scissors, then began to cut through the ragged pant leg.

"These are my best jeans," he whined.

"*Were,*" she corrected him and kept cutting until she could see the leg. Her breath caught and she had to look away for a moment.

"I always thought my legs were one of my better features," he managed.

She glanced up at him and nodded. *"Were."*

71

He tried to look down and she pushed him back. "Just stay still," she said and forced her eyes back to his leg.

It was like ground beef. All of the flesh had been flayed — ragged and bloody — and she could see deeper cuts, too. "I'm going to have to clean this," she murmured. Finding bandages in the kit, she turned to the stream, wet them, then came back to him and began cleaning the wounds.

Cobb turned in the seat, trying to get more comfortable. The wallet dropped to the floor. The badge and the I.D. showed. She looked at the badge and I.D. "Gerald Monroe," she read, then shook her head and kept cleaning the wounds. "I don't understand. Was he trying to arrest us?"

"No, he was trying to kill us. Run us off the road. His partner back there was the man I saw in the restaurant in Culpeper. They've been trying to set us up all along, to take both of us out and make it look like an accident."

"But he was a policeman."

"He was moonlighting."

"You mean as a . . ."

"Hit man, professional, mechanic."

"A policeman?"

Cobb smiled. "I arrested a pro once that turned out to be an elementary school teacher."

"I still don't understand. You're a policeman, too. Can't you —"

"I'm a deputy in Clear Creek County. If I go beyond the county on official business, I have to inform the authorities of that county. Or city, or whatever —"

"But can't you explain?"

He nodded. "Oh, yeah. I can explain: But there's going to be an official investigation. One helluva investigation. One cop just killed another cop, both out of their jurisdiction. I'll have to go through all the proce-

72

dures. I'll be relieved of my duties, and they'll hold you as a material witness. The problem is, with them holding you, another moonlighting cop will have easy access to you, and one morning you'll turn up dead in a cell someplace. A tragic suicide."

She paused and stared at him for a moment, then went back to work. "This is crazy," she said. "We really are in deep . . . what did you call it?"

"Kim-chee."

"Kim-chee?"

"Korean cabbage. Hot, fermented Korean cabbage."

"You're kidding."

"No. It's wonderful."

"I'll take your word for it." She looked at his leg. It was clean now, at least as clean as she could get it, but it was still bad. Mostly surface lacerations, but there were also some very deep cuts. She found a spray antiseptic and looked at him. "This is not supposed to hurt, but—"

He swallowed and nodded, then gripped the back of the seat and the dashboard. "Do it."

She sprayed the wounds quickly and Cobb stiffened, gripping the seat and dash until his fingers whitened. When she'd finished, he trembled, then the tension ebbed away slowly. He smiled grimly. "I'm glad it wasn't supposed to hurt."

Using clean bandages, she wrapped the wounds. "That's all I can do for right now," she said. "We can get you to a hospital—"

"No," he grunted. "No hospital. Don't you get it? We're out in the cold. And I mean *really* in the cold." He shook his head and wiped the sweat from his face. "What the hell did you see or do anyway? I mean somebody is going to a lot of trouble here."

She shook her head. "I don't know, but I hope I don't do it again." She ran her fingers through her hair.

"Yesterday . . ." She smiled with a weary amazement. "Yesterday. A Tuesday, less than twenty-four hours ago, I was driving around, looking for pictures, something with shadow and light . . ." She sighed and leaned back against the seat. "Sorry," she offered. "Rambling . . ." She looked at him. "What do we do now?"

He glanced at his watch. "It's . . . four-twenty. It'll be dark in about two hours. We'll move then."

"Where to?"

He shook his head and eased back in the seat. "I have no idea." He sighed. "I'm making this up as I go along." He eased farther into the seat. "I'm going to close my eyes for a couple of minutes . . ."

She looked around. "Two hours. That seems like a lifetime. I — " She looked back at him, and he was breathing deeply. Asleep.

"Unbelievable," she whispered and sat down next to the stream and stared at it. Sunlight glittered on the moving water, rustling with the shadows of the pine and oak. There was a painting there, she thought, and tried to click her mind into that mode. But it was no good. There was a wall there. An overwhelming weariness washed over her like lead. She found herself staring, lost in the reflections on the water, floating in a strange nothingness. She pushed herself up and walked to the Bronco, climbed into the driver's seat, and was asleep almost immediately.

The smell of coffee woke her.

Her eyes fluttered open to soft darkness. Cobb sat across from her, sipping from a thermos cup. He looked at her and smiled. A gentle smile, and in that moment in the darkness with the smell of coffee and the rustling of his coat, she felt an incredible intimacy with him. Something sexual. And something more, too.

74

He held the cup out. "Breakfast?"

Blinking, she sat up. "No kidding. Coffee?"

"From this morning," he explained. "It's a little old, but hot."

She took the cup. "Hot is all that counts." She sipped it, then looked at his leg. "How is it?"

He shrugged. "Stiff."

She smiled. "Stiff. That's it?"

"A little pain."

She shook her head. "A little . . . I'll bet it hurts like hell."

His lips pressed in a reluctant smile. "Only when I breathe."

She sipped again. "Is that a guy thing, not admitting pain? Stiff upper lip and all that?"

"Actually, it's not my lip that's stiff, it's my leg and foot." He glanced at his watch. "Time to move."

"What time is it?"

"Ten after nine," he answered, then reached for the radio.

"What are you doing?"

"Seeing how much trouble we're in." He pressed the button on the mike. "Ned, this is Bubba. Come in."

There was a pause, then: "This is control, Bubba. You seen anything of Cobb? These boys really want him."

"No."

"Seth wants him, too. Seth is really pissed."

"I can't say as I blame him. Bubba out."

He hung up the mike and looked at Jessie.

"Bubba?" she asked.

"Nickname. There are state police all over the place. And my boss, Seth Hardesty, is pissed."

"So no help that way?"

"No. He's very political. He'll do everything by rules. So . . . we can't go to Clear Creek, and I think

75

West Virginia is out. They'll find out about the cabin."

"Where then?"

He rubbed his chin. "Front Royal is the closest good-sized town. There, then D.C. Monroe was a cop in Jefferson, and your friend Kay is there. We can get the list from her. Plus the traffic and people — we need all the traffic and people we can stand." He opened the console and took out two clips of ammunition. "You're sure you can use that nine millimeter?"

"I'm sure."

He handed her the two clips. "Then keep these in reserve. There's another 9mm in here, and more ammunition."

She took the clips and put them in her purse.

He reached into the console again. "Now we need to take the antenna off."

"Why?"

"Because the wand will say I have a radio, and it's easy to spot."

He found a screwdriver and reached for the door, his breath catching with pain.

She took the screwdriver. "I'll do it."

"Can you . . . I mean . . . do you . . ."

"I can operate a screwdriver," she said. "Women can do those sorts of things."

She got out, removed the antenna, slipped it into the back, then climbed back in the driver's seat.

"I'll drive," Cobb offered.

"You're kidding."

"No, I'll — " He eased up and leaned across the console and his face went rigid with pain. He settled back into the seat, breathing deeply. He swallowed, "It'll take a minute," he whispered, "but I'll be all right."

She shook her head. "I'll drive."

The muscle in his jaw flexed, and he grasped the dash again. "I said — "

She started the Bronco and popped the clutch, roll-

76

ing him back in his seat. "And I said, *I'd drive.* Damn, you're hard-headed."

He eased back in the seat, his breath still coming hard, then he nodded. "You drive," he agreed.

With Cobb directing her, Jessie wound her way through the darkness until they found a main road that led to Front Royal.

She drove to the outskirts, and Cobb directed her to turn off into the first big motel.

"Drive around back," he directed.

"We're not going to check in?"

"No. We're just here to steal—"

She looked at him. "Steal?"

"Yeah," he nodded and as she drove around to the rear of the third building, Cobb reached into the glove compartment, found a screwdriver again, then pointed to a parking place. She parked and he handed her the screwdriver. "Take our plates off," he ordered.

It took her a few minutes, but she managed to get both plates off, then she climbed back into the Bronco.

"Watch for plates," he said. "We want anything but Virginia."

"But won't they notice when they come out—"

"Maybe. But how many times a day do you look at your plates? How many today or yesterday? Usually people come out and get into their car. They never look. They see what they want to see. And if they're tourists, most likely they'll be in another state before they notice they're gone. And stealing plates is petty larceny, not a big crime."

It was only a few minutes before a pickup drove in and parked.

"South Carolina," Jessie read.

"Good," Cobb said. "Now wait."

A man and woman climbed out of the pickup and crossed the sidewalk.

"No good," said Cobb.

"Why?"

"They could come back at any time. They're right in front of their door. Too convenient."

A Buick Skylark pulled in and parked. "Nevada," Jessie read.

They waited. A man got out, pulled a suitcase out after him, then walked to the stairs and went up to the second floor. He walked down the passageway to a door, paused, then went in. The door closed and the light went on. They waited.

The door didn't reopen.

"Okay," Cobb said. "I'll watch the door. If he comes back out, I'll tap the horn. Take his plates off. Put ours on his car, then come back and put his on the Bronco."

"Okay." Her voice sounded strange. Tight, nervous.

Cobb smiled. "You'll do fine," he said. "It's always best to do your first robbery with a Deputy Sheriff."

She smiled, then opened the door to the Bronco. The night air was suddenly very cool. She swallowed and looked back at him. "I have to tell you I've never done anything like this before."

"I thought you were a whiz with a screwdriver."

"You know what, Cobb?"

"What?"

"Sometimes you're an asshole."

"The truth hurts. Now go."

Pulling cold air into her lungs, she turned and ran across the parking lot.

She knelt down in back of the Skylark. Her fingers were cold, and it seemed to take a long time to get the license plate off. Down the walk someone came out of a door. She pushed down behind the car. Then another car started and she went back to work. The back plate came off. She replaced it, then moved around front. It

78

went much faster. It came off, she replaced it, then ran across the lot. The new plates went on the Bronco quickly and she climbed back into the cab with Cobb. Her heart pounded in her chest and she felt a little dizzy.

She looked at him. "I did it," she said, amazement apparent in her voice.

"Welcome to the wonderful world of crime," he replied. "Now let's get the hell out of here."

Twelve

Jessie drove to a Hardee's drive-through and they ordered burgers, fries, and soft drinks, then she wound her way toward I-66 and Washington, D.C.

They ate as they drove. When the traffic began to thicken around them, they both began to relax a little. She took the beltway around D.C. and turned off into Silver Spring.

They found a motel and Jessie checked in, asking for a room in the back on the ground floor away from the street. She drove around to the room, parked in front of it, then came around to Cobb's side to open the door, but he had already done it. He placed one hand on the dash and the other on the seat and tried to lower himself to the ground.

Jessie reached up to help him, but he shook his head.

"I can do it," he insisted quietly.

She stared at him for a moment, her mouth tightening, then she turned away and walked to the door, unlocked it, and went inside.

Another anonymous room. Two beds, lamp and table between them. TV set with HBO Guide on top. Metal racks for hanging clothes. Dresser. Bathroom beyond with small white towels. She wondered what archaeologists would think when they found all those undersized towels. She was sure they weren't biodegradable. She tossed her purse on the bed and turned to the door and looked out. Cobb had made it to the ground. He had also closed the door and was leaning against the fender. His face glistened with sweat.

"How you doing?"

He nodded heavily. "Fine. Good."

She nodded and turned to the TV. She switched it on, found CNN, tugged two pillows from under the spread on one of the beds, and placed them against the headboard.

Cobb hopped into the doorway and leaned against the frame. Jessie sat down and leaned into the pillows, watching the news. He hopped in the door and to the bed, dropped onto it, and sat, breathing heavily.

"You didn't close the door," she said.

He raised his eyes to her and frowned. "Sorry."

"Want me to do it?"

He looked at the door, sighed, then looked at Jessie. "Would you mind?"

"Not at all."

She got up, walked to the door, closed it, then sat back down on her bed.

"Thanks," Cobb said.

She looked sidelong at him. "Is this like a macho thing?"

He sighed. "I don't know, I never thought about it."

"That doesn't surprise me."

He stretched out on the bed. "Could we have this conversation some other time? I'm a little beat right now."

She looked at him, and her eyes softened. "Sure. What do you need — ?"

He shook his head. "Nothing," he started to say, then looked at her. "How about a pillow?"

Leaning from her bed to his, she uncovered a pillow and slipped it under his head. "Anything else?"

"A cold beer."

"Not a bad idea."

"Tomorrow," he said, his speech slurring slightly. "I'm buying." He blinked against the sudden heaviness in his eyelids. "Jesus," he whispered. "I never sleep this much. I don't think I'm operating at full capacity."

"No kidding."

"No, really . . . Oh—" he blinked heavily. "You're kidding when you said no kidding . . ." His voice trailed away, and his head fell to one side as he began breathing deeply.

She looked at him; smiling, she shook her head. This was the second time he'd gone to sleep on her.

She turned the TV and the lights off, stretching out on her bed. She closed her eyes, but the adrenaline still pulsed through her. She opened her eyes and sat up. Since Cobb had picked her up this afternoon, activity had kept the fear away. Now it returned darkly, breathing through her. And bringing with it a kind of replay video, running and rerunning conversations until none of it meant anything.

Cobb moaned. She looked at his dark shape. He said something, muttering, then held himself as if he were cold. She rose, pulled the spread up, and covered him with it. "He's got a piece, Danny," he whispered. "He's got a goddamn piece . . ."

She pulled the blanket up, too, and he quieted. She sat down on the bed watching him and remembered waking up in the Bronco with him. She felt that intimacy again now. A closeness—and a distance. Both at the same time. She found herself attracted to him, yet wary.

Frowning, she shook her head. This was no time for dating . . . she sighed, and lay back down and closed her eyes. They came open again. No good. The video in her mind kept running. She lay awake a long time, staring into the darkness, trying to make sense of what was happening, trying to find an answer. It never came.

She drifted in and out of sleep, and finally after four, she got up, found the key, and went out into the chill morning. Bright lamps washed a dark wet light over the parking lot. A heavy dew glistened and in the distance Jessie could hear the passage of tractor trailers. She took the thermos from the Bronco and walked around the buildings to the street. A Shoney's sign hovered in the darkness, and she turned toward it.

Inside, it was brightly lit, heavy with the odors of eggs, sausage, onions, hamburgers and coffee. A few people were scattered among the tables and along the counter. Weary faces. Smoking cigarettes, drinking coffee, peering at newspapers or staring into the night. All in between, waiting.

Jessie sat at the counter and had a sudden craving for waffles.

Knowing she would hate herself afterwards, she ordered them anyway, complete with butter, maple syrup, and coffee. She found a newspaper on the counter and began reading it, flipping through it idly. The waffles came; they were wonderful, and she was right, she hated herself afterwards. She felt like she'd swallowed a small tank. She had the thermos filled, and sipping her coffee, found another newspaper and wandered through it. It had been a dull day. Not much news. Nothing interesting.

She paused.

Nothing interesting?

Turning, she stood up and walked to the newspaper racks next to the register. She bought all the papers and went through them.

Nothing interesting.

A strange dread began to seep through her. Something was wrong. Terribly wrong.

Gathering up the newspapers and the thermos, she paid her bill and almost ran back to the motel room.

On the bed, Cobb stirred as she came in. Then his eyes blinked open.

"Hi," he said thickly.

Turning on the light, she dropped the newspapers on the bed. "Congratulations," she said. "You're not famous."

He blinked again, looked down at the newspapers, then back to her. He ran his fingers through his hair. "It's early," he said, "and I just woke up, so I can probably get away with a response that doesn't reflect a great deal of intelligence. So, what the hell are you talking about?"

Thirteen

Cobb drank coffee and went through the newspapers for a third time, then shook his head.

"You're right," he said. "We're not famous." He pushed the newspapers away and poured more coffee. "Not a goddamn word."

"Maybe there's been some mistake," Jessie suggested. "Maybe we—"

Cobb shook his head. "No. There's no mistake. I talked to my dispatcher, Ned, remember. No, we're wanted . . ." He looked back to the newspapers. "But Monroe's partner is keeping it quiet for some reason . . ."

"Why?"

Cobb shook his head. "I'm not sure." He paused, thinking, then went on. "He had to have a reason to be out there and a reason for his partner to die, so he told them I was running drugs . . . and he knows I can't go in because we know that he or somebody like him can get to you. He knows we're going to stay out. He wants us isolated . . ." He sighed and shook his head. "It's like some kind of insane game . . . Alice in Wonderland chess . . ." He raked his fingers through his hair. "Or maybe not," he grumbled. "Hell, I don't know.

Everything is guesswork." He smiled. "Danny would love this one . . ."

"Danny?"

"My old partner." He poured himself more coffee. "We need to move, but first we have to take some precautions. The papers may not have us but the cops do." He pushed his fingers through his hair again. "My hair is grayer when it's shorter . . ." He touched his mustache and frowned. "And I'll shave." He looked at Jessie. "You can . . ."

She stiffened. "I can *what?*"

"Let me see your driver's license."

She took her license from her purse and handed it to him.

"It's not a very good picture," she said.

"Good," he replied and looked at it, then nodded. "Your hair photographed dark. We'll lighten it, make it blonder—"

"Blonder?"

"And cut it."

"Cut it? Oh, come on, Cobb. Do you know how tall I am?"

"I've got a fair idea, yeah."

"And skinny?"

"Well, you're not really *that* skinny—"

"With short blond hair, I'll look like a bimbo stork."

"Look, we're not in the papers, but we'll be on circulars. It's not likely, but it's possible some cop will stumble across us. They'll use your license photo on the circular. Most people think the way to disguise themselves is to wear dark glasses—"

"Wrong?"

"Wrong. Change the color and style of your hair. Subconsciously, that's what we look at first."

She stared at him for a long moment, then nodded. "Okay," she grumbled. "Then what?"

He held up the wallet. "Then Gerald Monroe."

* * *

86

Jessie went out and brought back breakfast for Cobb — two egg biscuits and gravy from Hardee's and coffee. Then at eight o'clock Cobb called the police station in Jefferson.

From the News and Information Officer, he learned that he could send flowers to the Gish Funeral Home in Vienna.

He hung up. "He lived in Vienna."

"Now what?"

"We find out where he lived."

"Information?"

"Cops don't have listed phones," he said. "No. The utilities. You're going to be Mrs. Monroe. You've just moved and haven't gotten a bill. You want to know where the last one was sent."

She dialed the number for the utilities in Vienna.

A woman's voice answered. "Miss Allen. How may I help you."

Jessie adopted a worried, flustered tone. "Miss Allen . . . don't do that, honey . . . sorry, my little boy is fascinated by telephones . . ."

"I have a five-year-old."

"Davey is two and the term 'terrible twos' is most appropriate . . . Davey, sit down and eat your cereal. You like Fruit Loops . . . anyway, was it *Miss Allen* . . . ?"

"Yes."

"Miss Allen, this is Marilyn Monroe . . . not the real one, the dead one; actually, I was Marilyn Smith, then I married Jerry. It's really embarrassing, and now I go by Lynn . . ."

"I see . . ."

"Anyway, this is Marilyn . . . Mrs. Gerald Monroe, and we just moved and we haven't received a bill in like two months. What address have you been sending the bill to? I mean, do you have the new address?"

"Ahh . . . let me see. Your last bill went to 451 Ausband —"

"Well, that's the old address . . . honey, don't do that . . . excuse me, Miss Allen, I'm going to have to call you back."

She hung up. "It's 451 Ausband."

Cobb looked at her in amazement. *"Marilyn* Monroe?"

"I'm sorry, it was all I could think of."

Cobb shook his head. "No, it was wonderful. Great, as a matter of fact. You're a terrific liar."

"I was in advertising."

"That explains it."

Fourteen

Four-fifty-one Ausband was a one-story brick house on an oak-lined street.

Jessie parked the Bronco across the street. Cobb's eyes moved carefully over the Monroe house as he rubbed his smooth upper lip where the mustache had been.

Jessie had lightened her hair and felt like she should be standing on a street corner somewhere.

"Well, we might be in luck," Cobb said.

"Why?"

"No toys in the yard. No basketball hoop on the garage. Probably means no kids. The lawn hasn't been mowed and the hedge hasn't been trimmed in a while. No flowers, which probably means no wife." He looked to the neighboring houses. "No cars in any of the driveways," he added, "which probably means the wives work. Nobody home." He opened the glove box and after rummaging through it came out with a notebook, a pen, and the screwdriver.

"Ahh, the trusty screwdriver. I never knew how important a screwdriver could become in my life."

"New horizons. Yesterday it was license plates, today is B and E —"

"B and E?"

"Breaking and entering."

"I hope they give us cells close together."

He shook his head. "If they catch up with us, we won't make it to cells."

She nodded. "Tell me about breaking and entering."

He handed her the pen, the notebook, and the screwdriver.

"Walk around the house. Hold the notebook and the pen. Find the meters. Act like you're taking readings. Go around to the back, to the rear door. Cops fall into two categories: they're either fanatics or slobs about home security. It's either Fort Knox or a cracker box. From the looks of the outside, I'm betting Monroe was a slob. Go to the back door. If there's molding along the door, ram the screwdriver between it and the frame and into the door latch. It'll pop."

"And if there's a bolt?"

"If there's a bolt, we're dead."

"How about an open window?"

"At night maybe. Never in the daytime. Anyway, when you get inside, come to the front door and open it."

She turned to the door, then paused and looked back at him. "Are you a slob or a fanatic?"

"Just break in the house, Marsh."

She smiled. "Good. At least you're consistent."

"Consistent?"

"With that strong, silent, macho front."

He frowned. "Just —"

She nodded. "I know. Break in the house."

Opening the door, she stepped out into the cool morning. She slipped the screwdriver into her back pocket; then, holding the notebook in one hand and the pen in the other, she walked across the street to the Monroe house.

She angled to the driveway and back toward the garage. Her eyes went along the side of the house. No meters. She went through a gate and into the back yard scruffy with high grass and weeds. The gas and electric meters were between two windows. She took the readings, then turned to the back porch.

A full-sized charcoaler sat at the bottom of the steps surrounded by empty beer cans. There were more beer cans next to a lawn chair and table on the back porch. No magazines or books, no tape player or radio. Just beer cans. Jessie felt the sudden chill of an empty life. She walked up the steps and opened the glass door. Then she took the screwdriver from her pocket and, reaching for the knob, saw the keyhole for the dead bolt.

"Dammit," she sighed, but decided to try it anyway. She placed the screwdriver next to the frame and shoved it between the frame and the molding. She felt the latch give. She turned the knob and pushed. It opened. The bolt hadn't been set.

She almost giggled. Easing the door wider, she stepped into a small kitchen. It was made even smaller by the litter. Carry-out cartons, beer cans, unwashed dishes, overflowing trash bags.

Cobb was right. No woman lived here.

She walked down a short, narrow hallway to the front door.

She opened it, then left it and stepped into the living room. More of the same. Beer cans around a chair in the middle of the room in front of the TV set. Newspapers on the floor. Papers piled high on a desk on the far side of the room.

She heard Cobb thump onto the porch, then cross it. She looked back as he leaned against the door frame, breathing heavily.

"You're going to be in great shape when this is over."

"I'm in great shape anyway. I'm just used to having two legs."

He stepped inside and closed the door and looked at the room. "Jesus," he moaned.

"You were right," Jessie said. "He *was* a slob."

Cobb glanced at her. "Well, I didn't exactly mean it this way. I meant careless. But this . . ." he shook his head.

"I thought professional killers were . . ." she shrugged. "Cool, efficient."

"Some are. Most are just petty people looking for an easy way out . . ." His eyes roamed over the room again. "No, he just sleeps here . . . a lot of cops like that." His eyes kept moving. "Probably divorced . . . lived out of the station or on the road. So tired when he got back here, he just changed clothes, had a beer, watched TV, and took off again. A lot of us like that."

"Us?"

He looked at her. "Yeah, Marsh. Us." His eyes fell on the desk across the room and he stepped toward it, limping badly. He glanced down. "Look and see if he had a mop or a broom—"

"You're kidding."

"As a crutch."

"That would have been what he used them for," she retorted as she walked back into the hallway toward the kitchen.

There was a small closet next to the stove. In it were a mop and broom, both covered with dust and spider webs.

She lifted out the broom, and using a dish towel, cleaned it off and went back into the living room.

Cobb sat at the desk, leafing through the stacks of papers and sorting them into different piles. Jessie leaned the broom against the desk and watched him. One pile was phone bills. Another credit card bills. Utilities. Letters. Junk mail. When the phone bills began to stack up, he handed them to Jessie. "Start going through these. Look for in-state toll calls he often made."

Nodding, she took the bills and her pen and sat down carefully on the sofa, avoiding magazines and a dirty shirt.

She started through the bills, and Cobb began going through bank statements.

After six bills, she found a Jefferson number repeating itself. It was on each bill at least five times. She walked over to Cobb. "This one."

Cobb looked at it, then handed her the telephone. "Get the number of the Jefferson Library. Ask them to look this up in their Cole's."

"Cole's?"

"A cross-reference directory. If you have a phone number, you can get the name and address."

"You're a cop. Surely you can still use official channels."

He grimaced. "Yeah, well, couple of problems there. Official channels . . . I mean *real* official channels are slow. Paper work. Three days minimum. Usually what I do is call in and get a supervisor and say it's an emergency. Then they call me back at headquarters. Or I call somebody I know. Unfortunately, when Jerry Monroe hit the ground, my shortcuts went out the window."

"Where did you learn all of these . . ."

"Scams," Cobb said. "They're called *scams.*"

"When . . ."

"When I was undercover," he said, then looked at the papers.

"Undercover. What did you do undercover?"

"Life stories later," he replied. "Now call the library."

She called the Jefferson Public Library, asked for the information desk, and gave the librarian the number. After a few minutes, Jessie hung up and shook her head. "Bad news," she said. "No such number."

"No, that's good news. Unlisted numbers aren't in the Cole's. Remember what I said about cops."

She nodded. "They don't have listed numbers, so . . ."

"So, that's probably the number of his partner—" He picked up the telephone and dialed the number.

It rang several times. Then he heard, "This is Robert Swann; leave a message at the tone."

"Robert Swann," he repeated, handing her a check. It was made out to the Paradise Bar and Grill. "There are about ten of these so far," he continued, "and they went through the Nationsbank here in Vienna. I'm betting he does his drinking there. Look them up in the book and get an address and phone number."

She reached for the book as he kept going through the checks. When she found it, she read off the number and address. "In Jefferson," she added.

He looked back at Swann's number. "Same prefix. We've got to get out of here. There's too much to go through. See if there's another trash bag in the kitchen."

She went through the drawers and found an empty box for trash bags. Pausing, she looked down at one of the half-filled bags next to the sink, picked it up, and emptied it out on the floor. She took it in to Cobb.

He opened it, and began scooping papers from the desk into it. Then he looked inside. "There are coffee grounds in here."

"I improvised," she explained.

Shrugging, he scooped more of the papers into the bag as she helped him. She shook her head. "We're interesting burglars. Old papers and a broom."

"And trash bags."

"Big time."

Fifteen

At the wheel, Jessie shook her head. "Why?" she whispered.

"Why are they after you?"

She looked at him. "Oh . . . that, too. No, this time I was wondering why Monroe did what he does. I mean, he lived like a slob, but that doesn't make him a killer. And he had a nice house, or it could have been. And a good job . . ." She shook her head. "I mean . . ."

"You mean how can the monsters look just like us?"

She nodded. "Yeah, something like that."

He smiled grimly. "It's what my old partner, Danny Herbert, used to call *the parallel*."

"Parallel?"

"For parallel universe. In that universe a completely different set of rules is in effect. I've seen people killed for fifty cents. Or for a pair of shoes. I remember a mob boss who had a guy killed because he smiled at the wrong time while the boss was eating. Thought he was showing disrespect —"

"That's crazy."

"In this world. Not in theirs. They use their logic,

their rules to survive. They do what they do by following their instinct, and their instincts are completely different from ours."

"That's . . . weird."

"Isn't it. And when their world crosses into our world, suddenly everything seems askew, off balance, outside the realm of possibility. You . . . most of us are insulated from it and we come to believe it doesn't exist. We lead our everyday lives. Most cops live everyday lives and have good workaday jobs. Desk. Paper work. Traffic. Mortgage. Wife. Kids. The whole nine yards. Even in robbery and homicide you can stay average. Then the worlds cross and everything goes weird . . ."

"Like now."

He nodded. "Yeah, like now. You keep saying, 'This can't be happening to me. I'm a nice, average person. I've never broken the law, never stolen anything—"

"Well, I can't really say that anymore."

"No, not anymore. But your mind is still in the other mode . . . you're still trying to operate by the old rules, the old logic. The old certainty. And all of that is gone."

"You make it sound like science fiction."

He grinned widely. "I said that to Danny once, and he looked at me, and said, 'That's just it, life *is* science fiction.' "

The Paradise was a small place in a strip mall that had seen better days.

From the Bronco, Jessie read the hours on the door. "They open at eleven." She looked at her watch. "About an hour."

"Then let's do something else," Cobb suggested and pointed at his foot.

Jessie drove to a convenience store, where she found the yellow pages. Then they drove to a medical supply store and bought crutches. From there they went to a bank machine and both drew out their maximum.

When they pulled up in front of the Paradise again, an OPEN sign was in the window.

Cobb almost fell out of the Bronco, but when Jessie came around to help him, he glared at her.

"Sorry," she said, holding up her hands. "Impulse. Just impulse."

Inside it was dark and smelled like men — sweat and cigar smoke. There was a small area with a few tables to the left, but most of the room was taken up by the bar. A couple of men sat at tables, drinks and burgers in front of them. A big, barrel-chested man sat behind the bar, a beer in his hand. He looked like he'd just gotten out of bed.

"Two drafts," he said.

Jessie shook her head. "That's okay, I — "

Cobb glared at her again.

She nodded. "Right. Two drafts. Sounds great."

The bartender stood down from his stool, drew two drafts, and carried them to Cobb and Jessie. His eyes rested heavily on Jessie. She knew she wasn't welcome.

Cobb tasted the beer. "That'll get your motor running."

The bartender nodded. "Does mine."

"Guy asked me to meet him here," Cobb said. "Swann, Bob Swann. You know him?"

"Bob? Yeah." His eyes narrowed. "You're a cop, aren't you?"

Cobb nodded. "How'd you know?"

"As many cops come in here, I can tell. You a friend of his?"

Cobb shook his head. "Never met him, except on the phone. I'm from the Southside. Chatham. Talked to him yesterday and he told me to meet him here at eleven."

"Never known him to be up at eleven in his life."

"I'll bet that's it. Called a few minutes ago and got

97

his machine." He looked at his watch again. "Listen, we've got some errands to run. "I think I'll just go over to his place. What is it, a couple of blocks?"

"More like six or seven."

Cobb reached into his pocket and pulled out the phone number and read it off. "I thought the address was on this." He looked at Jessie. "You have the address?"

"I thought it was with the phone number."

Cobb looked at the piece of paper with the phone number again. "Goddammit . . ."

The bartender frowned. "It's that complex there on Highland. Six, seven blocks."

"Thanks." Cobb paid for the drinks, then pushed another five across the counter. "I'll buy you one."

They drove to the apartment complex and Jessie checked the mailboxes. "Number 6," she said and drove around back. Six was upstairs and the parking slot numbered 6 was empty. There was an alley between the buildings, and Jessie could see the bottoms of stairwells. "They have back doors."

Cobb frowned. "There are also a lot of cars in the lot." He shook his head. "Let's try it later. After dark."

Sixteen

They found another motel room, this time in Alexandria. They spread towels on one bed, then put the trash bag on it and went to work. Cobb and Jessie sat on opposite sides of the bed separating the contents into various piles. Telephone and utility bills on the dresser. Bank statements on the coffee table by the window. Credit card statements on the lamp by the window. The rest went on the other bed.

After three hours they were close to the bottom of the sack. Jessie picked up a piece of paper, shook off the coffee grounds, and frowned.

"On second thought," she sighed, "maybe it would be better to look for another sack."

Cobb smiled. "Are you trying to apologize, Marsh?"

"Let's just say I made a slight error in judgment." She looked at the paper. "A . . . phone bill . . . no, a . . . bill from an answering service."

Cobb looked up and took it from her. "Handy . . ." He turned to the telephone and took stationery and a pen from the drawer. He dialed the number on the bill.

A woman answered, and Cobb coughed and sniffed. "Jerry Monroe," he rasped. "Anything?"

"Sorry."

Cobb coughed again. "Cold," he said, clearing his throat. "Jerry Monroe. Any messages?"

There was a pause. "Two," she answered. One was from a garage telling him his car was ready and the other was from Misty saying she could take him at four o'clock today.

Cobb wrote them both down, hung up, and frowned.

"Well, we can see what was wrong with his car, or find out what Misty is going to do for him at four."

"Haircut?"

Cobb paused. "No, he seems more like the barbershop type, doesn't he?" Shrugging, he turned to the telephone and dialed the number.

A woman's voice answered breathily.

Cobb smiled. "Sorry, wrong number."

He hung up. "Misty is your friendly neighborhood hooker. Taht was her service. At least now we know where some of the money has gone."

"Certainly not on home improvement."

He paused, then picked up the phone book.

"What are you doing?"

"Looking up the motel next door . . ." Then he picked up the telephone, called the motel, booked a room, hung up, and called Misty's service back. "This is Jerry Monroe," he said. "I have an appointment with Misty at four. I need to change the meeting place." He gave her the motel and room number.

"Now we're meeting hookers?" Jessie asked after he hung up.

"They tell great tales."

They went back to the trash bag. When they had finished, Cobb leaned back in his chair and looked at each of the piles.

"What next?" Jessie asked.

Cobb sighed. "We start through everything and try and find some pattern in all of this. Dates, places, phone numbers."

They worked for an hour. Glancing at his watch, Cobb nodded. "Almost time for Misty."

They drove next door and Jessie paid for the room.

It was almost exactly like the one they'd just left.

Twenty minutes later there was a knock at the door.

"Just a minute," Cobb called, motioning Jessie into the bathroom.

Getting up on his crutch, he went to the door and opened it.

A pretty young woman stood there. A halter top accented her large breasts and a pair of blue jeans were almost molded to her legs and hips. Her hair was dark and teased, and her eyes were brown somewhere under the shadow and make-up. They were also surprised when they saw Cobb.

"Sorry," she said. "Wrong room."

Cobb shook his head. "No, right room. Misty?"

Doubt filled her gaze. "Yeah . . ."

"Jerry'll be here in a minute."

She paused. "Two is double."

He nodded. "Okay." He stepped back into the room. She followed him, and he closed the door behind her.

"You want to start now?" she asked, "or wait till Jerry gets here?"

"Neither," Cobb replied as he showed her his shield.

"Shit," she grumbled and slumped down in a chair as Jessie stepped out of the bathroom. Frowning, she shook her head. "I'm not carrying, there's no reason to search me."

"I don't want to search you," Cobb said.

She glared at him. "You don't?"

"No. I'm not arresting you. I just want to talk to you about Jerry."

"You're not arresting me?"

"No."

She looked from Cobb to Jessie, then back to Cobb again. "How much?"

"I don't want money, either. I just want to talk about Jerry."

She gained a little confidence. "Maybe you should pay *me* then."

101

"How much did Jerry pay you?"

"A hundred."

Cobb nodded. "All right."

She opened her purse, took out her cigarettes, and lit one. "Information is more."

Cobb leaned forward. "Don't push it, Misty. You do and I'll take you downtown and book you and you can spend the night in jail and pay. Okay?"

She sighed her bravado away. "Okay. What do you want to know?"

"Just about Jerry."

"We didn't do a lot of talking, you know."

"When he did talk, what was it about?"

She shrugged. "Mostly about his job, and how his ex-wife was screwing him. Only not so much about that any more. Lately he was talking about retiring, going to Mexico. He even asked me if I wanted to take a trip to Mexico with him."

"You say *lately*. How long is *lately?*"

She drew on the cigarette. "Year, year and a half. Like that. He started calling me more about a year and half ago. Taking me to dinner sometimes."

"How long have you been seeing him?"

"Couple of years."

"So a year and half ago, he started having more money to spend?"

"Yeah."

"Did he say where he got it?"

She smiled. "He was on the take."

"You're sure?"

"I'm sure. Before that he never had money. Gave it all to his wife for child support. Then all of a sudden he had a lot, spent a lot. And I can tell you, he really liked being the big man."

"What did he work?"

"Vice. Narcotics."

"Was he out of town a lot?"

"Yeah. A lot more in the past couple of years."

"Since he started making more money?"

"Yeah."

"Did he talk about what he did?"

Her eyes darkened. "No. It was usually the opposite. He talked less. Got real quiet, almost like he was working at not saying something. I remember one time we were having a drink with that partner of his and Jerry started saying something and all of a sudden Swann says, 'Shut the fuck up.' Just like that. Then, 'She could be wired.' Me. Wired. Anyway, Jerry shut up."

"Did he ever say where he'd been?"

"No. Like I said, he got more quiet. Funny."

"Funny?"

"Sometimes quiet. Sometimes jumpy. Sometimes mean. He was always mean when he was around Swann."

"Did you ever do Swann?"

"Shit, no. That guy is weird. I mean, really weird. He hates women. I saw one after he got through with her. Paid her, then beat the hell out of her." She shook her head. "I don't do that." She swallowed. "And I'll never have to. I'm getting out of the business in two years. I'm getting some modeling jobs, and I'll be out of this in two years . . ." She drew in a breath. "Older ones do it, you know. When they're not good-looking enough. Or some chicks just like it. Get off on it. Not me. I do blow jobs, and up the ass, but not that shit. No golden showers and no sado."

"Did you see it?"

"What?"

"What Swann did?"

"No. We were at a motel. I set it up and all. Jerry and me in one room, them in another. I just did Jerry's usual—blow job, then straight if he could get it up again. Anyway, I go next door for Cindy and she's on the bed crying. Not too many marks on her face, but her boobs and ass were like black and blue, you know. I helped her home, and she said he grabbed her boobs

103

real hard, I mean like a vise or somethin', then whacked her on the ass. Couldn't even get it up hard enough to get it in her. He got real mad then and whacked her around more, and she finally got him off with her hand and mouth. She thought he was never goin' to get a round off. But he paid her good. Real good. She said it was worth it."

"God . . ." Jessie whispered with disgust.

Misty smiled grimly. "That's nothin', honey. I can come up with weirder than that."

"No thanks."

"Was there ever anybody else? Anybody other than Swann?"

Her eyes darkened. "Yeah," she said, her voice tight with fear.

"Who?"

She shook her head. "They never said his name. He made sure they didn't say his name. Swann started to introduce him, and he looked at Swann and said something like 'Don't be stupid.' And Swann shut up real fast."

"But you remember him?"

"Oh, yeah, I remember him."

"Why?"

She swallowed, trembling. "Because he was . . ." she took a breath. "Well, Swann is like a sado, you know. He hates women, likes to hurt them. That's easy because you know what you're dealing with — "

"But this other guy was different?"

"Yeah. Scary."

"How?"

"It was me and this other girl. Dawn, I think. Anyway, we were there in a hotel suite. Nice one. There was booze and some sandwiches. Not hamburgers, fast food, but good stuff from a deli. So anyway, there we are drinking and everything, and I offer to get another girl for this other guy. And he just keeps eating, like I wasn't there. I asked him again, and he looked at me

104

real quiet and flat, like a snake would. Then he goes back to eating. Then a little later on, Swann gets a little drunk and starts getting rough with Dawn. Jerry laughs nervous-like, tells Swann to go to one of the bedrooms. But the other guy doesn't do anything. No reaction. It was like it wasn't happening—or it wasn't worth noticing. He just goes on eating. Later Jerry and me go into the other bedroom and he's still there eating and watching TV."

"But he didn't do anything to you."

"No."

"Then what frightened you?"

She trembled. "I guess it's kind of hard to explain. People react, you know. Especially to people getting slapped around. They either laugh and get off on it, or get pissed, or something. But it's something. I mean, Swann hit her, and she was crying, and this guy just goes on eating, like there's a wall around him. Like he's someplace else . . . like he's not human . . . that and the way he looked at me . . . I mean, I exist, you know. I'm not just a scrap of paper . . ."

"You only saw him once?"

"Yeah, thank God."

"What did he look like?"

She shrugged. "Average. I meet a lot of guys, you know. They all start to look alike. All I really remember is how he looked at me."

Cobb rubbed his smooth upper lip, where his mustache had been. "Did Jerry ever say anything," Cobb went on, "that might tell you where he had gone?"

Misty puffed her cigarette. "Not really. Listen, I wasn't really into getting this guy to talk to me. Time is money, you know?"

Cobb nodded. "Yeah."

"How about names?"

Misty drew on the cigarette and gave him a weary look. "You really think I'm going to remember names. Like I said—"

105

" — Time is money." Cobb reached into his pocket and took out his wallet. He counted out a hundred dollars.

Misty stuffed the money into her jeans. "Hey, anytime. And I mean anytime." She put out the cigarette and went to the door, then paused. "You're on Jerry, aren't you? What are you, Internal Affairs?"

"You don't want to know."

She nodded. "You're right, I don't."

After she left, Jessie drew in a deep breath. "And this guy Swann is the one that's after me."

"Yeah."

"And the other one?"

"Most likely."

"Another cop?"

"That'd be my guess . . . except cops don't run in threes. Usually a guy and his partner . . . partners are like . . . well, they say it's the next closest relationship to a marriage."

She took another breath, trying to quiet a sudden hammering in her chest. "That scares me, about Swann, what he likes to do to women . . . and the other one."

Cobb nodded. "It would scare anybody," he said. Then, using his crutch, he pulled himself up to his feet.

Jessie ran her fingers through her hair.

"You okay?" Cobb asked.

She tried to smile. "I'm just beginning to see what you mean by a parallel universe."

Seventeen

They went back to the neighboring motel and started going through papers again.

Jessie pushed them away. "I can't do this," she said. "I'm having a really strange reaction to Misty."

"What?"

"Hunger."

Cobb smiled. "Not so strange. I get that way sometimes—just glad to be alive, glad to be who I am. After seeing something so damned destructive, you want to do something life-affirming, like eating—"

"Stop being so goddamn intellectual and let's eat."

"Do you like Chinese food?"

"I'd kill for kung pao chicken, extra hot."

"Really? Extra hot?"

"You don't like hot food."

"I love hot food."

She nodded to his foot. "Can you . . ."

"For kung pao chicken, extra hot, I'll dance."

"I'd like to see that."

He struggled to his feet. "So would I."

They found a small Chinese restaurant a few blocks

away. The tables were plastic, the walls decorated with paper dragons, but the smells coming from the rear were the real thing. They ordered kung pao chicken, scallops in garlic sauce, fried rice, beef noodles, and Tsing Tao beer. The beer was cold, the food hot. Perfection. They ate, sipped beer, and halfway through ordered two more beers; for a while, what was outside the restaurant didn't exist.

The food finished, Jessie turned sideways in the booth and leaned against the wall; she picked up what was left of her beer and looked at Cobb.

"You never did tell me."

"Tell you what?"

"Whether you're a slob or a fanatic."

He frowned. "Why do you want to know?"

She shrugged. "Curiosity."

"Nosiness."

"Probably."

He sipped his beer. "In Philadelphia, a fanatic. In Clear Creek, a slob."

"You changed."

He nodded. "Yeah. I changed. I even have a cat now."

"A cat! Really?"

"Yeah."

"What kind?"

"A mutt. Found him alongside my road one day. White cat, part Siamese, part dumb-shit. All appetite."

"What's his name?"

"B.C."

"B.C. After the comic strip?"

"No. Bad Cat."

She smiled. "I like that."

"To tell you the truth I couldn't think of anything else."

"Aren't you worried about him? I mean, leaving him—"

Cobb shook his head. "He's an outside cat. Besides, he takes off without telling me where *he's* going."

108

She sipped the beer. "You don't like to talk about yourself."

"I'm talking about myself."

"No, you're talking about your cat. I think you brought the cat up to keep from talking about yourself."

"You should carry your psychology degree with you."

"I rest my case."

He frowned. "No. I don't like to talk about myself."

"Why?"

"If I tell you why, then I'll be talking about myself."

"Okay."

He sighed. "You're really nosey, you know that?"

"Yes."

"Okay."

A silence drifted between them. They both drank their beer.

"Habit," Cobb said.

"What?"

"Habit. Training. Whatever you want to call it. When you're on the streets, undercover, you don't tell anybody any more than they have to know. You don't volunteer things. One, you might slip and blow your cover. Two, you might tell them something they could use against you. The more you talk, the better your chances of dying."

"Is that why you quit?"

He shrugged. "I'm still not sure why I quit."

"But you kept the training."

"Yeah." He shrugged. "Spooks never change."

She blinked and stared at him for a moment. Then suddenly, he felt the mood change. The air seemed to chill.

Jessie finished the beer and put the bottle down.

"Time to go," she said, looking at the bill. "What's my half?"

Cobb grabbed the ticket. "I'll buy."

"No. I want to pay my half. I don't want you to buy."

"Why?"

"I just don't."

Looking at the amount, she reached into her purse and pulled out a few bills and dropped them on the table, then got up.

Watching her with amazement, Cobb shook his head. "Women," he sighed. He paid his half and limped outside. Jessie was already in the Bronco. Cobb got to the car and climbed in.

Without a word, Jessie started the Bronco and they pulled out into the quiet street.

Cobb looked at her.

"You want to tell me what's wrong?"

"I'm just . . ." she swallowed against the emotion rising in her throat. "This is the second time I've been disappointed in someone in a very short period of time."

"Disappointed?"

"Yes."

"How did I disappoint you?"

"There's no use going into it. People who use that kind of language, do . . . intelligent people . . . and . . ."

"Language? What kind of language?"

"Racial language."

"Racial language?"

"Slurs."

He stared at her, completely dumbfounded. "Racial slurs? When did I use racial slurs?"

"Back there."

"Back where?"

"In the restaurant."

"In the . . ." he shook his head. "What the hell did I say? What word did I use?"

"I . . . *spook* . . ."

He blinked, staring at her. Then he suddenly laughed.

She glared at him. "It's not funny."

"I'm sorry, I'm not laughing at you . . ." He shook

his head. "I wasn't using it that way. In law enforcement and espionage, *spook* is a slang expression for spies. Or people who work undercover. Or in surveillance. You know, tap phones or follow people . . . that kind of thing."

Her eyes came around. "You're kidding."

"No. There's nothing racial about it at all."

She stared at him for a moment, then paled slightly. "I . . . don't know what to say, I . . ."

"It's okay. I don't like people who use racial slurs either. I might have reacted the same way."

"No, really. I should have known you wouldn't . . ."

"It's okay. Crisis passed."

They drove into the parking lot of the motel and she parked in front of their room, then came around to help him out of the Bronco.

He stepped down and held on to her shoulder as they walked toward the room.

Then he paused and turned to her.

"You said that was the second time," he said.

"What?"

"That was the second time you were disappointed."

"Oh . . . yes."

"The second time somebody used the word *spook?*"

She nodded. "Yes."

"When was the first time?"

She thought about it for a moment. "The day I went to Rappahannock."

Eighteen

An hour later, Jessie and Cobb were on I-95 headed south.

In the motel room, they had packed hurriedly keeping the piles of bills and statements separate, they had put them in marked envelopes, washed off the trash bag, then dried it and placed the papers into it. Then they stored the bag in the back of the Bronco.

With evening coming on, Jessie pushed the car south and Washington, D.C. began to scatter back and away behind them.

"Okay," Cobb began. "You've had time to think about it. Anything else?"

She shrugged. "Not really. It just wasn't that important."

Cobb nodded. "Yeah, I know how you feel. It's like trying to remember what you bought in the grocery the day before. You made out a list, you needed the stuff, you bought it, you used part of it. But if you sit down and try to rewrite the list, you can only get about half of it."

"Exactly."

"Then tell it to me again."

"You mean go through it all again?"

"What else do you have to do?"

She sighed.

"I drove down to Rappahannock. I stopped at Port Royal and bought film. Looked around and didn't really see anything I wanted to paint so I drove on down 17 and through Rappahannock, then started going off onto the side roads, dirt roads over to the river. I had a flat and this man Early came and I —"

"Take more time," Cobb urged. "Give me more detail. Act like you're painting. Give me as much as you can."

She nodded. "The more I try to get at details, the more I'll remember."

"Right."

"Okay." She sighed. "I was on a dirt road, going through a patch of oak and pine, lots of sunlight and shadow, when I noticed that the steering was a little mushy. I got out and looked, and I had a flat. I opened the trunk to get the spare, and it was flat, too. I was really pissed at myself for not checking it, and I knew 1 was going to have to walk.

"It's mostly farming country down there, and I remembered going by a couple of houses, so I started walking back the way I'd come. It was a nice day, a light breeze, a little cool, and I was sort of enjoying it. I took my camera with me and was watching for pictures. I must have really been concentrating because I only noticed the pickup when it pulled in behind me.

"It startled me a little, and I jumped. The man behind the wheel smiled and said he was sorry and asked if I needed a ride. I was a little hesitant at first. I looked at the pickup and the boat he was pulling. The pickup was old and beat-up. It had started out being white, or something close to it. Now it was just mud and rust. So was the boat. Fishing equipment in it. Poles. Buckets. Nets. An old lawn chair with a couple of bands broken. That all looked pretty ratty, but the man was different."

"Describe him."

"Late fifties or early sixties. A bulky man. Heavy, but

not fat. He was wearing one of those fishing vests and a baseball cap. He was scruffy, but not dirty. Glasses. He had good eyes, smiling eyes. He must have sensed my hesitancy because he said something like, 'I saw your car back there and the flat, I can send somebody back if you'd rather.'

"I thought about it for a second, then said no, and got into the truck with him and he started driving."

"And you talked," Cobb interjected.

"Yes," she replied, sighing. "What about . . . what about . . ." She frowned. "It's funny, you know, how one thing can overshadow everything else."

"The *spook* remark — "

"Yeah, my brain just seemed to turn him off. Go cold. I was there but not there. Just wanting it to be over." She frowned. "All I can remember is that thing about spooks and feeling like a fool."

"Why?"

"Because I had liked him, and then he said that, and I knew I had been wrong about him." She sighed again. "Except that maybe I wasn't wrong about him."

"Kick yourself later. Try and remember what you talked about."

She shrugged. "I'm really not sure. The weather. Painting. Taking pictures."

"How did the comment about spooks come up?"

"We had talked a lot about me." She glanced at Cobb. "He was a little like you in that he kept the conversation on me. Away from him. When I asked about him, he just said he was retired, that he was going to work on becoming the perfect fisherman and home repair man. I guess I asked him again, because he said he had been in electronics, and I started asking him about stereos and things like that. That's when he laughed and said, 'You would have made a good spook.' " She shook her head. "And after that I kind of turned him off. Turned it all off. I really don't remember much else about the drive. He took me into Rappahannock — "

"You're going too fast. Slow down. He made the re- mark about spooks, then what?"

"We . . ." she said with a shrug, ". . . drove. Took a wrong turn and were lost for a bit. I think that's when he said something about having just moved down there. We saw a small farmhouse, back off the road, so we drove up and he got out and asked directions of a man and his son. Then we drove to 17 and he stopped again at a bait shop, actually a roadside stand, and bought blood worms."

"Did you go inside?"

"No."

"How long did he take?"

"A few minutes."

"How long were you at the farm?"

"Probably even less time. Mr. Early got out of the truck, asked directions, and got back in.

"And after the bait stand?"

"We drove into Rappahannock and he dropped me at a service station where he knew the man. He was also Triple A. I was worried about getting back to my car be- cause we'd gotten lost, but Mr. Early remembered the number of the road and the nearest intersection and was able to tell him where the car was. The station man went out with a tow truck, hauled it in, and fixed the flat."

"You didn't go with him?"

"No, he knew where Mr. Early was talking about, so I stayed in town."

"What did you do?"

"I walked down to the harbor, then went to a place called The Mainsail for a bite."

"Did you take any pictures at the farm or the bait stand?"

"No. There was really nothing to take a picture of. The farm had a nice barn, but nothing unusual. The bait stand was definitely not the stuff of great paint- ings."

"Did you see Early again?"

"No . . . oh, well, yes I did. At The Mainsail, but not to talk to him. He was sitting in the back with some other people and I made it a point to stay out of his line of sight. I took a booth and ate and left."

They drove for a while, then Cobb asked, "You're sure that's what he said, that you would have made a good spook?"

"Yes. Or something close to that."

"And he said it when you started asking questions about him, probing his past?"

She nodded. "Yes. I'm sure of that."

"That fits . . ."

"You're sure?"

"Yeah. Look at the context. Not about race, but about curiosity, investigating, nosing into other people's business. Oh, yeah, it fits. And the remark about electronics makes me think he was in intelligence or surveillance. Maybe CIA. Camp Peary isn't that far away."

"Camp Peary?"

"It's where they train CIA agents. Nicknamed 'The Farm.' It's a marine base, and the other is supposed to be secret, and it is to everybody except those who read spy novels." He rubbed his upper lip, then glanced down and realizing what he was doing, stopped.

"Do you think that's what happened, that I got in the middle of some kind of espionage thing?"

"I . . . don't know," he replied. "It doesn't sound like it. If he was working, he wouldn't have picked you up."

"Why? It was just a courtesy—"

Cobb shook his head. "Business. Nothing comes before business. And you might get in the way. Or get hurt. Or you could be a plant—"

"A plant?"

"Planted by the other side to stop him. Kill him. Compromise him."

"How?"

"The most common thing is to have sex with him.

116

Make sure pictures are taken. Threaten to show them to his family."

"Nice people."

"To paraphrase Mae West, 'Nice has nothing to do with it.' " He looked at her. "You're sure he didn't talk about himself? Being overseas, something like that?"

"I'm sure. I never knew what he did. Like I said, I thought he was in electronics." She frowned. "Is that enough to go to Rappahannock?"

Cobb nodded. "When it's the only good lead we've got, it is."

Nineteen

They stopped for gas just outside Fredericksburg, then took 17 south. Soon the four-lane was gone, and the build-up around it, and they were in open country. Deep woods, tulip poplars, farmhouses set back from the highway on long stretching roads, grain feeders, fields of Christmas trees and asparagus, and dairies. A quiet settled over them as they rode, and for the first time in a long time, Jessie began to relax. She enjoyed driving—it was what she did to think, sort things out.

As if he had read her mind, Cobb asked. "You like going, don't you? Driving."

She felt herself flush a little. "Yeah, I guess I do."

He nodded. "Me, too. It's what I do to mull things over. If I've got a problem sometimes I take a drive, think it through."

Her flush deepened. "That's weird."

"What?"

"That's exactly what I was thinking."

He smiled. "They'll probably find out that it has something to do with the shape of Broncos and the type of metal they use. It induces alpha waves and communication with the collective unconscious."

She glanced at him and laughed. "By God, Cobb, you really do surprise me sometimes."

118

"The depth of my knowledge?" he teased.

"No, the lengths you'll go to to keep from talking about yourself. Now we're into Jung and New Age philosophy. What next, flying saucers?"

"Well, I do happen to know a little about flying saucers . . ."

"Jeez," she sighed in surrender. "Okay. Let's talk about flying saucers."

He stared at her for a moment, then shrugged. "I think I like driving because my dad liked driving. Maybe it's genetic."

She looked at him warily. "You're surprising me again."

He smiled. "I know. Would you rather talk about flying saucers?"

"No. Tell me about your father and driving."

Cobb shrugged. "Maybe he liked to drive because he was a mechanic. Loved cars. Loved everything about them. He grew up on a farm near Clear Creek and started working on Model T's when he was a kid. That's when cars had about six moving parts, not counting the tires. And he loved to go. That's what I remember most about being a little kid, between five and ten, is the going. He owned his own garage, and for two weeks in the summer, we took off. It was like a ritual. We always had to get up at four o'clock. Breakfast was already cooking—bacon and eggs and biscuits and gravy, and coffee. We ate, then they piled my sister and me into the car. And the car always smelled like coffee because my dad had made a thermos of it, and he started out with that metal cup in his hand. And we drove. Well, he drove. Never my mom.

"And it was like a war. We had a schedule and we had to stick to it. There were no freeways then, so going through the mountains was slow. But we stayed on schedule. My sister and I had to regulate our bladders to the gas stops. All of us had two-hundred-mile tanks—the car, my sister, my mom, my dad, and I. There were no rest stops, and no stopping. Then there was gas roulette.

119

When we needed gas, we drove into the town, and Dad would start looking to see if there was a gas war. We never bought gas at the first station. Always had to go on through—"

"And if he missed it," Jessie said, "he would buy it at the last station, no matter what the price because he wouldn't turn around."

Cobb looked at her. "Right. Your dad, too?"

"Oh, yeah. He's still that way."

"Never turn around and never ask directions. We had family in California, and we went a couple of times. It was a real journey, almost five days in the car. For those trips we took a month. We drove Route 66 when there was a Route 66. We drove and drove so we could hit the California desert at night. Because of the heat. That's when most people did it, and it was like a communal event. If anybody had pulled over to the side of the road, we stopped and helped them. We got water in Needles. For the radiator, in these canvas canteens we carried on the front of the car. And in these air conditioners we put in our window. Then we bought a piece of dry ice and put it on the floorboard on the passenger side. It was hot in the Mojave, even at night. We pulled a rope on the air conditioner to soak a kind of roll in there, and if we pulled it hard enough and quick enough, the water would spray out on us. That cooled us off, at least for a while.

"It was wonderful out there. Like a moonscape. No vegetation. Nothing but moonlight and shapes. My mom slept, but my sister and I stayed up and kept my dad company. We told stories or sang. Then toward morning, Bobbie, my sister, and I would go to sleep and we would wake up in California."

Jessie nodded. "Sounds like my father. I was raised in Colorado, and we made a trip every summer. I remember maps. Daddy had a stack of them in his workshop and when we took a trip, he would get the appropriate maps to put into the glove compartment. When we went into the gas stations, and the man was filling the tank—this was before self-serve—Daddy and I would go into the station and look at the rows of maps. It was like . . ."

"Collecting," Cobb interjected.

"Yeah. Stamp collecting. We stood there looking up at all the different names of the states. And the pictures on them. The further we got from Colorado, the more the maps changed. I remember in Washington state, I found a map of British Columbia. We had just studied it in geography in school, so I knew that this was a map of another country. *Another country.* It was like finding a map of the moon."

"And maps of the Eastern United States and the Western United States—"

"No good," Jessie replied, laughing. "Well, not to Daddy. No back roads. No shortcuts. But I liked them because they put things into perspective. Until then I thought the Atlantic Ocean was just beyond St. Louis."

Cobb smiled. "That's all right, I had the impression the Pacific was on the other side of Denver until we went to California."

Jessie watched the night and the highway rush toward them.

"The world has gotten smaller, hasn't it?"

"Not if you count the parallel," he replied.

Ahead of them, the headlights pushed into the darkness.

Twenty

They drove into Rappahannock. Down the quiet main street, past the post office, the Dollar General Store, The Virginia Street Cafe, The Mainsail, then around the curve, down toward the harbor.

The service station was on the left. There were lights in the window as they pulled into the gas pumps.

Cobb turned toward the door and winced. Sighing, he looked to Jessie. "You do it," he conceded. "I'll wait."

She got out and walked into the office. It was empty.

"Back here," a voice called from the bays.

Jessie walked through the door. There were two bays and both had disemboweled cars in them. Their viscera lay strewn over the dirty floor and benches.

A man's head came from under a hood. He wasn't the man who'd been there last Wednesday.

"What can I do for you?"

"I was in last Wednesday," she began. "I had a flat—"

"Go flat again?"

"No. Where is the man who fixed it?"

"That's Dawes, the owner. He's not here now. Went home, won't be back till morning. What's the problem?"

"No problem really. A man gave me a ride in and Mr. Dawes towed my car in — "

"Yeah?"

"The man who gave me a ride was named Joe Early and I left my purse in his car. I was hoping to get his address from Mr. Dawes. Maybe you can give it to me."

"Early," he said, leaning against the car he was working on. "Don't think I know him."

"About sixty . . . retired . . . husky, wears glasses, drives an old white pickup truck. Kind of rusty and worse for wear . . ."

The mechanic nodded. "Yeah, I do know him. We work on that pickup all the time. I've picked it up a couple of times." He gave her directions and she hurried back out to the Bronco, then wound her way through the town's shady streets and modest houses. Early's house was on the outskirts, near the river. It was a small ranch-style with a neatly-trimmed yard. The old white Ford pickup was parked in the drive. The boat was beyond it. As they pulled up in front, Jessie looked worried.

"No lights on," she murmured.

He looked at his watch. "Nine-forty," he said. "He could be in bed."

"I'll try," she replied, and went to the door. She knocked several times, but got no answer. She walked back to the Bronco. "No answer."

"You sure this is the same guy?"

"It's the same truck."

Cobb sighed, then glanced up and down the street. There were lights on in a house across the way.

"Ask over there," Cobb suggested. "They might know something."

Jessie climbed out of the Bronco and hurried across the street through the cool night. She almost tripped over a concrete lawn sheep in the front yard.

She walked up on the porch and could hear a TV inside. She knocked once, then again; then the door opened and a tall woman in her late fifties peered out. "Yes?"

Jessie smiled. "I'm sorry to bother you, but I'm looking for your neighbor across the street. Joe Early."

The woman's blue eyes shadowed. "Mr. Early—?"

"Yes."

"Are you a friend or family?"

"No. We just met a few days ago, and I stopped by to say hello."

The darkness in the woman's eyes deepened. "Well . . ." She was hesitant.

"Is something wrong?"

"Well, I hate to be the one to tell you—"

"Tell me?"

"Mr. Early's dead," she said. "He was killed in a fall Saturday morning."

Ten minutes later, Jessie and Cobb sat in the woman's living room. It was a clean house; the furniture was worn, but well kept. On the walls were prints of flowers and pictures of the Pope and Jesus. A rerun of *Cheers* was on, but the woman, Mrs. Scott, turned it off as Jessie sat on the sofa and Cobb lowered himself into a chair.

"I'm so sorry," Mrs. Scott said. She was attractive, her gray hair cut short around a long face. She wore an old, but clean and well-ironed house dress. "But I don't know what I can tell you."

"You said he was killed in a fall," Cobb prompted. "What kind of fall?"

"Kind of a freak accident, I guess. At least that's what the policeman said."

"What happened?" Jessie asked.

Her voice tightened. "He . . . fell off his boat and broke his neck. Like I said, kind of a freak accident. The policeman said he must have hit just right. They,

124

well, they said it looked like he tripped over his fishing box because it was overturned, and gone over the side, and . . . hit, you know, just right . . ." Her eyes glistened and she took a tissue from a box on the lamp table beside her. "I found him, you know . . . it was almost noon, and I noticed that his boat was still there, and I thought that was kind of funny; he always went fishing early in the morning. Then I was out in my flower bed and I . . ." her voice broke. "He was just lying there. At first I thought he was doing something under the trailer—then I saw that he was lying there kind of funny, his head twisted. I walked across the street real slow, I mean, I couldn't believe it. Then I saw his eyes . . ." She wiped her eyes. "It was awful. It was the worst thing I've ever seen . . ."

Cobb looked at Jessie, his eyes skeptical, then to Mrs. Scott.

"Did you know him well?"

She blushed slightly. "Well, fairly well, I suppose. I'm a widow and Mr. Early wasn't married. We went to dinner a few times, and I cooked for him a few times . . ." Loneliness edged her voice. ". . . You might say we were just getting to know each other. Nothing serious, you understand, just friendship, just . . ." She swallowed. "Getting to know each other."

"How long had he lived here?" Cobb asked.

Mrs. Scott paused. "A little over six months."

"He retired here?"

"Yes."

"Where from?"

"Virginia Beach."

"What did he do there?"

Mrs. Scott smiled for the first time. "Now that's funny, you know."

"Funny?"

"Yes, well, Mr. Early, Joe, was a kind of quiet man. Friendly, but quiet. He didn't talk about himself very

125

much. Not that he didn't talk, but he talked about other things. Fishing, shows on TV, movies. That kind of thing. And when he first came here, I asked him that, too, and he told me electronics. Then one night we were out to dinner and Mr. Early had had a few scotch and waters and he said something about a case he'd worked on. And I said something like, 'A case? You mean an electronic case?' And he laughed and said, 'Well, no.' Then he told me he hadn't been completely honest with me. He said he had been a policeman. I asked him why he was hiding it, and he said he wasn't hiding it exactly, but he didn't like to talk about it. When people knew you were a cop, he said, they liked you to talk about being a cop and he didn't want to do that anymore. He didn't want to tell cop stories because it brought it all back. And that was all he ever said about it."

"He never talked about it again?"

"No . . ." She pressed her lips together thoughtfully, "And you know . . . I had a feeling that something bad had happened back there. Something that made him want to forget about being a policeman."

"When he mentioned the case, did he say what it was about? What kind of case it was?"

Mrs. Scott thought for a moment, then frowned and shook her head. "No. I don't remember how it came up. Like I said, he'd had a couple of drinks, two out of his three. He always had just three drinks, and he was talking, and it just sort of came out, I think."

"Did he buy his house, or was he renting?" Cobb asked.

"He bought it."

"Did he have many visitors?"

She shook her head. "No. Not many. His sister once. A friend from Virginia Beach once."

"Man or woman?"

"A man. A nice man. I met him."

"Was he a policeman, too?"

"He didn't say, and Joe didn't either. He came up one day and Joe introduced us, then they went fishing. I only met him that one time."

"Do you remember his name?"

She grimaced. "No, I'm sorry, I don't. I'm not very good at names."

"Anybody else?"

She nodded slowly. "A couple of other men. I didn't meet them. I saw them when they went fishing with Joe."

"Did you ever go fishing with him?"

She laughed. "No." She looked a little ashamed. "I hate to say this, but I can't stand fish. Living this close to the water and all, you'd think I'd love seafood, but I can't stand it. Give me a nice bloody steak any day."

"Since Early moved here, did he stay here most of the time, or was he gone a lot?"

"Well . . ." Mrs. Scott started to answer, then suspicion tinged her eyes. "You're police, aren't you?"

Cobb smiled. "Yes, ma'am, we are." He reached into his corduroy coat and pulled out his badge. "Sorry, I should have told you right off."

"Is there something wrong? About Joe's death, I mean . . ."

"No, ma'am. Not really. I hope you'll understand, but I can't discuss it with you."

"Of course, police rules and all that."

"Something like that," Cobb said, slipping his badge back into his coat. "I'd like to ask you a few more questions."

"All right."

"What were his days like? What did he do?"

She shrugged. "Well, he fished. And watched sports on TV. He loved baseball. I've never understood that. It's so slow. Like watching paint dry—"

"What else?"

She sighed and paused. "Well, he liked to go have a drink in the evenings. Down at The Mainsail."

"The Mainsail?"

"It's a restaurant and bar on Virginia, the main street when you come in."

"Has anyone come for Joe's things. I mean to take care of the house?"

"No."

"Do you know his sister's name?"

She frowned. "No. He only mentioned her a few times. She lived in Virginia Beach, too."

Cobb leaned forward and rubbed his chin. "I'm going to ask you a favor, Mrs. Scott—"

"All right."

"I'd like to look through Joe's house. You can come along if you want, to make sure we don't take anything. Do you know if he kept an extra key around? Maybe on the back porch, or—"

"Under a flower pot on the back porch," she offered. "And I don't need to come with you," she added. "You're a policeman. I'm sure it's all right. Besides, it's funny. You remind me a little of Joe."

Twenty-one

Jessie found the key under the flower pot on the back porch. There were other flower pots on the porch, all arranged carefully.

As they turned to the door, she whispered, "A freak accident?"

Cobb nodded. "A little too convenient, isn't it?"

"But she said he *was* retired."

"No, he *told* her he was retired."

Jessie unlocked the door and she stepped into a kitchen. Cobb hobbled in after her. She turned on the lights.

"What are we looking for?" she asked.

He shook his head. "We won't know until we find it."

"Gosh, that's helpful," she said wryly.

There were dishes in the sink, but they were filled with water and arranged. Bowls in bowls. Plates on plates. Silverware in one of the bowls. The counters were clear.

Jessie went into the next room and turned on the light.

A living room. Again, neat. There was a sofa against the wall, an easy chair, and a huge recliner with a coffee table and reading lamp next to it. Newspapers were stacked neatly on the coffee table. Books lay next to them, again stacked carefully. Early was a very neat man, Jessie determined. The only thing out of place was a newspaper beside the chair on the floor. Even it had been folded. Against the other wall was a console television and a VCR. The tapes were arranged neatly in small wooden crates. Next to the TV was an expensive stereo set-up. Amplifier, cassette player, turntable, and CD player on shelves holding records, tapes, and CDs. Jazz, big band. Ellington. Glenn Miller. Benny Goodman. Miles Davis. Gerry Mulligan. The books on the table were mysteries and thrillers. Thomas Harris. James Lee Burke. Carolyn Hart. Patricia Cornwell.

She walked on through the living room and into a short hallway. Bathroom. Bedroom. Probably a guest room. There was only a bed and a dresser. Another bedroom, this one larger. The master bedroom. There was another TV, a clock, and a chair. The next room had a desk and chair, cardboard filing cases stacked next to it.

"Here's something," she said.

As Cobb made his way down the hallway, Jessie crossed to the desk. Papers were sorted across the back in a plastic organizer. Phone bill. Utilities. Letters. Checkbook.

Cobb sat down at the desk and began going through the drawers. More bills, all arranged.

Leaning over, he opened the cardboard files. Tax returns.

The bottom one was house papers, repair bills, credit card bills.

He rubbed his lip and picked up the letters in the arranger. He gave half of them to Jessie. She frowned. "Now I'm violating somebody's privacy."

"Joe has no privacy left," he said grimly and opened one of the letters.

Jessie sat on the edge of the desk and began going through her stack.

The first was really just a sparse note from some-body named Mac. He was coming to go fishing on the 25th. If Joe provided the fish, he would provide the Bud. There was no return address.

The next letter was from a woman who signed the letter "Ellie." She hoped he was enjoying retirement. It was hard to believe that he was old enough to retire, even harder to believe that she was getting close to that age. Megan and the kids were coming to stay for a week. She wished she felt more like a grandmother instead of just a baby-sitter when she came.

"I think this is the sister," Jessie remarked. "Sounds like family."

She looked at the envelope. The address was Virginia Beach.

Cobb nodded. "Somebody named Ellie?"

"Yeah."

"I have one, too."

She went to the next letter. It was from Ellie. It was brief, containing more family news.

"Well, hell," Cobb sighed and put the letters down.

"What?"

"He *was* retired. This is a letter from the retirement fund. Gives him the balance of his account, shows payouts he's already taken and what he has coming."

"That's not good, is it?"

"Well, it means that whatever he was doing that day, it wasn't official. Unless he was working in the private sector."

Jessie pointed to the desk. "Anything else?"

"A letter from his sister, and one from a friend in Montana saying that the fishing is great and he should come up."

Cobb found a sheet of paper, made notes of the names and addresses they had found, then sat back in the chair rubbing his upper lip. He looked down and shook his head. "Dammit," he whispered.

"You miss it?"

He laughed. "Can't you tell? Jesus, I feel naked. I've had that mustache for twenty-five years."

Jessie looked at the papers on the desk. "So how are we doing?"

"Not great. But not bad either. How about a drink?"

"A drink?"

"Yeah. At The Mainsail."

She paused, then nodded. "Where Joe drank."

"You're catching on."

Jessie helped Cobb back through the house and drove to The Mainsail.

It was in an old building with high ceilings. A long oak bar ran the length of one side of the room, and the wall panels were dark-hued. It was about half full and the air was thick with the smells of frying fish and onions. Jessie left Cobb at a table near the door, then walked to the bar. The bartender was a tall, handsome man in his early twenties. Blond and tanned, well-muscled. Jessie leaned against the bar and as he came toward her a smile started on his lips and she felt an uh-oh coming.

"Hi," he said and leaned on the bar so she could see the muscles in his arms. He glanced at her face, then his eyes floated down to her breasts.

"Hi."

His eyes flickered from her breasts to her eyes and back.

"What'll it be?"

"I'm looking for someone."

The grin widened at such a great straight line. "You found him."

She ignored it. "Did you know Joe Early?"

"Joe Early?"

"He was new in town. In his late fifties or early sixties. From Virginia Beach. Fished a lot. Probably drank Bud or scotch and water."

He frowned and shook his head. "Sorry, I don't remember guys. And especially not old guys." He pointed to a man at the end of the bar. "That's Eddie. He knows everybody."

Eddie looked up as she approached. A small man in his sixties, dressed in work clothes. "Eddie?"

He smiled. "Yes, ma'am?"

"I was told you might know Joe Early."

He rubbed his chin. "Joe Early. Joe Early . . ."

"He had just moved here. He was about your age, from Virginia Beach . . ."

His eyes flickered. "Oh, yeah. The fella that was killed fallin' out of his boat."

"Yes. Did you know him?"

He shook his head. "No. Can't say I did. Had a drink with him one time. Tell you who did, though. Brian Tuck." His eyes roamed over the room. "Was in earlier. Guess he went on home."

"Brian Tuck?"

He nodded. "That's right."

"What does he do?"

"Real estate. Office is just right there across the street."

As they sipped their beers at the table, Jessie filled Cobb in on what she had learned. He glanced at his watch and frowned. "After ten. A little late to call. I guess we might as well—"

"Eat," Jessie said.

"Eat? Are you hungry?"

"A little, but that doesn't matter. We're talking soft-shell crabs here. Sport eating."

"Soft-shell crabs?"

"You've never eaten soft-shell crabs?"

"No."

"How can you claim to be from Virginia?"

"I don't like the beach."

She blinked, nonplused. "How the hell can you not like the beach?"

"I don't."

"That's un-American."

133

He shrugged. "I never could see the point of getting a chair and sitting in the sun and getting burned."

"But you fish. I know you must fish."

"Why?"

"Because you hunt."

"And one naturally follows the other?"

"Well, yes . . ."

He shook his head. "Wrong."

She stared at him for a moment and sighed. "You never cease to amaze me."

"Good."

"We're having soft-shell crabs."

He frowned. "Soft-shell . . ."

"Yes. They take them when they're molting, when the shell is soft. Take their undersides off, sex organs I think —"

He winced. "Tear off their sex organs?"

"Yes."

"Is this a Women's Lib recipe?"

She ignored that. "Then peel back the soft shell and take off the gills, sometimes called dead men's fingers —"

"Why?"

"I have no idea. Then scrape off little green and yellow bits of fat —"

He grimaced. "Green and yellow?"

"Yes, dammit. I can't believe this from the man who eats fermented cabbage."

"That's a delicacy."

"Sure. Anyway, after all that you roll them in flour and garlic powder then drop them in hot grease and cook them."

"Okay. That part sounds good."

"Then put Tabasco on them."

"And that part sounds good."

"You're having soft-shell crabs," she said. "No more arguments. You'll love them."

They ordered the crabs and two more beers. The

crabs came and Jessie watched Cobb as he took the first bite. He smiled. "Tomorrow you eat kim-chee."

"You don't like them."

"No. I love them. Just like you're going to love kim-chee."

Twenty-two

They found a motel on the edge of town, overlooking the river, and checked in. It was small, with two beds, a bathroom, and a kitchenette to one side. A second door opened onto a porch. Beyond it, the water glistened in the night.

Jessie sat down on one of the beds and looked up at Cobb.

"I was just wondering—"

"What?"

"Why didn't you tell Mrs. Scott? She cared for Early. She has a right to know."

He half-fell on his bed and shook his head. "Maybe, but for one thing, we don't really know yet. And the second and most important reason is, I want to keep this contained. I don't want people calling the police in a few days wondering how the investigation is going. We want to make as few waves as possible."

She nodded. "I see what you mean," then ran her fingers through her hair. "Hot water," she said. "I'm going to bathe." She looked down at herself. "Clothes," she added, "tomorrow, we get fresh clothes."

"Agreed."

She bathed and slipped her shirt back on, then opened the door. The light was on and Cobb was asleep on top of the covers.

She walked out, switched the light off, covered Cobb with a blanket, then crawled into her own bed.

The next morning they ate breakfast at a small diner; then at half-past eight, Jessie called Brian Tuck's office number. No answer. She tried the home number.

A woman answered and Jessie asked for Tuck.

"Well . . ." The woman hesitated. "He's busy right now."

"I hate to interrupt him," Jessie replied. "When will he be in his office?"

The woman laughed. "He won't mind being interrupted at all," she explained. "He's trimming the hedges. I'll get him."

"It might be better if I spoke to him in person," Jessie countered. "Would it be all right if we came to the house?"

"He'd love it," Mrs. Tuck said and supplied directions.

The house was an old Cape Cod farmhouse set off the road.

As Jessie drove up the dirt road, she could see a tall man in his sixties dressed in shorts, a baseball cap, and an old sweatshirt. He stood next to a long hedge, an electric trimmer in his hand.

He let go of the trigger, and set it down on the grass as Jessie parked the Bronco.

He tipped the baseball cap back on his head and eyed Cobb's foot as he made his way across the driveway on the crutch.

"You bust it?"

"Cut it." He tugged his badge out of his jacket and showed it to Tuck. "My name is Davis," he said, "and this is Lynn Monroe."

Jessie glanced at him, surprised, and hoped she could remember her name.

"—We'd like to talk to you about Joe Early," Cobb went on. "If you have a few minutes."

Tuck grinned. "Are you kidding? I've got all the time you want." He glanced at the hedge and shook his head.

"Boxwood." He sighed. "Jesus, I hate boxwood." He turned back toward the house and gestured toward the lawn. "And grass. What the hell does modern man find so threatening about grass, that we have to cut it?"

"His neighbors," Cobb retorted.

Tuck laughed. "Most likely." They walked to a set of lawn chairs and a table under a tulip poplar. "Marge is bringing some coffee, if you'd like some," he said as they sat down. "You're asking about Joe's accident."

"That's right."

He took his cap off and ran his fingers through his sweat-heavy salt and pepper hair.

"So it might not have been an accident."

"No, actually this has to do with another case that Joe was involved in that we're trying to clear up. Did he ever mention a woman named Jessie Marsh?"

Jessie glanced at him.

"—Did he ever talk about her? Or any of his old cases?"

Tuck rubbed his chin. "Old cases? No. He was so damned careful; no, controlled is the word. Controlled."

"How so?" Jessie asked.

A woman approached from the house. She was heavy set, but had a pretty face. She carried a tray of cups, a carafe, sugar, and cream to the table. Tuck introduced his wife, Marge, then she went back inside. Coffee was poured and Tuck sipped his coffee. "How so," he mulled. "How so . . . well, like his drinking. It was always either three or five—"

"Three or five?"

"Three scotch and waters or five Buds. Never more. Sometimes less. And when we talked, he guided the conversation, kept it on track."

"Away from his past," Cobb supplied.

"That's right. Or at least he limited it. He was here for over three months before I found out he'd been a cop. One time I asked him what it was like being a cop. He just shook his head and said, 'That's the past, Brian. I'd really rather leave it that way.' He wasn't trying to hide it, just didn't want to talk about it. Funny part of it is, he did talk about it, though, but in bits and pieces." He smiled. "If you'd like some two-bit psychology, I think there was something back there he'd just as soon forget, something that . . ." He shrugged. "I don't know, the only word I can think of is *haunt*. Something kind of haunted him. We'd be drinking and I'd be telling some fishing lie, and I'd look over at Joe and he'd be staring off into space. Now there's a lot of things I am, but one of 'em ain't a dull storyteller. I can't be—I'm a salesman. I get dull, and I start losing some serious weight. Hell, I might have to do yardwork for a living."

"Did he ever say what the case was?"

Tuck shook his head. "No. Just one time we were talking about serial killers, and Joe was at the far end of his three scotch and waters and said something about serial killers getting all the press. That there were other crazies out there. People who look sane but do unspeakable things. Things you could never understand. Those are the ones that make you wonder whether man as an experiment isn't an absolute failure. His words, not mine."

"But no specific reference."

"No. But he was thinking about something specific. The way he said it, you could tell he was seeing it again when he talked about it."

"Did he ever say what he did on the force?"

"No. Just those oblique references."

"Just before he was killed, did he seem troubled? Did he get any bad news, visitors, anything?"

Tuck thought about it and sipped his coffee. "No. Well . . . yeah, maybe he was a little preoccupied, but it was hard to tell with Joe. He was always a little distant."

"But he didn't talk about it?"

He shook his head. "No."

"Did he mention a week ago Wednesday?" Jessie asked.

"No."

"And you're sure he never mentioned a Jessie Marsh?"

He shook his head. "I don't think so . . ."

"She's a painter. He picked her up on a back road—"

"Oh, yeah. The woman with a flat. Yeah, he did mention her. Joe said she was a real looker. Made him wish he was twenty or even ten years younger."

Jessie blushed. "Did he say anything else about her?"

"Not much. Just how good-looking she was, and she was interesting, but a little distant. You know, cold. I don't think he told me her name, though."

"Did anything else happen that day that he talked about?"

"Wednesday . . . Wednesday." He shook his head. "No. I wouldn't even have remembered about that woman if you hadn't brought it up. No. We probably just talked about fishing."

"How about Thursday?"

Tuck frowned. "Sorry . . ."

"But you said he seemed more distant, a little distracted. More than usual."

"Yeah, but . . ." He shrugged. "Nothing I can put my finger on."

"You had a drink with him Wednesday evening?"

"Yeah."

"What did he talk about?"

"The woman he'd picked up . . . fishing . . ." He frowned. "Sorry, it all kind of runs together."

"Did he seem preoccupied that night?"

"No. That was Thursday or Friday. No, he didn't come in Friday night. It had to have been Thursday."

"But you don't remember what you talked about?"

Tuck frowned. "No. Wish I could."

They finished their coffee, then thanked Tuck and left him back at the hedge with the trimmer in his hand.

As they pulled back on the highway, Jessie said, "I'd like to know what he was preoccupied about."

Cobb nodded. "So would I."

"How about Mrs. Scott?"

"Good idea."

They drove back through Rappahannock to Mrs. Scott's house. Her driveway was empty.

Cobb shook his head. "Well, maybe we can . . ."

"Clothes," Jessie said.

"What?"

"Clothes," she repeated. "Remember—"

"Oh," he nodded. "Yeah—"

They found an outfitting store along the boat docks on the river. Jessie bought two desert shirts, a pair of jeans and another pair of shorts, and panties. No bras.

She changed in the store. The new clothes felt wonderful—crisp and new-smelling. She wrapped her old clothes separately; after paying, she walked out to the Bronco.

Cobb was leaning against the fender, looking out over the river. There were sacks on the hood, but he seemed to be wearing exactly the same clothes.

"You going to change later?"

"I did change." He looked down at his clothes. He was wearing a blue shirt, jeans, and his corduroy coat. Looking closer, she saw that the shirt and the jeans were new.

"You bought clothes exactly like the ones you were wearing?"

"Why not?"

"Variety."

He frowned. "Variety is in the mind. Besides, I like blue."

They got in the Bronco.

"Something else Tuck said," Jessie brought up as she started the car.

"What?"

"The case that haunted him."

Cobb shrugged. "There's always one like that. One if you're lucky."

Jessie drove to the street. "Mrs. Scott's?"

He nodded. "Mrs. Scott's."

This time she was there. She invited them into the living room.

"Something to drink?" she asked as they sat down. "Tea or coffee?"

"No," Jessie replied.

"Thanks, Mrs. Scott." Cobb smiled. "But we'll only take up a few minutes of your time."

"It's no trouble."

"No, thanks. We talked to Brian Tuck and he told us that Joe seemed to be preoccupied just before his death. Do you remember that?"

She touched her chin with her finger. "Preoccupied . . . well, yes, now that you mention it, he did seem to have something on his mind. As a matter of fact, he didn't go fishing on Thursday. He stayed around his house. We had coffee Friday morning, and he just sat there staring. I asked him where he was and he blinked and looked at me and kind of smiled, and said he was sorry. Then a few minutes later, I asked him if he wanted more coffee and he was just staring again. And apologized again."

"And that was all he said?" Jessie asked.

"Yes. Later on he went out for a drive."

"A drive, not fishing."

"No. He left the boat in the drive."

"What time did he leave?"

She shrugged. "About two, I guess. I came out in the yard to do some work and his truck was gone."

"What time did he get back?"

She shook her head. "I don't know. I don't think he was back when I went to bed and that was ten."

"So you didn't talk to him when he got back."

"No. That time he had coffee with me was the last time I saw him. He was killed the next morning."

142

Twenty-three

They got into the Bronco, and Cobb sighed. "Tuck said Joe didn't come into The Mainsail Friday night —"

Jessie nodded. "Right."

"And Mrs. Scott said he wasn't back at ten when she went to bed. Ten, say eleven o'clock. Nine hours." He shook his head. "Hell, he could have gone anywhere in nine hours. If it's even connected. Maybe he was really just preoccupied. And maybe he *did* just take a drive." He sighed wearily. "There's no center to this whole thing, nothing to anchor onto. Nothing solid. All we've got are feelings, moods. Nothing specific. I'm fairly certain Joe wasn't working on anything, that he really was retired. That most likely means something from the past."

"The case that haunted him?"

He nodded. "Maybe. Let's drive back to Joe's. We need to know about his old cases. Maybe he files them at his house."

They drove back to Early's and searched again and found nothing. Jessie helped Cobb back to the Bronco and they sat there for a moment.

"I think something happened," Jessie said, "maybe something I said to him. Or something he saw along the way when we were driving."

He looked at her. "Did his mood change anywhere along the drive?"

She frowned and shook her head. "No. I mean, I don't know. Like I said, after he made the remark . . ."

"You turned off."

"Yeah. But I don't think so. He just kept talking. After what Tuck said, I think maybe he was coming on to me a little bit. But no, I don't think his mood changed. If there was anything, it began to nag him later."

"Or it happened after he dropped you off."

"Maybe." She started the Bronco and pulled onto the road.

"Where are we going?"

"I'm going to drive the route we took again." She frowned. "Maybe it'll remind me of something."

She drove back to the station where Early had let her off and went inside. Dawes, the man who had gone after her car, gave her the route back to the place she'd had the flat.

On the road again, she said, "The bait stand was only a few miles back, off the side of the road."

She rounded a curve and saw the stand on the shoulder under a giant oak tree.

"There," she said and angled the Bronco off the road. She parked in front of the small, shed-like building and helped Cobb from the car. The inside was made up of homemade cases with ice in them. Somewhere, Jessie could hear water running.

A skinny man in his late forties looked up from a lawn chair. He wore a pair of loose overalls with no shirt underneath. His hair was long and tied in a ponytail and his face was covered with a long, untended beard that looked like wild ivy. He wore an old Yankee baseball cap with a scratched "Flower Power" button on it.

He nodded at her. "Yes, ma'am, goin' fishin'?"

"I just need to ask you a few questions."

"Directions?"

144

"About one of your customers. A man named Joe Early."

His eyes narrowed. "Joe who?"

"Early."

He shook his head. "Sorry, I don't think I know him."

"He was in his late fifties, early sixties. Heavy set. He recently retired and moved here from Virginia Beach."

He grinned. "Escaping the megalopolis, huh?"

"Something like that, I guess. We dropped by here a week ago Wednesday."

He shook his head slowly. "Sorry, I kind of lose track of the days, if you know what I mean. Only time I get a break is when I can get my kid to spell me." He frowned. "And that isn't often. Kids today, you know."

"Yeah. Well, thank you."

"Why are you looking for this guy?"

"It's a family matter," Jessie replied as she left.

On the road again, Jessie sighed. "No hotbed of activity back there. One old hippie who thinks the kids of today are going to hell."

Cobb grinned. "I'll bet his old man said the same thing. What goes around comes around."

Jessie drove until she found the county road going off toward the river. She turned down it, then drove slowly. The road led to a gently shifting landscape of hills, deep woods of oaks and pine, swamps, pastures, and fields. Jessie missed several turns and doubled back on herself. "It would have been toward the river," she said, "because that's how we knew we were lost."

Coming out of a stand of woods, she smiled. "There it is!" She pointed to an old two-story frame house standing well back from the road in a field. It was surrounded by poplar and oak with a huge barn and outbuildings.

"I remember the barn. It's got wonderful lines."

She stopped at the drive, and Cobb read the mailbox.

"Atherton," he said, as she turned up the drive. A

145

pickup stood at the back porch. The yard was well-kept, but not neat. A tire stood against a tree, shovels and rakes leaned against a tractor.

Jessie parked. "Doesn't look like anybody's here."

Cobb looked at his watch. "It's . . . one-thirty. Lunch hour is gone. Most likely working."

She opened the door and stepped out into a chilly wind brushing across the fields of hay.

She glanced around, then walked up on the porch. There were two lawn chairs and a wooden table between them. She crossed the porch and opened the screen door, squinting through the glass into a large kitchen. She knocked, then knocked again. No answer. Using her hand to create a shadow, she looked into the kitchen again. Table. Chairs. Stove. Refrigerator. A package of meat on the sink.

She turned and walked around the porch, looking at Cobb and shaking her head. She knocked again at the front door. Still no answer.

In the Bronco again, she sighed. "You're probably right. They're most likely at work. Looks like they came home for lunch and put some meat out for dinner. So six or so. Sundown."

"Yeah." Cobb glanced around. "Anything jog your memory?"

Her eyes roamed over the yard. House. Barn. Tractor. Truck. She frowned. "Not really. Looks like a farm to me."

"How about on the way here?"

She shook her head.

"And the bait stand?"

"It looked the same to me."

Cobb nodded. "Where did you have the flat?"

She thought for a moment, then pointed toward the river. "Back over that way."

"Let's take a look," he said cheerily, "and see if we can sustain this level of excitement."

Twenty-four

She turned the Bronco back to the road.

"You come over here a lot, don't you?"

She nodded. "Yeah. I like the landscape."

"Why?"

"It's gentle. Quiet. Good lines. Variety. And not far from the ocean. Well, the Chesapeake."

"You like the water?"

"I like the vastness. The motion. It's always changing."

"But you live in the mountains."

She smiled. "Seems a little contradictory, doesn't it—"

"That doesn't surprise me about you."

She glanced at him, then went on. "I like the mountains, too. Another kind of space. An incredible negative space—"

"Negative space?"

"What's there because of the valleys or mountains, what's in between."

"Why not Colorado?"

She shrugged. "I don't know. I guess I've become attached to this. I've spent most of my adult life here, and it would be hard to leave. I met Bill at Charlottesville in school, and we just stayed."

"How long were you married?"

"Nine years."

"Long time."

"Longer than you think."

"How long before you knew—"

"Knew?"

"Knew it wasn't going to work."

She shrugged. "I don't know. A year or so. After the glow wore off." She smiled. "Funny . . ." She glanced at him. "You ever notice how people say *funny,* when they don't really mean *funny?*"

"Oh, yeah."

"Funny. It was all there from the first time I met him, but I saw it differently at first."

"How so?"

"The things that attracted me to him were his looks and his ambition. That drive. And in the end those were the things that I hated about him."

"You hated his looks?"

She grinned. "No, I hated the fact that it was so easy for him to play around."

"He cheated on you?"

"Again, *cheated* is one of those funny words. Cheated. No. Because I don't think it had anything to do with me. Bill likes the game. I think that's what the whole money-making thing is about. For him it's about power."

A slow smile pushed through Cobb's lips. "Oh, it's about power all right," he said, "but saying that it had nothing to do with you . . ."

She looked at him, then sighed, "You're right. It did have to do with me. I let him get away with it because I wanted it safe. Secure. And I didn't want to fail."

"Who does?"

"Nobody, I guess. It was only when it started to affect my work, what was at the center of me, that I knew I couldn't do it any more."

"You could have done it. But when it came down to

it, you had the guts to let it go. To save yourself." He looked out the window. "I wish I had."

Her eyes came around, settling on him, and she felt the vulnerability again. "You, too, huh?"

"Yeah, me, too."

"How long were you married?"

"Eight years."

"And she cheated on you?"

He shook his head. "No. And I didn't cheat on her. I wish it had been that simple." He rubbed his lip. "The job was part of it. I think cop's wives should get danger pay. Emotional danger. She lived with it for eight years; then my partner, Danny Herbert, took one—"

"Took one?"

"Got himself shot."

"And his death was too much for her?"

"No. He didn't die." He smiled. "He caught one in the hand. In the hand, of all places."

"How?"

"We were checking our messages, talking to our snitches. Informants. Prostitutes. They always make the best snitches—"

"Why?"

"Because they're always on the street and most of them are junkies and because of that they always know exactly what's going on. They don't want to do time because they not only lose money, but they can't feed their habit. Anyway, we saw one of our girls score some boy from this guy—"

"Boy—"

"Heroin. Heroin is cheaper than coke, which is known as girl. Anyway she scores and we see it. We'd known this guy Skinny was a dealer, but never been able to catch him either dealing or with it on him. And he was a smart ass, which Danny hated more than him being a dealer. So we see him do a deal and follow him back into an alley. He's scared to death. 'Don't arrest me,' he pleads, 'I'll deal, I'll deal.' Danny says, 'We'll talk downtown,' and all of a sudden he's got a piece in his hand. 'I'll kill you, motherfucker. I'll kill you.' And if anything he's even more frightened. Danny and I start trying to talk him down, separating, walking away from each other. Skinny's eyes jerk back and forth, back and forth, and Danny raises his hands to say something, and Skinny, I guess seeing only the movement, swings and shoots him in the hand. I got him down and the weapon away from him, but Danny was — is — the luckiest man alive. Mandy came to the hospital and we were sitting around the hospital room and it turned funny. Danny started joking about it. He said his sex life was over unless he could become ambidextrous — "

Jessie smiled in spite of herself. "That's awful."

"Anyway, we were all sitting there joking and laughing. When he walked out of the room, Mandy just looked at me, and it was all there in her eyes. Pity, and horror, and weariness, and most of all, fear. We had talked about it before. All of it, but in that instant I knew it was over." He swallowed and straightened in the seat. "We talked about it, discussed it, but in the end, we both knew it was over. She didn't even ask me to quit."

"Why?"

"Because it's what I do."

"Good lady."

"Yeah."

"You still miss her, don't you?"

"Not that way. I . . . just wish it could have been different, you know what I mean?"

She nodded. "Yeah, I know what you mean."

They drove the back roads for another half an hour before Jessie rolled the Bronco down into a wooded glade.

"This is it," she said. "There's the stream."

She rolled to a stop and Cobb's eyes combed the area. Pine and oak blended into each other and into their shadows. Shades of green, brown, and black. Shapes crawled across the sky and the floor below. The bright sunlight made darker shadows. It was like a labyrinth.

He sighed. "Well, it's not the most dangerous looking place I've ever been." He turned in the seat. "The river is —"

"Back there." She pointed down the stream, then paused. In the shadow shapes of the trees her eyes picked out another shape on the top of a hill.

"What's that?" she asked.

Cobb followed her gaze and shook his head. "I don't see anything."

"There," she directed. "Follow the stream down, then to the left on top of the hill."

Cobb squinted, then nodded slowly. "Yeah, I do see it. There's something back there. A cabin maybe."

"Maybe."

He looked at her. "How the hell did you see that?"

"It's a different shape. There are tree shapes and man-made shapes. Whatever it is back there, it doesn't fit the natural shapes around it."

He smiled. "That's not bad."

She drove down a few feet and came to a twisting dirt track that wasn't much more than a path.

She turned off the road and onto the track. They did a slow bounce through the woods and up the hill. As they approached it, a small building began to emerge out of the other shapes. Set up and away from the path, it was an old collection of weathered wood that almost seemed to lean in two directions at once. A shovel and a ladder were propped against one side. Both were old and covered with leaves and cobwebs.

Jessie climbed out of the car and walked through the brush to the building. Peering through the dusty cracks, she could see another ladder, a work table, a small handsaw and a larger crosscut saw. The rest was in shadow. She touched the old door that was kept shut by a block of wood nailed into the frame. It had been that way a long time.

She looked back at the Bronco. Cobb had climbed out and was hobbling his way down through the brush.

She frowned. Of course, she thought.

Walking back toward him, she shook her head. "It hasn't been used in years. Everything is covered with leaves and mold and dust."

He smiled grimly. "Another of our great clues."

They turned back toward the Bronco.

"We need to —" he began.

She felt the engines roar before she heard or saw the white car, an Oldsmobile, flashing through the trees below them. Then it swerved, skidding, and hammered onto the path. Coming straight for them.

She looked to the Bronco. It was too far. They would never make it.

Twenty-five

"The woods," Cobb growled. Pivoting on the crutch, he slashed through the brush down the slope toward the creek.

Jessie was right beside him. They barreled through the branches of an apple tree, and trying to run, Cobb caught the crutch on a root. He stumbled and stepped on his wounded foot. Screaming, he slammed into Jessie. She caught him, and managed to keep him on his feet. He dropped the crutch, and they kept running.

Behind them, Jessie could hear the tires on the dirt, then the brakes and the solid thunk of car doors.

Cobb and Jessie pushed further into the brush, angling toward the water. The ground steepened under them. Reaching out, Cobb grasped her shoulder, trying to steady himself. The angle of the slope increased.

Jessie's foot went out from under her, and she almost went down. Cobb dipped over, but she caught him, pushed him up, and they ran down around the slope of a hill, through the brush and down into the fold of another creek joining the first. The brush thickened even more.

Jessie rammed through it and they slipped down the bank into the creek. Cold water seeped up through her running shoes. Her eyes went up and down the creek.

An oak had fallen over the creek a few yards below them — its branches still held leaves and they covered the creek.

"There," she whispered, and before he could say anything, she was hauling him through the water. Coming to the trunk, they knelt and crawled under the sheltering branches. Leaves and twigs scratched over them. Then they pushed up against the bank and lay still. Jessie smelled the wood and dirt mixed with her own odor of sweat and fear.

Above them, she could hear the heaviness of men moving through the brush.

Cobb reached down and tugged his 9mm free. He thumbed the hammer back slowly, then his eyes moved from the hill above them to Jessie, then to his foot, and he shook his head.

The sound of movement above them slowed, then stopped.

An interplay of voices, barely perceptible above the rush of the stream around them.

Jessie started to whisper, but Cobb shook his head and held his free hand up, then pressed his finger to her lips.

His touch was almost electric.

And there, under the canopy of leaves, their bodies touching, the water rushing by, she felt an incredible rush, a bond with him. He stared at her, then brushed his hand over her cheek gently. The rattle of bushes tugged his eyes away.

They were moving again. Away.

Cobb and Jessie pressed into the cool dirt. He brought the pistol up and they lay still, listening.

Then it was quiet again.

That was almost as bad as the sound of movement.

She looked up and started to ease up to take a look.

Cobb touched her on the shoulder and shook his head. Then he motioned her to him, and leaned into her until his face was pressed next to hers. She could smell his sweat and the newness of his blue shirt and feel his warmth as his breath feathered the back of her neck. He pressed his lips to her ear.

"Get out of here while you can," he whispered. "I'm slowing you down."

She closed her eyes for a moment. Part of her wanted to do exactly that. Get the hell out and never look back. But there was another part that said something else.

She shook her head slowly.

"Do it," he growled.

She shook her head again. "Let's get one thing straight. I'm not leaving you, you pig-headed macho sonofabitch."

He eased back and looked at her. His eyes spoke regret, anger, and fear. Then they softened, and he leaned back into her.

"Pigheaded?" he whispered.

They both smiled, then almost laughed. He shook his head and they lay back against the bank. Waiting.

The sun eased through the sky, changing the shapes of the oak and pine, lightening shadows in one place, deepening them in others. She drifted. Her heart pounded and she felt both incredible anxiety and calm at the same time. And she listened. To the breeze through the branches, and the birds and insects. But no movement. The wind stirred, rustling the leaves as a shower of rain pattered over them.

After a long time, she eased over to Cobb and pressed her lips against his ear.

"Have they gone?" she whispered.

"No."

Jessie was about to nod off when suddenly a car engine growled to life. She started, bolting upward. Reaching out, Cobb grasped her and eased her back down. After such a long time, the car sounded completely foreign in this setting. It hammered for a minute, then she heard it shift into gear and ease away. Back to the road, then away.

She looked to Cobb.

He pressed in next to her ear. "Now it really starts," he whispered. "One of them is waiting up there, hidden in the brush, near the Bronco. They're hoping we'll think they've given up, and we'll go back to the Bronco."

"And?"

"And we are. In a while."

He motioned her back down. They waited. Slowly the evening began to steal the light from the woods and underbrush.

Cobb leaned back into her. "You're going to have to do something."

"I'm not leaving you —"

"Only for a bit. He's most likely in front of, or in back of, the Bronco — someplace he's got a view of both sides and both doors. I think he's in front because the path's in back. Cover is a little light there. Can you place the Bronco from here?"

She nodded. "I think so."

"Ease away from here. Stay low. And quiet. Do not, repeat, do not, hurry. Take all night if you want to. Work your way to a line in front of the Bronco, then work your way forward. Look to the trees first, then to both sides. Move a few feet, then do it all again. Look at everything twice or three times. You're good at this. It'll be like spotting the shed from the road. Just do that again. When you spot him, come back and we'll go from there." He swallowed. "I hate to send you out there, but I'm running a little low on stealth."

"It's all right."

"No, it's not, but it's all we can do right now."

She slipped back and away from him. In the dying light, it was difficult to see his face. Reaching up, he started to touch her face, but his hand hesitated and he gripped her shoulder instead. He squeezed it gently and she nodded, then turned and slipped from under the

156

branches and through the water and up the bank into more underbrush.

She paused for a moment, her eyes probing the half-darkness, and she felt a sudden isolation. Aloneness. She wanted to turn around and go back and hide next to Cobb there until . . . She swallowed. Until what?

Frowning, pushing against the fear, she crawled up the slope, staying to the low spots, taking her time.

Twilight moved in around her, and soon the light was gone. She was thankful for that, even though she knew it would make it harder to spot the gunman.

It took her nearly forty-five minutes to get around the hill and in line with where she thought the Bronco was parked.

Rising up off the ground a little, she tried to see the shack. No good. Then the Bronco. Nothing.

She looked up into the nearest tree, trying to pick out any kind of irregular shape. There was nothing there. Lowering her gaze to the ground, she combed through the undergrowth. Bushes, downed logs, branches. She could see nothing unusual there. She eased out, staying on her stomach, slipping through the brush quietly. Stopping again. Dividing the area into quarters. Examining it. Moving on.

She had done this several times when she caught an odd shape to her left, about thirty feet away. Her breath caught, then she realized that it was the shack. Easing her eyes to the right, she finally caught the sloping lines of the Bronco. She moved even slower now. Quartering the area, she went over it once. Twice. Three times. Seeing nothing, she walked her way forward on her elbows. Then paused. She had forgotten the oak tree just in front of her.

Lifting herself on her elbows, she eased her eyes up over the contours of the trunk. Then the branches, then the patchwork of the leaves, then the —

Movement stopped her eyes.

But she couldn't see anything. Nothing moved now.

157

She looked again, trying to sort darkness from darkness, shape from shape.

Still nothing.

She frowned. She knew she had seen movement. A bird? No. It wasn't that kind of motion. It was hard. Stiff.

Slipping to her side, getting a different background of sky, she looked again. Slowly. Slowly.

Then she saw it.

A gun barrel. And seeing that, she was able to pick his shape from the leaves.

About six feet up, in the notch of the oak.

Waiting.

Twenty-six

It took Jessie thirty minutes to get back to Cobb. She moved through the undergrowth quicker and easier this time. But she still took it slowly.

As she ducked under the branches, the 9mm was leveled on her.

Her breath caught, then the pistol nosed down, and Cobb sighed.

She eased in beside him, and they placed their lips next to each other's ears. As she brushed his cheek, felt his breath and his touch, a warmth stirred through her.

She told him where the gunman was waiting. Cobb listened, then eased back against the bank, thinking. Then he pushed back into her.

"I'll take your route," he whispered. "You go around the other way, back to the shed. Make sure you stay behind it. Then find something, rocks, or twigs or gravel and toss them at the Bronco. Make noise. Not big noise, but noise. Anything to draw his attention."

"To keep him looking away from you."

"That's right." He looked at his watch. "Forty minutes from now."

She looked at her watch too. It was nine forty-seven. She nodded. "Forty minutes from now."

They slipped from beneath the canopy of branches

and into the underbrush. Cobb moved fairly well on his hands and elbows. They paused, then he smiled, and turning, he faded into the darkness and branches.

A hollowness seemed to open, then widen inside her, and she felt emotion struggling in her throat.

Not now, she thought. Dammit, not now.

Turning, she crawled up the slope toward the shed.

Again, she moved slowly, carefully. Pressing her weight down on the leaves, then shifting forward. Around the hill. Through the tangled vines and branches. The shed gradually took shape from the shadows. Straight lines and angles.

The pain started immediately as Cobb crawled through the brush.

Each time the foot touched the ground, it was like an electrical pulse jolting through him. Sticks and branches brushed it and it was like touching a live wire. Sweat beaded on his face, in his arm pits, and down the small of his back, but he kept moving. He told himself he would get used to it. He never did. The thing he had to watch was his breathing. He concentrated on keeping it regular. And he crawled, the pain throbbing through him.

He tried to think about what he was doing, but the pain was always there.

He stopped several times, resting, then moving on, but by the time he neared the oak tree, he was trembling.

Wiping the sweat from his eyes, he eased his gaze up through the branches, searching. Trying to pick out the shape. About five feet up, she had said. In the first fork of the tree. Nothing. Frowning, he shifted up on one shoulder to get a different perspective. Still nothing. He eased back down and wondered if it was the wrong tree. The shed was to the left. The Bronco to the right, in clear view. This had to be it. It was the only tree big enough to hold a man that was in a straight line with the Bronco.

His eyes went back to the oak. To the fork. A chill began to spread through Cobb.

He wasn't there.

He had moved.

Jessie circled wide of the shed, then when the small building was between her and the oak, she pushed herself up into a crouch. She looked at her watch. Ten-sixteen. Eleven minutes to go.

She looked down. There were several dry and broken twigs around her. She picked them up, then stuffed them into her shirt pocket. When she thought she had enough, she eased through the brush and to the wall of the shed. Pressing against the old wood, she edged forward. The smell of dust and mold was heavy. Just up the slope, through the brush, she could see the Bronco clearly. She took another step toward the front of the shed.

Her breath quickened suddenly, and from somewhere deep and primal, a warning jolted through her.

Then two things happened at the same time. She smelled him. Sweat and after-shave and cherry-fragranced tobacco. Swann.

And the dark form exploded from the front of the building where he had been crouching, waiting.

His movements were sure and quick and deadly. He rushed into her, one hand slamming into her face, the other grasping the back of her head. The hand on her face closed over her mouth and nose, thumb and forefinger pinching her nose, closing off her air. The hand behind her head pressed her into the other one and kept her head steady. Her hands came up, clawing against his, but he was incredibly strong. His hands were like stone.

Her trapped breath struggled in her throat. She pulled back, but he jerked her to him. His hands stayed where they were. She jerked from side to side. It was no good. The air was bursting in her lungs. She was dying. She struggled, but he just pulled her closer. Almost like an embrace. She looked into his face.

He smiled.

He was enjoying this.

A white-cold rage washed through her and her hands fluttered and touched the twigs in her shirt pocket. The twigs. Her hands went back to them. More out of instinct than thought, her hands fumbled over the sticks, found one and grasping it, she tugged it free. She looked into his shadowed face.

Darkness swarmed behind her eyes and she knew she only had one chance. Bringing the stick up, she drove into where she thought his eye would be.

Swann howled with surprise and pain and stumbled backwards, his hands loosening, and she drove the stick into his face again, and at the same time, rushed into him, using the surprise and the little bit of momentum, bringing her other hand up, hitting him in the chest with it. He pitched backwards. Twisting, she jerked free and slammed into the side of the shed. Instead of stopping her, the old wood gave, crumbling under her weight as she tumbled head-first through splinters and dust and spiderwebs into a nest of handles and metal. A sharp edge sliced into her shoulder, and a handle whacked her in the back. Rolling on the dirt floor, she fought to get air into her lungs. She made a pitiful moaning sound, but no air would come. She tried again. Air and dust seeped into her.

Then Swann was there. Filling the hole in the wall.

Coming for her.

The handle that had hit her was still across her back.

Reaching around, she grasped it. It was a shovel.

He bulled through the hole in the wall. Holding the handle, she dragged the blade of the shovel around and stood up at the same time. He rushed toward her in the small dark space, and she brought the blade of the shovel up, swinging the flat side of it into the side of his

162

head. It made an almost comical ring. He gave a grunting sound and went down suddenly, quickly, as if his legs had been jerked out from under him.

She stood over him with the shovel, and a deep, thick silence washed over them. Her breath cawed through her, raking her lungs.

Her breath.

The shed, the darkness, the tools, everything seemed to float around her, the night tilting as she continued to stand and stare at the man lying sprawled. Awkward in his stillness, his head at an odd angle.

A numbness began to spread through her, a strange non-feeling.

"Oh my God," she whispered and knelt down beside him. She rolled him over.

"Jessie—"

She jerked around, bringing the shovel up into Cobb's face.

He stood at the broken wall. He looked from her to the body on the ground.

She stared at him, still floating.

Reaching out, he took the shovel and set it down.

"Jess—"

"What?"

"Are you okay?"

"Yes," she lied. "I'm okay."

The numbness tingled through her and she welcomed it, wished for it. She looked back at Swann. "I think he's dead."

Cobb knelt beside him and leaned in close, then felt the pulse in his neck. He shook his head. "No. He's alive." He stuck the 9mm into his belt and bent down. "Help me—"

"Help you what—"

"Get him to the Bronco," he said. "He knows what's going on—"

"You think he'd tell us?"

"I can persuade him to—"

163

He tried to lift Swann, but Cobb's leg gave. Jessie leaned down and tried to help, but he was too heavy. She tried again, then heard something.

A car engine.

"We've got to get out of here," Cobb said.

"But —"

"Now!"

They stumbled their way down the slope and clambered into the Bronco.

Jessie started it, and turned on the lights.

"No —" Cobb barked.

She turned them off, then swerved around through the brush, down the track, and to the road. Headlights topped the hill to her left.

She turned right, speeding away.

Twenty-seven

Driving, Jessie began to feel something strange whisper through her. It was a little like a chill breeze or walking into an air-conditioned room on a hot day. Around her, the night seemed to gain incredible detail. Branches in the headlights, gravel in the road, her hands on the steering wheel seemed to have a light and life all their own.

She smiled, then found herself giggling. Coolness exploded through her. "Wow," she murmured. laughing.

"Marsh—"

She looked at Cobb. She could see him very clearly in the half-lit cab. The lines of his jaw. The texture of his skin. The gray in his hair. His blue eyes narrowing with concern as he looked at her.

"Marsh—"

"I'm fine," she said. "Really, I feel great."

She pressed the gas pedal down. The Bronco eased forward and she smiled. The speed felt good.

"I'm hungry," she said. "Are you hungry? I mean, I could really put away some food. Soft-shell crabs. Or shrimp! How about we go back to The Mainsail and get some crabs and shrimp. Or kim-chee—do you know where we can find kim-chee? I'm game—"

Cobb reached over and touched her hand. "Slow down," he said softly.

"I'm only doing thirty-five."

"On this road, it's too fast. Slow down . . ."

"No really, I've got it."

They passed a side road.

"Better yet," Cobb said, "pull in here."

"But—"

"Do it."

She shrugged and pulled off onto the side road. They rolled into the woods and she parked.

Jessie swallowed, her hands gripping the wheel. Hard.

"So what is it?"

"You're high, Jess—"

"What?"

"You're high. And it's okay."

"High? You're crazy. I haven't been taking anything—"

"Listen," he said calmly. "Are you listening?"

"Yeah. Hey, what else can I do?"

"Jessie, you're high because you survived. It's an adrenaline rush. It's natural."

Darkness tinged her mood. "You're saying I'm high because I almost killed somebody—"

"Yes."

She shook her head from side to side. Deliberate and hard. "No, nobody can be happy about killing somebody—"

"I didn't say *happy*, I said *high*. Because you're alive."

She shook her head against it. "No."

"It's all right, Jess, it's all right."

Anger exploded through her, searing white-hot through her blood and brain. "That sonofabitch!" she screamed. "That stupid sonofabitch! Why did he have to do that? Why did he have to—"

Reaching out, Cobb took her hands from the wheel and pulled her over to him. She tugged against him at

166

first, then sank into his chest and let him fold her into his arms.

"Are you coming on to me?" she asked.

"Not right now."

She trembled. "I . . ." she whispered. Then the tears came. "I never cry," she sobbed, and pushed her face into his shirt. "I never cry . . ."

"Now's a good time to start."

Her fingers clawed into his shirt. "It all happened so . . . fast. So goddamn fast. He was trying to kill me." Her jaw tightened. "And enjoying it." She sat up a little and looked at him, her eyes bewildered. "He smiled at me, Cobb. The sonofabitch smiled at me. His hands were so hard, and so goddamned strong . . . and he smiled at me, like a child pulling the wings off a fly, relishing its pain." She trembled. "And when he went down and I thought he was dead . . ." She swallowed. "I was happy. I wanted him to be dead. I wanted to claw that smile into . . ." She trembled. "Damn . . ." she whispered. "I never thought I could hate like that. I wanted to hurt him. Wanted to . . ."

He swallowed. "I know."

She shook her head. "I thought he was in the tree . . . why did he move?"

"He may have heard you. I don't know. We'll never know."

"So fast," she sobbed. "He went down so fast . . ." She kept talking and crying until she was exhausted, then she slumped into his arms and fell asleep.

Cobb stared at her and frowned, then shook her awake.

"Jessie—"

"No," she murmured, "I just—"

Sighing, he opened the door and climbed out of the Bronco, easing her over onto his seat.

Then he went over the Bronco several times, but found no bug.

No bug.

His eyes moved to the sky, searching it, then back toward the country road they'd just come from. It was quiet. It had been since they'd gotten there.

That was interesting.

He turned back to the passenger door and opened it. Jessie was still asleep.

Smiling, he tugged his 9mm from his belt and leaning against the Bronco, he made his way back to the rear tire and sat down.

And listened.

But he heard nothing.

She awoke slowly. Her arms and legs seemed to be made of rubberized lead. She could move, but there was no center to it. Her brain was thick.

She pushed herself over and sat up in the driver's seat.

Then realized Cobb was gone.

Panic exploded through her.

"Cobb—"

She opened the door and got out.

"Cobb—"

"What?"

She looked around, squinting in the darkness.

"Where the hell are you?"

"Back here," he replied.

She walked around the Bronco and saw him sitting against the rear tire.

"What are you doing?"

"I got out to check for bugs, then didn't want to wake you."

She sighed. "You scared the hell out of me. Next time wake me up."

"I don't know if I could have."

Leaning down, she helped him up and into the Bronco then walked around and climbed in the driver's side.

"How you doing?" he asked.

"I. . . ah . . ." She shook her head. "I don't think I have any verbal skills." She rubbed her tongue against the roof of her mouth. "And it tastes like I've been eating nails . . ." She ran her fingers through her hair and closing her eyes, she could hear the meaty whack of the shovel hitting the man's neck. "Damn . . ." she whispered.

"You're going to be depressed." Cobb said. "It may be pretty bad for a while—"

Her head jerked up. "Goddammit, I know that. Do you have to be so fucking intellectual?"

"Sometimes."

She shook her thick mane. "Wow," she whispered. "Damn. I'm sorry. But you keep saying you know, and you don't know."

"Yeah, I do. I've been through what you're going through. I did kill a man, remember? Monroe. And one before that."

"You didn't seem to react."

"I reacted, just in a different way. My way."

She swallowed and pushed the hair from her eyes and sighed. "Okay."

"Can you drive?"

"I think so. Where to?"

"Back to the motel," he said. "We'll get some sleep and figure out what to do tomorrow."

Twenty-eight

They slept until nearly noon the next morning. After showering and dressing in fresh clothes, Jessie and Cobb went to the same restaurant for breakfast.

Waiting for her food to come, Jessie let her eyes roam over the people sitting talking, eating, smoking, laughing. They seemed to be from another planet. Or another universe. One she used to live in. Smiling grimly, she looked at Cobb.

"All I could think of all night," she said, "was Danny's parallel universe." Her eyes darkened "I saw it last night, Cobb. For the first time, I really saw it. In Swann's eyes."

"I'd say 'Welcome,' but I'm not sure I'd mean it."

She sipped her coffee. "How did they find us?"

"They knew where to wait. But that's the good news."

Her eyes narrowed. "The good news?"

"Now we know for sure that we're on the right track."

"Where did they pick us up?"

He shook his head. "That I don't know. Somewhere along the line. The town, the road, somewhere along there."

"The shed?"

"Maybe. Early didn't come from the shed, did he?"

She frowned. "No. Down the road. The way we came."

"And there's more good news."

"More?"

He nodded. "There aren't cops all over us."

"I don't understand."

"I realized it last night after I didn't find a bug on the Bronco. Swann lost us. Didn't have a bug on the Bronco. He could have found us by using the locals. He had the description of the Bronco, and probably the license plate—"

"Then why didn't he?"

Cobb shrugged. "I think it's what I said before. He's trying to contain this. But more important, if the cops have us, the first thing we'd do is give them his name. They wouldn't believe us, but after we were dead, he's the first one they'd go looking for."

"He would have to go under."

"Right."

"And wouldn't have access to police channels anymore."

"Right again. So they want to do this as quietly as possible. But this way we're still isolated. Still operating on our own."

"But we can't go in."

He shook his head. "Not really. We don't have any more than we did. Nothing solid. And going in, what we do have would get fouled up in procedure. Then Swann or somebody else would have an easy way to us. And make no mistake, if that was the only way to do it, he would. Even if it meant having to go under."

She looked out the window. "You know what really bothers me?"

"What?"

"You're guessing. Using logic. What if you're wrong? What if this is just more of Danny's parallel universe?"

He paused, then nodded. "Yeah. We'll change the license plate again."

She smiled and sighed. "Two steps forward and three steps sideways. It gets worse as it gets better."

The waitress brought their breakfasts—platters of eggs, sausage, biscuits, gravy.

Cobb tore a biscuit apart and buttered it. "Its time we found out more about Early."

"Virginia Beach."

He nodded. "Yeah."

She frowned. "Great, we get to load all that crap back in the Bronco."

Cobb shook his head. "No. We'll be back here. We'll keep that room as a base. We'll just leave it."

After stealing another license plate, they drove on south to Newport News and through the tunnel to Norfolk. And the beach frenzy started. Freeways, bridges, tunnels, parking garages, hotels and motels, shopping malls, miniature golf, but mostly fast-food chains. Instant biscuits, hamburgers, chicken sandwiches. Miles and miles of instant gratification.

After winding their way through the freeways, they came off the toll road and into Virginia Beach. Jessie asked directions at a convenience store and they found the address on a shaded street near the beach. It was a modest two-story, freshly painted white with a neatly trimmed yard. On the door, Jessie found a handwritten note giving another address and a telephone number if you were interested in a rental.

The other address was a small cottage a few blocks from the beach. Jessie could see a deck in the rear, and the front porch was screened in with chairs and a daybed on it.

They entered through the screen door. The front door was open and from inside, Jessie could hear the rattle of dishes and pans.

"Hello," she called.

"In the kitchen," answered a female voice.

They stepped into a sparsely furnished living room. The smell of cleaners soaked the air. The furniture was cheap or plastic, utilitarian. No pictures on the walls. No plants. A transitory place, a place where people just passed through, drank, slept, partied, made love, but

172

didn't live in. They walked on to the kitchen. At the sink, washing dishes, was one of the most attractive women Jessie had ever seen. She was tall—taller than Jessie, probably six-one—her long, willowy body clad in cut-offs and an old sweatshirt. Her blond-gray hair was tugged back into a ponytail, and she turned and smiled. If she had seen her at a distance, Jessie would have guessed she was in her twenties, thirties at most, but closeup, her face showed the wear of years in the sun.

"Hi," she said. "Looking for a rental?"

"Are you Ellie?" Jessie asked.

She nodded. "Ellie Griffin." She looked at the sink and dishes. "Pardon me for not shaking hands, but I'm doing a little clean-up for some folks."

"Was Joe Early your brother?" Cobb asked.

The woman's face darkened and her hands stopped moving as the smile drifted from her face. "Yes," she nodded. "Joe was my brother. We just buried him."

Cobb showed her his badge. "Could we talk to you for a few minutes?"

"You're not from here—"

Cobb shook his head. "No. I'm a deputy from Clear Creek County."

She dried her hands on a small blue towel. "Where is that?"

"Northern Virginia in the Blue Ridge."

"And you're asking questions about Joe?"

Cobb nodded, then smiled. "You mind if we sit down?" He looked at his foot.

Ellie Griffin nodded. "Of course."

In the living room, Cobb and Jessie sat on a cheap sofa. Ellie pulled up a plastic chair and glancing down at it, she frowned. "Have to keep things to a minimum," she explained as if she were self-conscious. "But people tear things up. Folks think having rentals is the easiest thing in the world. Just hand people a key and they give you money. But I'll bet I've cleaned up more messes than most people ever imagined." She was rambling, Jessie realized, because she was nervous. "God," she sighed. "I wish I had a cigarette. I quit smoking twenty years ago, but it comes back on me when I'm tense, you know . . ."

"A death in the family can do it," Cobb remarked.

She smiled. "That, and other things. Maybe just how tenuous life is. How fast it goes. I'm a grandmother," she said. "And I'm fifty-eight years old."

"That's hard to believe," Cobb replied.

She nodded. "Thanks, I'll take that as a compliment. It's like somebody has played a joke on me. I'm still in good shape. Run five miles a day. Can still do most of the things I've always done. But then I look at my face. Or my hair. And it's like somebody snuck in in the middle of the night and put all this old folks makeup on me. I'm beginning to look like my mother." She smiled. "Fifty-eight years old." She shook her head. "Then Joe's death . . ." She swallowed against the tears. "That really brought it home. And such a stupid way to die. After all he'd been through, to fall out of a goddamn boat . . ." She swallowed. "Either of you smoke?"

"No," Cobb answered.

Jessie shook her head. "No. Sorry."

"Don't be. I'll be glad later. Saved by circumstance."

Jessie leaned forward. "You said, *after all he'd been through*. What did you mean?"

"Oh, you know, being a cop."

"What did he do?"

"Surveillance. Electronic stuff, bugs and cameras. Jody always liked to tinker with things even when he was a kid."

"Where was that?"

"Here. Except when we were kids it was like a small town. Now . . ." She shook her head and smiled. "They used to worry about the communists taking over the world, but I think it's California. Everything close to the water is beginning to look like California, have you noticed that? High rises. T-shirt shops, fast food." She laughed. "Now I do sound like I'm getting old."

174

"Did Joe like being a cop?"

She nodded. "At first, yeah, he did. He loved it."

"But it changed," Cobb prompted.

"Yeah, it changed. Through the years. Slowly. Like somebody cut pieces away from him—or glued them on. He started drinking, and drinking hard. Putting on weight. And the more weight he put on, the more he kind of walled himself away from the world.

One time he was sitting right where you are. I was cleaning up the place, and he came in with a six-pack of beer—he carried a six-pack with him kind of like a brief-case—he was sitting there having a beer, and he said it was dealing with the scum all the time. At first it was guys beating up on their wives, or kids. Kids were the worst for him. Some guy would lose his job or get loaded and come home and beat the hell out of his kids. That got Joe his first suspension. Some guy came home and beat one of his kids, a girl, into mincemeat. Joe had arrested the guy before, several times, for the same thing and they always let him out. Joe got the call and went out there. The girl, about eleven, was all huddled up in the bathroom, down between the tub and the toilet. Her face looked liked a Halloween mask. Joe tried to help her, but she was so scared, she wouldn't let him touch her. The father came up behind Joe in the hall, his breath reeking of beer. He belched and took a sip from a can in his hand, and said something like, 'Little bitch . . .' and Joe came unglued. He remembered hitting him that first time, the can of beer the floor and spraying up, the father stumbling back into the living room. Joe hit him again and again and the next thing he remembered was his partner pulling him off. They put the father in the hospital. They didn't even prefer charges on the father, but Joe was suspended. The father got out of the hospital, went home, beat the girl again, and this time he killed her. And this time the court put him away.

"Anyway, Joe went into surveillance after that. I think it was because he didn't have to deal with people directly any more. He watched them and listened to them, was removed from them, but in a way it was worse."

"How?" Jessie asked.

"Before when he dealt with them, the bad guys, they would at least put on a face for him. Say they didn't do it. Make some kind of excuse. And he could bust them, do something about it. But this way, listening to them, watching, he saw them the way they really were. 'An obscene purity,' is how he put it. He had to watch them or listen to them, and let it go. He couldn't do anything about it because that might blow the whole deal. He felt more and more impotent, useless. And he drank more."

"But he cut down lately," Cobb said.

She nodded. "Yes, he did." She smiled. "I told him he was an alcoholic, and he got pissed off. Started limiting himself to three hard drinks or six beers. And because he limited it, that meant he wasn't an alcoholic. At least to his way of thinking."

"Was he married?"

"No. He never married."

Jessie leaned forward. "He mentioned a particularly bad case he was on to his neighbor in Rappahannock—"

"Mrs. Scott—"

"Yes. Did he ever say anything about that case?"

She sighed, letting her mind go back, then shrugged. "Well, not exactly. He didn't talk about it, but about a year ago, he fell off the wagon for a while. He was very depressed. All he would say was that he'd come up against somebody who didn't qualify as human. A true sociopath. Somebody that really frightened him."

"No names? No references?" Cobb asked.

She shook her head. "No. Joe didn't talk much about his work. Less and less as time went on. The only person he talked to was Russ MacDonald."

"His partner?"

"Yes."

"Do you have his address?"

"I can't remember the number, but it's over on the corner of Atlantic and 73rd. A small, white frame, two-story on the east side of the street."

"Do you know his hours with the department?"

She shook her head. "He's not with the department anymore. He quit not long after Joe did. He has his own business now." She smiled. "He calls it a security business, but he's doing what he used to do, but making more."

"What's the name of it?"

"MacDonald Security. He runs it out of an office down on Atlantic."

"When was the last time you saw Joe?"

She shrugged. "I guess about three weeks ago. I felt like taking a drive and went up to see him."

"And the last time you talked on the phone?"

"Hmmm . . ." She shook her head. "I'm not certain. Two weeks ago? Something like that." Her eyes narrowed. "Why are you looking into this? Joe's death was an accident, wasn't it?"

Cobb frowned. "Mrs. Griffin, you're a cop's sister—"

"Was."

"Was. Then you'll understand when I tell you I can't discuss it. All I can tell you is we've got a cross-reference on a case. Joe was mentioned. As far as I know, Joe's death was an accident. Do you know where he kept his old files?"

She shook her head. "No. They're in Rappahannock, I guess." A frown began to cross her brow. "I need to get up there and clean all that out. But I've been putting it off—" For the first time tears glistened in her eyes. "But that will be the final thing, you know, getting rid of his clothes, his records, all that goddamn fishing gear . . ." She swallowed. "Damn," she sighed. "Damn . . ." She cleared her throat and lifted her head. "Well, I need to get back to work. Got some people coming in tonight."

Twenty-nine

Following Ellie Griffin's directions, they found Russ MacDonald's house easily. Jessie knocked at the door but got no answer, so she drove to the business district.

MacDonald Security was across the street from one of the large hotels. In the front was a small partitioned waiting area with a few chairs. No secretary, no receptionist. As Jessie closed the door behind them, a voice called out from behind the partition.

"Back here—"

They went through a doorway and behind it was what looked like an electronics junkyard. Tape decks, VCRs, television sets, wires, and microphones littered tables and metal shelves. A balding man with a mustache and a sharp, hawklike face sat behind a desk with a screwdriver in his hand, working on a jumble of wires. He glanced up at Cobb and Jessie. His eyes stayed on Jessie and he smiled.

"Russ MacDonald?" Cobb asked. "Mac?"

He reluctantly looked to Cobb and paused, the screwdriver in the air. He nodded. "Yeah, I'm Mac."

Cobb showed him his badge. "I'm John Davis, and this is Lynn Monroe. We're from northern Virginia and we need to talk to you for a minute."

He smiled. "You've got the wrong man. I'm retired. Well, sort of retired."

"It's about Joe Early," Jessie declared.

178

His eyes narrowed questioningly. "Joe? Joe's dead."

Cobb glanced down at his foot. "You mind if we sit?"

"No, sorry," MacDonald said. Standing up, he cleared papers off one chair and a receiver off another. After Jessie and Cobb sat down, he asked, "You said this is about Joe?"

"In a roundabout way," Cobb answered. "We found a woman dead in a motel room in Manassas. Joe's name and phone number were on a pad next to the phone."

"What was the woman's name?"

"Jessica Marsh."

MacDonald shook his head. "Never heard of her."

"I know that Joe was supposed to be retired, but could he have been working on something privately."

MacDonald shook his head. "No. He was retired, and I mean *really* retired. It's too bad—he was the best I've ever seen. He could put infinity bugs in a room so everybody could be heard. I mean really lit up—"

Jessie shook her head. "I'm sorry, I don't know a lot about electronics."

MacDonald smiled patiently. "Most people think bugging is putting one mike in a room and everything comes through crystal clear." He tugged a box of small cigars from his pocket. "You mind—?" She shook her head, and he went on. "Anyway, it's not that way. You've got to account for distance, corners, furniture, all of that. And Joe was the best. He would locate the bugs around the room in such a way that it sounded like a talk show. You could hear everybody perfectly. He was the best. He could hard wire a place in less time than—"

"Hard wire?"

"Infinity bugs use a phone or an outlet as a source of power. Hard wiring uses conductive paint. But it's got to be placed, painted, then painted over." He smiled. "He was an artist." He lit the small pencil-like cigar and sighed. "He really was something. Taught me most of what I know."

"But he got tired of it?" Cobb queried.

179

Mac puffed the cigar. "Got tired?" He shook his head. "No. He got to where he hated it. Hated everything about it."

"Why?"

MacDonald shrugged. "A lot of things. Small things adding up. Time. Listening to people who really are not what they pretend to be." He puffed the cigar. "Listening to them talk about killing people. The method. Place. Time. All that, like some kind of business deal or commodity. Or they'd joke about it. Laugh about the way some guy took it. That and, strangely enough, the violation of it—"

"Violation?" Jessie asked.

"Yeah. Not everybody we listened to was a bad guy. Some would turn out to be ordinary people having very private conversations. Like one guy we tapped was a guy that found out he and his wife couldn't have children and it was him, not her. He just sat there and cried. Then the wife starts drinking, and hammering him, making fun of him, ridiculing him because, before, he'd put it all off on her. I got up and left, but one of us had to stay and listen, so Joe did it—"

"Why?" Jessie asked.

"What?"

"Why did you have to listen after that?"

"Because that was our job and he still could have said something we needed. He was a lawyer, supposedly connected to the mob. So we listened." He shook his head. "Or listen to or watch people . . ." his face reddened slightly. "Well, you know, make love. That's probably the worst. It's funny, in the movies when that happens, they make it comical. Like everybody wants to watch or listen. Not true. That's when you really feel like some kind of pervert. And a guy and girl is bad enough, but when it's two guys going at it—" He shook his head with disgust.

"Couldn't you just listen to the tape later?" Cobb asked.

"Not Joe. What if your equipment goes on the fritz?

You've got to kick in the backup. Or replace it as soon as possible. So somebody listens. Like I said, he was the best. He didn't do sloppy work, and that's why he quit. He couldn't do it any more."

"So you don't think he could have been working on something on his own . . . private?" Cobb asked.

MacDonald shook his head. "I know he wasn't. The last time I saw him, a couple of weeks ago, I asked him to come in with me. He said no, that retiring was the best decision he'd ever made, that finally some of the ghosts were beginning to go away. Not gone, but beginning to go away. No, guys go private for two reasons: they need the money or they miss the life. I got back into it for a little of both. Retirement bored the hell out of me. But Joe sure as hell didn't miss the life, and Joe wasn't rich, but he had enough to get by on. To fish and do a little drinking. No, he didn't go private."

"Then this must be an old case."

"It would have to be. But like I said, I never heard of a Jessica Marsh."

"Did you work on everything together?"

"Sometimes, not all the time. We were spread a little thin."

"Could it be in his old files?"

He puffed the cigar. "Could be, sure."

"Did Joe keep his own files? It would make things a lot easier."

He smiled. "You know we did. For backup."

"Do you know where they are?"

His lips pressed around the cigar. "Well, no. He didn't take them to Rappahannock with him." He puffed the cigar and rolled it in his fingers, thinking. "Maybe his sister, Ellie Griffin; she lives over on—"

Jessie shook her head. "We checked with her."

"No. Okay. I think he did leave some stuff in storage. But I don't know whether it was here or in Rappahannock. Most likely here. Why move it there to put it in storage?"

"You said you kept your files—"

"Yeah, and you're welcome to go through them. Problem is, they're not referenced by what was mine and what we worked on together. Just by name. You'd have to go through all of mine, too—"

Cobb shook his head. "No, I'd rather have Joe's files. He might have made some personal notations. But if we can't find them, we might just take you up on that."

Jessie leaned forward. "Ellie and Mrs. Scott up in Rappahannock both said he'd mentioned one particularly bad case he'd been on."

MacDonald's lips gripped the cigar filter grimly. "There was more than one bad case, believe me—"

"Ellie said he'd come up against somebody who didn't qualify as human, a true sociopath—"

The smile widened. "Same song, second verse. There was more than one."

"Which were the ones that got to him the most?" Cobb asked.

Sighing, MacDonald settled back into the chair. "Well, the first one that comes to mind is Martin White. He was probably the last straw."

"Why?"

"The guy was a monster." He shook his head. "You come across some pretty bad folks in this line of work. This guy was the worst."

"Crazy?"

"Maybe. I don't know. We came across him smuggling aliens in from South America as slave labor. We got a lead on him, that he was bringing some people in down the coast. The feds called us in to do a peep for them. They had spotted a van, not one of the small ones, but a bread truck van. Joe got to the van and wired it—two mikes and two eyes, video bugs. Anyway this guy White and another guy, Bendix, brought the aliens in by boat and put them in the van." He grinned with pride. "I mean, it was beautiful. We had a view into the back, into the cab. Everything. And we could hear everything." He puffed the cigar, then stubbed it out and lit another, drawing heavily on it. "But something went wrong . . . maybe somebody was following too close." His jaw hardened. "Maybe . . ." He started to say something else then let it go. "We'll never know. Anyway, this guy White is driving and he pulls over into a rest stop all of a sudden, takes out a Mac 10, and looks at Bendix. 'It's blown,' he says to Bendix. Then he turns back into the van." MacDonald swallowed and the cigar trembled in his fingers. "There were eleven people back there. Men and women. He shot them all." He shook his head. "We watched it, right there on the monitors. In a kind of warped black and white—"

"Warped?" Jessie wondered.

"The lenses were fish-eye, wide angle and that distorts it all, bows it in the middle—"

"I know about lenses," she replied.

"Anyway, we watched it all. Watched him . . ." He cleared his throat. "It was like Hell for a minute. Screaming, the slugs impacting the bodies, and them going down. The walls of the van splashed with black and white blood. It was all kind of unreal. And quiet. Unbelievably quiet. Then the other guy, Bendix, starts screaming and White turns to him. 'No loose ends,' he says, and shoots him. Blows him right out of the door onto the ground. The guy he was working with. Then White took off. He must have had a car stashed someplace close because we never found a trace of him." He shook his head. "Twelve people. Twelve people, just like that." He placed the cigar between his teeth and bit down on it. "Anyway, Joe wasn't the same after that. He never said it, but I kind of think he wondered if White hadn't spotted the bugs somehow. Wondered if he fucked up and got those people killed." He shrugged. "After that, this guy White became an obsession with him. Then, a month or so later, it was all over."

"Why?"

"This guy White was killed up in D.C. Another deal

went bad, but this time the cops got him. Funny, you'd think Joe would be relieved, but he wasn't. He'd wanted to take him. Kill him himself. But again, it's not like the movies. It didn't work out that way." He looked at Jessie. "That was the final thing, I guess. The thing that finally finished it for him because he retired about six months after that." He puffed the cigar and shook his head. "We want things to balance out, to have some kind of logic to them, but sometimes they don't, you know. They just don't." He shrugged. "He did get something out of it though, in a way, I guess."

"What?" Cobb asked.

"Rappahannock. It was one of the stops the van had made on the way down. We found a gas ticket from up there in the van. Along with a restaurant receipt from Rappahannock. Joe backtracked, hoping to find something, but he never did. Then White got himself killed and it didn't matter anymore."

"That was the first time he was there?"

"No. But it hit him just right this time. Later on, he decided to retire there. The last place you've been is always the best, I guess."

"Did he have any other cases there?" Cobb asked.

Mac bit on the cigar thoughtfully. "A murder case, I think. Yeah. A guy named . . . what the hell was his name? Norton? . . . No. Norris? He killed his wife. Claimed a burglar did it while he was out of town. Investigators didn't believe it, and had us put a directional bug on his car. Followed him up to Rappahannock and to a girlfriend's house. And all the stuff that was supposed to have been stolen in the robbery." He shook his head. "Guy was really stupid, you know. Greedy. Should have deep-sixed it all; instead, he gave it to the girlfriend. Was still claiming he was innocent when he went to jail, that the girlfriend had framed him. Nice guy."

"And the girlfriend?"

"She got off. Never could prove a case against her."

"Do you remember her name?"

Mac grinned. "Yeah." He laughed. "I'll never forget it. Hooker. Donna Hooker."

Jessie and Cobb laughed, too, then Cobb leaned forward on the table. "You said a couple of cases came to mind when I asked about the ones that bothered Joe the most. What was the other one?"

Mac puffed his cigar. "You're really out in the cold on this one, aren't you?"

Cobb nodded. "Yeah. The woman seems to have been killed for no reason — "

"Robbery?"

"Nothing taken."

"Ex-husband?"

"No."

"Old boyfriends?"

"We're looking into it, but so far, nothing. She was an artist. Led an ordinary, quiet life. The only thing we have is Joe's name, but there doesn't seem to be any kind of connection."

Mac picked up his screwdriver and turned it in his fingers.

"The other one I remember really got to him was a mob lieutenant. Lou Kelly. We had enough wire around him to run a three-foot fence from here to California. Got him, too. Got him dirty. A federal investigator, his wife, and kid were murdered and we got him saying he did it on tape. Then, the feds, in their infinite wisdom, got him to testify against his bosses. They put them away, then put Kelly in the witness protection program."

"They let him go?" Cobb asked in disbelief.

He nodded. "They let him go. Joe got good and drunk. Talked about trying to find him, and taking him out himself, but his chances of doing that were slim and none. Not with somebody in the program. The bad guys had won again. But what else is new?"

Thirty

Jessie stopped at a pay phone and called Ellie Griffin.

"A storage locker?" Ellie sighed. "Well, it's possible. I think he left a couple of boxes in the garage. You're welcome to look through them if you like."

They went through the boxes. They were filled with old fishing equipment. A few papers. Books. But nothing about a storage locker.

Before they left, Cobb got Early's old address from Ellie, then thanked her.

In the Bronco, Cobb sighed. "Well, we actually have to do some police work."

"Check all the storage lockers," she affirmed.

Cobb nodded. "Yeah."

"Won't we need a search warrant?"

He grinned. "Not if we do it right."

They found a small motel near the beach, with an even smaller restaurant. Jessie ordered grilled tuna with artichoke hearts and Cobb decided on steak.

He shrugged apologetically. "Sorry, I'm too tired to be adventurous tonight."

Jessie smiled wearily. "And I'm too tired to nag you." She shook her head. "And discouraged. I thought I would get more from MacDonald."

Cobb sipped his beer. "I know. I was hoping one of those old cases would pay off, too." He shook his head.

"But with one guy dead and the other in witness protection, I'd say we're batting zero."

"What about Kelly? Maybe Joe saw him, and—"

Cobb shook his head. "The last thing the feds would do is put him so close because of that very thing. Somebody he knew would have a better chance of stumbling across him. No, Kelly's in Iowa or Montana or Oregon working at some good-paying job and no mortgage on his house."

"Crime does pay."

"Sometimes, yeah." Cobb leaned back in the booth and looked out the picture window at the boardwalk and the beach. Bicyclers and runners flickered through the evening twilight. Others walked holding hands, and some just sat and watched the dying light on the water. Finally he shook his head. "I've never had a case like this before. One without any handles at all . . ."

"And I got you into this."

He smiled. "True. But don't you think you're up against enough without bringing guilt into it?"

"Still . . ."

"Still if Seth Hardesty hadn't brought me in from Philadelphia, none of this would have happened, either. And Seth's an asshole about half the time, so let's blame him."

She shrugged. "I'm still sorry."

His gaze rested on her. "I'm not," he said, and his eyes held hers for a moment more. A moment too long. A warmth exploded through her, and she felt that proximity again. The intimacy. Of lying in the creek under the canopy of leaves, of brushing his skin, of sleeping on him in the Bronco. She swallowed against the tightness in her throat. "Are you coming on to me?"

"Yeah," he answered. "This time, I am."

They didn't wait for their food. They left money behind on the table and rushed out into the soft, cool night fragranced with the sea. Cobb stumbled on his crutch and almost fell on the hood of a car. Jessie grabbed him, and in doing so, she almost went down, too. They started giggling like children, and the giggling turned to laughter. They bounced their way down the short sidewalk. Jessie pulled the key out, dropped it, and Cobb almost went down again. By now, he was sobbing with laughter. She scooped the key up, managed to open the door, and they fell into the dark room. And the laughter stopped. Abruptly. Hands pulled at clothing, fumbled with buttons. With her shirt halfway off, her mouth found his, and kissing, they fell against the wall. Their hands kept moving, undressing themselves and each other, then with the clothing gone, the hands found lips, wonderfully naked skin, each other. They tumbled onto the bed and Cobb winced with pain. She eased away. "Should we . . ."

"Don't worry about it."

She didn't.

For a brief time, everything went away. Fear, death, yesterday, time, all sloughed away into the soft darkness. There was only their motion, touch, mingling, focusing into a soul-searing pinpoint of happiness.

Later, in the night, drifting, exhausted in each other's arms, she smiled. "Wow."

"I agree."

"You mean we agree on something?"

"A couple of things, it looks like."

They drifted a while longer.

"Funny," she said.

"*Funny's* not quite the word I'd use."

"I mean, how you find something after you stop looking for it."

"Metaphysics again?"

"I guess. I'm not sure."

"If you're not sure, it must be metaphysics."

They drifted again. Then slept.

Thirty-one

The next morning Cobb and Jessie tried showering together. Before they touched the soap, they were tumbling, wet and giggling, back into the bed. Then, calling a truce of sorts, Jessie showered, then Cobb, and they hurried over to the motel restaurant.

Then they went to work.

Using the yellow pages and a city map, they wrote down each storage facility, starting with the closest, then fanning outwards.

With the addresses marked on the map, they started their slow trek. They were well into the afternoon and getting close to Norfolk when they found it.

They walked into the small air-conditioned office, and Cobb flashed his badge to the skinny young man behind the desk, whose eyes widened a little.

"Cops?" he asked.

Cobb nodded. "We're looking to see if a man named Joe Early stored anything here."

The young man fumbled through his cards, stopped and nodded.

"Yeah. Joseph Early. Rented 772 in December. He's paid for a year."

Cobb leaned on the counter. "Now, what's your name, son?"

"Terry—"

"Now, Terry, we can do this the long or the short way.

189

We can get a search warrant, but this is Sunday; trying to get a judge will take time, and I'm not sure we have the time."

The young man's eyes widened a little more. Jessie could see the question bubbling up from his skinny throat, slipping by the sharp adam's apple. He didn't want to ask, but duty overtook him. "Why?" he squeaked.

"Well, this Early may have stolen a considerable amount of ordnance from the naval base."

"Ordnance? You mean like . . ."

Cobb nodded. "Explosives."

"Oh, shit."

"About seven hundred pounds of it."

"Oh, shit."

"Let me ask you a couple of questions."

"Oh, sh . . . okay . . ."

"Does 772 get a lot of afternoon sun?"

"Ah . . . yeah, it would."

Cobb frowned. "Not good, Terry."

"Not good?"

"No."

Terry gulped. "How come?"

"Sun. Heat. This is very old ordnance. Heat makes it extremely unstable. Have you ever seen the movie, *The Professionals* with Burt Lancaster and Lee Marvin?"

"About the guys going into Mexico?"

"That's the one."

"Yeah."

"You remember the scene on the train where the dynamite sweats pure nitroglycerin?"

"Oh, shit."

"You could have puddles of nitro in there."

"Oh—"

"Would it get pretty warm in there?"

"Probably, yeah."

"Do you know what seven hundred pounds of explosives could sweat? What it could do?"

"No."

"Well let me put it this way: this business won't be here anymore if it goes off. You do have insurance for all of this, don't you?"

"Oh, shit."

"Now like I said, a search warrant will take time. Maybe a day or so. And it's been hot the past couple of days . . ."

"You're a cop, aren't you?"

"Yes."

"Then who gives a damn about a warrant?"

"I was hoping you'd say that, Terry. Now I'd like you to accompany me back there and—"

"Accompany?"

"Yes."

"You mean go with you?"

"That's right. That way you can be surer everything stays legal, and—"

"Legal. Fuck legal. I'm not going back there."

"Well, I can't force you, but—"

"I've got a crowbar—you need a crowbar?"

"No, I don't think so. Now if you'll just show me back there."

"Seventh row. You sure you don't need a crowbar? It's a big crowbar—"

"No, thanks, Terry. We'll just go on back. What's the code on the gate?"

"Five, twenty-four, thirty-four, three."

"Thanks." They turned toward the door. "Oh, and Terry—"

"Yeah?"

"You might want to stay down for a bit."

"Oh, shit."

His head disappeared behind the desk.

They walked outside and Jessie had to struggle to keep from laughing.

"That was mean."

Cobb nodded. "You're right. And I feel bad about it."

He limped to the Bronco while Jessie punched in the code at the gate, then came back to the Bronco and drove through. They found 772. Cobb got out and looked at the lock. It was a regular hardware store issue. He took what looked like a key packet from his pocket and opened it. Inside were various lengths of thin steel. "Picks," he told her, then turned to the lock.

"You have picks?"

"Of course."

"Is that legal?"

"It's legal to have them."

"But—"

He glanced at her. "This place may blow any second."

She nodded. "I'll shut up."

He returned to the lock, slipped a pick into it, turned his wrist. It popped open.

Smiling, he raised his eyebrows, took the lock off, and opened the door.

The air was thick and close. Jessie turned on the light. The room was small and nearly empty. A chest of drawers. An old chair. Old 78's. And a stack of cardboard files. Seven of them.

"Bingo," said Cobb.

Jessie loaded the files into the Bronco. Then they relocked the door and returned to the office.

Jessie got out and opened the door.

"Terry?"

From behind the counter. "Yeah."

"It's all clear."

"All clear?"

"Yes. Everything's fine."

They heard a long, relieved sigh, then "Oh, shit."

They drove back to the motel and started through the files. Bugging, wiretaps, video surveillance on drug runners, smugglers, murder suspects, mob connections, child molesters. First, they divided the cases into years—

192

that was fairly easy. Then into those that had to do with Rappahannock—that took a little longer. Staying within the last year, they found five: Norris, murder. McClure/Rodriguez, smuggling. Miller/Sullivan, smuggling. Glebov, burglary, transporting stolen goods. White, murder.

Then they started reading and Cobb smiled.

"Figures," he said.

"What?"

He shook his head. "Oh, nothing. Character, that's all."

She stared at him, slightly perplexed, and he pointed to the report he was reading. "Joe," he explained. "He was a closed, reticent person—it even shows in his reports. Look at them. He hated doing this. They're all short, clipped, business like. Nothing extra in them. It must have been like pulling teeth for him."

Jessie looked back at the report in her hand. It was on Albert McClure and Juan Rodriguez. "Subj R entered the house at 370 Maple at 7:26 P.M. Conversation between R and M. 26 min. See trans." She looked. There was a long transcript in the folder. She read it. At the end was the entry, "JE/LB." Somebody else had typed the transcript of the conversation between McClure and Rodriguez. She smiled. He really did hate this.

"Jeez . . ." Cobb sighed, and Jessie looked up.

"The report on the incident in the van.

"What—"

"Seven Hispanic males, one white male Caucasian, four female Hispanic females were shot at close range. Approximately fifty rounds of ammunition were discharged." He nodded. "MacDonald was right. This White was a cold bastard." He flipped the pages. "Transcript. Photocopy of a gas receipt. Restaurant receipt." He read through it and smiled. "Well, he did get personal every once in a while. At the bottom of the page, he wrote, 'Got the bastard.' "

He continued to look through it, then placed it aside.

"Nothing?" she asked.

"Like Mac said. Dead. And the guy with him, Paulson, is dead. All of them. Like White said, 'No loose ends.' An easy one."

She read the file on Elliot Norris, the man who had killed his wife, then tried to blame it on his girlfriend, Donna Hooker, in Rappahannock.

Norris was a computer software salesman. He called in on June 7 at 3:30 a.m. to report that his wife, Sharon, had been murdered. When the police got there, Norris told them that he had come in from the road late and found his wife dead. Upon searching the house, the investigating officers found jewelry missing. It looked like Mrs. Norris had been killed during a burglary, and would have passed that way if one of the officers, Miles, hadn't noticed that there was a VCR and CD player left untouched in the same room. And the intruder had gained entry through the back door. The plate had nearly been torn off by a screwdriver. There were a couple of things wrong with this: a good burglar would have just shoved the screwdriver between the doorframe and the door and popped the latch. The bolt wasn't set. If the burglar was a slob and ripped it open, that meant he wasn't the kind that would concentrate just on jewelry. Probably on drugs. He would have taken the VCR and CD player and gotten out in a hurry. Miles reported this to the detectives and they decided to put a bug on Norris and follow him. This went on for a few days; then he made his trip to Rappahannock and the detectives found the girlfriend and the jewelry. Donna Hooker said she didn't even know Norris was married. When Norris accused her of doing the killing, Hooker was able to provide an alibi. She was a student at Rappahannock Community College in Glenns, and was studying with a girlfriend, Janet Buchanan, until twelve midnight. The ME fixed the time of death for Sharon Norris at between eleven and twelve.

When she was finished, she handed it to Cobb. "He

says he didn't do it. Maybe he didn't."

Cobb took it and read through it, then shrugged.

"I don't know." He sighed. "I think he did it. Maybe Donna was lying about knowing he was married, but her alibi is solid. People saw her at the library at eleven." He shook his head. "But, it is a maybe, I suppose."

They read on, going from the Rappahannock cases to the others. From one of the folders, Cobb pulled out a photo and handed it to Jessie.

"Lou Kelly."

She looked at the man in the photo. Light hair, round face, pudgy jaw, flat eyes.

She shook her head. "No. I haven't seen him."

"He might have had plastic surgery," Cobb urged. "Just look at the shape of his head, the—"

She looked up at him. "You forget what I do for a living."

"What?"

"I deal with shapes for a living. That's the first way I looked at him. The round face, soft jaw, ears . . ." She shook her head. "And the eyes. Plastic surgery can't change the eyes. I'm fairly sure I haven't seen him." She shrugged. "I could be wrong, I suppose, but I just don't think so."

They went on, and finally, late in the afternoon, Cobb dropped a sheath of papers onto a pile he'd made in front of him.

"I just don't think it's here," he said glumly. "There was nothing left pending, except what he turned over to Mac-Donald. Joe was a very neat guy. Everything's all rounded off, caught up, taken care of, thank you very much." He frowned. "Dammit," he growled and stood up. "We're missing it. Whatever happened, we're missing it." He paced the floor. "An ex-cop out fishing picks up a woman who's had a flat and gives her a ride. They get lost, ask directions at a farm. They drive to a bait stand where the ex-cop buys bait, then they drive on to town where he lets the woman out. She sees him one more time in a restaurant, but there's no exchange between them. And that's it. But somebody kills the cop and tries to kill the woman. What the hell did he or they see?"

Jessie paused for a moment. "Well, we know it wasn't a crime."

Cobb's eyes narrowed questioningly, and she went on. "Because if a crime had been committed, say—the bait stand operator was selling dope, Joe would have turned it over to the local police. He didn't want to be a cop anymore. He hated it. He wouldn't have become involved in something. Ellie and Mac gave us that."

Cobb nodded. "Yeah, but he became preoccupied with something. Saw something that . . . reminded him of something . . ."

"Which says to me that it had to be a past case."

Cobb looked at the files. "Which leads us back here. A dead end."

"Other than Elliot Norris and Donna Hooker."

Cobb looked doubtful. "Like I said, maybe. But to tell you the truth, I don't think so."

Jessie sighed. "Well, that was a nice trip." She shook her head. "You know, this is a really frustrating line of work."

He smiled slowly. "Well, I have a remedy for frustration."

She smiled, too. "I like the way you think, Cobb."

Afterwards, stretched out on the bed with just a sheet over them, Jessie eased over on her elbow and looked at the files scattered around the room. "I've got a feeling your remedy was only short term."

"I've got a feeling you're right."

"Okay, what's the plan?"

He shook his head. "Check out Donna Hooker. And if that goes the way I think it will, start all over."

Thirty-two

They were on the road early the next morning, taking the highway to Hampton Roads, then north up 64 to 17. Slowly the city and its outskirts began to scatter away and Jessie felt better. There were fishing boats and yachts on the York River skimming through fog and into the glistening sunlight.

They pulled into Rappahannock a little after nine. A cool breeze blew off the river and the sun was bright.

They stopped at the motel room and unloaded the files, then looked up Donna Hooker's address in the phone book.

It was a small apartment complex near the river. Jessie knocked on the door as Cobb eased his way out of the Bronco.

An auburn-haired woman in her early twenties answered the door. Tall, angular, and pretty in a quiet way, she wasn't what Jessie expected. Mistresses didn't look like this. They were supposed be sexy and blond with big breasts. So much for expectations.

When Cobb told her why they were there, her face hardened and the prettiness faded away.

"I thought that was over with," she said tightly. "Do we have to go over all this again?"

"I'm afraid so," Cobb informed her. "It won't take but a few minutes."

Turning, she nodded. "Okay," she said, and a weight

seemed to settle through her. "Let's get it over with — I've got a class at eleven."

The apartment was furnished with various styles of chairs and a sofa. Posters of Garth Brooks and Clint Black hung on the wall. There was a rack stereo on a bookshelf made of bricks and boards.

She gestured them to the sofa, and she sat in one of the chairs. Wearing shorts and a T-shirt with Elvis on the front, she pulled her knees up into her chest, then wrapped her arms around them. It was a protective motion, and suddenly Jessie felt guilty about being there. This was Donna Hooker's nightmare come back again.

Her arms tightened around her legs, and she said, "I loved him, you know." Her eyes glistened. "I still do, I guess." She shook her head. "Dammit . . ."

"Even after he said you did it?" Cobb asked.

She looked up, then smiled grimly. "Yeah. Isn't that crazy? I mean, here's this guy who tells me he's lonely. Lives on the road. Is single, and I'm his dream. I'm the one he's been looking for all his life."

"Where did you meet?"

"I had a part-time job at a computer store in Williamsburg a couple of days a week and he was a salesman. I met him there. God, he was nice, you know. Sweet to me. Not all that good-looking, but he was so sweet to me."

"How often did you see him?"

"Once, twice a week. Something like that. It wasn't real regular." Her lips pressed together. "Now I know why."

"Didn't you think that was odd?"

She shrugged. "He was a salesman. On the road all the time."

"Where did he say he lived?"

"In Virginia Beach."

"And you never went there?"

"No. He said it was kind of an in-between place, and he lived with two other guys, and it was a pigpen. He always said he wanted another place. A couple of times we looked at apartments together, but he always found something wrong with them."

"So you always came here to your apartment . . ."

Her eyes hardened a little and she stared at Cobb. "You mean to have sex?"

"Well . . ."

Anger edged her voice, and the muscles in her arms tightened around her legs. "That's not all we did, you know." She shook her head. "That's what the other cops asked about, too. I heard them making a joke about my name. Hooker. Like a whore. Well, I'm not a whore."

Jessie knew it was time to step in. "We didn't mean to imply that, Donna."

"The other cops sure as hell did."

"We're just trying to figure out what happened, and why."

"Why? I fell in love, that's why or what." The tears drifted down her cheeks. "I fell in love . . ." she whispered. Surrendering her grip around her legs, she wiped her tears by rolling her shoulder up and touching her cheek and eyes with the cloth of the T-shirt. *A rustling stirred in the back of Jessie's mind. Something in the motion was familiar. Something just out of reach.* "He was so sweet to me. Gave me all that stuff. I never had stuff like that before." She sniffed. "I always thought I'd grow up and find somebody nice. Then I met Elliot, and I thought it was all going the way it was supposed to go, you know. Meet somebody, fall in love, get married, have kids." She shook her head. "Then a couple of cops come to the door . . . and it's all over with. They jammed Elliot up against that wall and handcuffed him, then tore up my apartment looking for the stuff. And it wasn't like it was hidden. It was there. All they had to do was ask me, but they tore my house up . . ." Trembling, she looked around. "This is where I live. But even that wasn't the bad part. It was when they said he was married, and he killed her. *Killed her.* Do you know what that was like? I . . . I shared a bed with him. Ate with him. Let him touch me. And they tell me that this person I love has killed somebody. It's like nothing makes sense. Nothing is real. But even that wasn't the worst part . . ." She sobbed and used the arm of her T-shirt to wipe her face.

Taking a tissue from her purse, Jessie crossed to Donna Hooker and handed it to her. She looked up, then took it.

"The worst part," Jessie said, "was when he said you did it."

Donna's eyes widened a little. "Yeah . . . if I hadn't been studying that night, they might have thought . . ." She wiped her eyes. "He said I did it. He would have let them put me in jail . . ." She dabbed her nose and looked to Jessie. "I loved him, and he did that." Her bewilderment was making her sound like a child. "He did that."

Sitting back down, Jessie asked, "Do you know a man named Joe Early?"

"Ealey?"

"Early. Joe Early."

She shook her head slowly. "I don't think so. There are a lot of people in my classes, but I don't remember that name. Is he a student?"

"No," Cobb said. "Where were you two weeks ago Wednesday?"

"I . . ." she sniffed. "I don't know. Wednesdays I have an eleven o'clock, a twelve o'clock, and a chem lab in the afternoon."

"Then you weren't in Rappahannock from, say, one to four?"

"The lab is from one-thirty to three-thirty. I usually get home about four."

"What about that Wednesday?"

She shrugged. "I . . . don't know. That was what, the sixth?"

"Eighth," Cobb said.

"I had classes," she said. "And I went to lab. I think I got finished early and came home about . . . it would have been about three-thirty . . . and I met some friends at The Harbor for a drink."

"The yacht harbor?"

"No, a place called The Harbor, down at the yacht harbor." She nodded. "It seems like it was two weeks ago. Yeah, I think it was."

"Who did you meet?"

"Cindy Baker and Lou Anne Larson."

"How long were you there?"

"Two hours or so."

Cobb nodded and pulled himself up on his crutches. "Thank you, Miss Hooker."

She blinked. "Is that all?"

"That's all."

She walked them to the door, and as Jessie climbed into the Bronco, she saw Donna closing the door, wiping her eyes with the top of her T-shirt.

Cobb shook his head. "I don't think so."

"No," Jessie said absently. "I don't either . . ."

Cobb's eyes came around. "What?"

Jessie looked up and shook her head. "Oh . . . I'm . . . not sure. One of those little nagging feelings in the back of my mind."

"About what?"

"That's just it, I'm not sure. When she wiped her eyes, it reminded me of something."

"What?"

She sighed. "If I knew, it wouldn't be nagging me. Just a feeling." She sighed with frustration. "It probably has nothing to do with this."

"Maybe. Maybe not. When I get that feeling it's like a tune to a song I can't remember."

"Yeah . . ."

"Could you have met her before?"

She shook her head. "No. I don't think so."

"She said she was at the marina. Could it have been there?"

"I . . ." She shrugged. "I don't know. But you're right.

Maybe I saw her there, passed her in a store, something like that."

"But she seemed familiar?"

"Yes . . . no, what she *did* seemed familiar." She ran her fingers through her hair. "Hell, I don't what I mean." She sighed with frustration. "You know what I think?"

"What?"

"I think all of this is driving me crazy and I'm grasping at straws. As a matter of fact, a straw would seem like a major coup right now." She looked at him. "So, where to next?"

"The bait stand."

"Why there?"

Cobb shrugged. "We have to start somewhere, and that's as good a place as any."

They drove to the stand, then past it to a Laundromat parking lot.

They sat and watched. The man in the overalls, the aging hippie, occasionally came outside, stretched, smoked a cigarette, then wandered back inside. Pickups pulling boats came and went. Sitting there, Jessie's mind kept wandering back to Donna Hooker and the motion of her wiping her tears. *Dabbing her eyes with the cloth of the T-shirt on her shoulder. Rolling her shoulder up. An awkward motion* . . . Frowning, she shook her head. What the hell did a motion have to do with anything? She let her mind wander to other things; after a while, she had to fight to stay awake. It all gave boredom a new meaning. After a while she decided it was providential they were in front of a Laundromat, so she did the laundry and read magazines. *Time, Newsweek.* They were a little out of date. The Berlin Wall was just coming down. There was still a USSR. When she finished with the laundry, she settled back into the Bronco and an odd emptiness slowly settled over her. She hadn't painted in . . . how many days? Six days. And she missed it. Missed the concentration. The focusing. The smell of the paint. The lines and shapes. Of course, what she was doing now was a little like that — trying to find form and line and shape. But before, she had known where to look. Not anymore.

She must have been dozing because Cobb touched her and she jumped.

He smiled. "I've fired guys for that."

"I wish I could get fired from this job."

He looked at his watch. "There's nothing happening here. It's almost twelve — let's go take a look at that farm again. Maybe they'll come in for lunch."

Nodding, she started the Bronco and pulled out of the parking lot and onto the highway, and she breathed a little easier. Moving felt good.

Winding their way through the farmland, it took them almost twenty minutes to get to the farm. As they approached it, Jessie's eyes roamed over the fields, then the barn and two-story frame house under the poplars and oaks.

"Doesn't look like anybody's home," Cobb said.

The pickup still stood at the back porch. The tire leaned against the oak and the shovels and rakes were propped against the tractor.

"Let's try after eight," she said. "They should be home by then."

Cobb rubbed his chin. "Yeah," he nodded. "Then let's go back to Joe's. Go through his stuff again. Closets, under the bed, everything."

"You think we missed something?"

He shrugged. "I don't know. To tell you the truth, I just can't think of anything else to do."

The key was still under the flower pot on the back porch. Stepping inside, she felt an odd chill. The dishes still in the sink. Still arranged. Counters clear. Everything exactly the way they had left it. It was as if they had chanced on a place where nothing ever changed, moved, or breathed.

"I'll do the study, you take the living room," Cobb said.

He limped away on the crutch, and she walked into the

living room. The chill brushed her again. Everything was the same. As if she'd stepped into a photograph.

Easy chair. Recliner. Coffee table. Books. Records, CD's, tapes. Everything neat. Arranged. In place.

Except the newspaper beside the recliner.

It was funny. The newspaper bothered her. Walking to it, she picked it up, folded it, and looked at it. Friday. The day before he died.

She put it down on the recliner, then turned to the records, CD's, and tapes. She went through them. Then the books. Then the magazines and newspapers.

Then she paused and looked back at the newspaper on the recliner.

She picked it up again and began going through it. Her eyes combed each page.

The front page was a mixture of local and national news. Inside were editorials, columns, more local news.

She stopped at each crime report.

A burglary. Boating accident. Neighbor dispute. Car theft. A fistfight in a local restaurant. Another burglary. Farm equipment stolen.

And that was it.

She read them all again, but found nothing.

Then she started through the paper again. Carefully. Going through each article.

Fishing reports. A feature on a local artist. The monthly fish fry from the volunteer fire department. How the druggist used a computer to find lost relatives. High school track teams. A new coach coming to the high school. A new bridge. She read them all.

Then did it again.

Her eyes moved over the pages, taking in each word. Then she realized she was skipping the photographs and the captions under them.

She went through the pages again.

And this time she found it.

Thirty-three

"It's thin," Cobb said as Jessie pulled the Bronco into the driveway leading to the farmhouse and looked back at the newspaper they had taken from Early's living room. His eyes went back to the story about the volunteer fire department holding its monthly fish fry. In the picture above the story were two men standing behind a stove in front of the firehouse. The photograph had been taken to show the outside stoves, tables, and the firehouse, and the men in the picture were not clearly detailed. Under the photo the caption read, "Carl and Larry Atherton make sure the stoves and deep fat fryers are ready for the fish fry Saturday, 9 to 5 at the Firehouse."

He looked at the mailbox as they drove by it. "Atherton," he said.

"It was the last newspaper he read," Jessie said. "Saturday's was still wrapped up and on the kitchen table where Mrs. Scott had put it. She said he usually went fishing first thing in the morning, then came home, ate, then settled down and read the newspaper and a novel in the afternoon. That morning he didn't go fishing, but he probably didn't read this until Friday afternoon. When he went for a drive."

She drove up behind the pickup and parked. "And

the newspaper was on the floor," she said. "Out of place. It was the only thing out of place in that house. I think he made some kind of connection and hurried out to check it."

Cobb rubbed his chin. "Could be."

Leaving the Bronco running, she opened the door and stepped out.

The chill washed over her again because for the second time that day she had the feeling of stepping into a photograph. Nothing had changed since they had been there on Friday.

She walked up on the porch and to the screen door. She knocked, then opened the screen and peered through the glass into the large kitchen. She knocked again. No answer. Raising her hand to create a shadow, she looked into the kitchen again.

Nothing out of the ordinary. Nothing . . . then her eyes stopped.

Turning, she ran back to the Bronco and got in.

"Friday when I looked in the kitchen there was a package of meat on the counter. Put out to thaw, it looked like," she told Cobb. "I just looked and it's still there."

"You're sure it's the same one?"

She nodded. "Same one, same place. Exactly."

His finger rubbed the spot where his mustache had been. "Nobody's been here for four days."

"Do we go in?"

He thought about it for a moment. "No. Not yet." He twisted in the seat, looking up and down the road. "Let's find a neighbor first."

Jessie drove back to the road and turned away from the river. She went to the first crossroads and turned right. She drove another mile before they saw another farmhouse. It was a small brick ranch with a barn and a silo beyond it. Jessie pulled into the short driveway and parked behind an old Buick Electra.

Jessie got out and walking up on the small concrete

front porch, she knocked on the door.

A small, pretty woman in her twenties opened the door and smiled cautiously. "Yes?"

Jessie showed her the badge. "Hi," she said. "I'm Lynn Monroe with the Sheriff's Department in Clear Creek. I'm sorry to bother you, Mrs. . . . ?"

"Yearwood," she said. "Darlene Yearwood."

". . . But I've been trying to contact your neighbors, the Athertons. Have you seen them lately?"

Darlene Yearwood's eyes followed the badge down as Jessie slipped it back into her purse. "Is there some kind of trouble?"

Jessie smiled and shook her head. "No. They witnessed an accident a few months back and we need to talk to them about it."

"Well, Grant and I wondered . . . Grant's my husband—"

"Wondered? Why?"

"Their alfalfa. They started harvesting last week, cut it and left it lying in the field. Now it will rot and they're going to lose the whole thing. And over toward the river about ten head of cattle are out and on our land. We don't mind, you know, but when Grant called them, he couldn't get an answer. Even went over, but nobody seems to be there."

"When was the last time you saw them?"

She shrugged. "I don't know . . . over a week ago. They were supposed to be at the fish fry at the fire department, but they never came." Her mouth settled into disapproval, making her face seem older. "I just don't think that's right, you know, to say you're going to do something, then not do it. Grant ended up havin' to do extra duty because of them. Right thoughtless, if you ask me. They even got their picture in the paper. Grant sure didn't."

"Does this happen often?"

"You mean them goin' off?"

"Yes."

207

Her mouth settled again. "Well, no, not like this. They go off sometimes, on trips, things like that. Vacations. Usually that Larry. I always kind of thought they were more gentleman farmers, if you know what I mean, but they never let this kind of thing happen before. They never just went off and left a crop in the field."

As she talked, Cobb eased out of the Bronco and limped toward them.

Darlene looked at him. "Why, you've gone and hurt yourself—"

He shook his head. "I'm all right, ma'am."

"This is my partner," Jessie said. "Would you mind if we came in and sat down?"

"Well, of course, didn't mean to keep you standin' out here in the sun."

They went into a modest living room. It was furnished with cheap or second-hand furniture, clean but a little littered. Picking up a newspaper and cable guide from the sofa, she gestured for them to sit down. Darlene took the overstuffed chair.

"You were telling me about the Athertons," Jessie said.

"Oh, just that they go off sometimes, but they never just leave a crop in the field."

"Are they not married?"

"Well, Carl was, of course, but she left him a long time ago. Went off with a Jehovah's Witness, they say. I never knew her."

"And the son, Larry?"

Again, the settling of the mouth. "Well, now that one probably never will get married, the way he runs around."

"Runs around?"

"Kind of plays the field, if you know what I mean. He's the one always going off down to Virginia Beach. Tell you the truth, Grant and I have never been able to figure how they make it through the year on what they

208

raise. We work this place a lot harder than they work that one, but they always seem to have money. Oh, they act like they're just makin' it, but they've got money. Grant thinks they inherited it. Investments, something like that."

"How do you know?" Cobb asked.

"What?"

"How do you know they have money? I mean, do they drive an expensive car, or have—"

She shook her head. "No. Not like that. But Larry likes clothes. Has a pair of ostrich skin boots. Grant swears they must cost right much. Five, six hundred dollars, at least. And every time you see him he's wearin' a new shirt."

"But not Carl?"

"Oh, Carl, no. He goes two or three days wearing the same thing. The only thing he cares about is hunting."

Jessie leaned forward. "You said Larry dated a lot. Who does he go out with?"

"Oh, that Trish Forman in Rappahannock. And I saw him once with Carrie Rush from Urbana. All in the space of about two weeks. And there's talk about other girls down in Williamsburg and Virginia Beach. Playin' the field's what he's doin'. Needs to settle down."

"How long have you known them?"

"Seven years. That's when we bought this place. Grant always wanted a place of his own, and we finally got one. 'Course, we have to work it day and night, but it's ours. And the bank's."

"Do the Athertons have a hired hand?"

Darlene shook her head. "Not regular. Hard to get hired help any more. Ever' once in a while you see one over there, but they come and go."

"No one lately, somebody we could get hold of?"

"No, I haven't seen a hand over there for a couple of months."

"When they're gone, do they usually tell you?"

209

"Sometimes, if both of them are leavin' and they're goin' to be gone a while, they ask us to put feed out for the cattle. But not often. They come and go as they please."

"Where do they go on their trips?"

Darlene sighed, thinking. "Virginia Beach. That's where Larry goes. He almost commutes, if you ask me."

"And when they go together?"

She shrugged. "Usually huntin' someplace. I know they went to Colorado elk huntin' one fall. Like I said, they come and go as they please."

Cobb pushed himself to his feet. "Mrs. Yearwood, we're going to go back over to the Athertons' and try to get in. I'm telling you this so you won't be alarmed."

"Do you think something's happened?"

"No," Jessie answered. "We just need to get this traffic accident cleared up, and the sooner we find them, the sooner that will happen."

"Well, you let me know if there's anything else I can do."

Thirty-four

In the Bronco, Jessie said, "Joe was killed on Saturday and the Athertons didn't show up for the fish fry on Sunday."

Cobb nodded. "Yeah."

Jessie drove back up the driveway of the Atherton farm and parked behind the pickup.

"You have the pistol I gave you?" Cobb asked.

She nodded. "In my purse."

They climbed out of the Bronco and walked up onto the porch, Jessie first, Cobb limping after her.

She opened the screen door and looked into the kitchen.

Empty.

The meat package was still on the counter beside the sink.

Cobb tried the door. It slipped open.

He looked at Jessie.

"Who goes on a trip without locking their door?" she asked.

He shook his head. "Not many."

They stepped into the kitchen. From the top of the house, Jessie could hear the drone of an attic fan. Warm air rustled in the kitchen, thick with the taint of spoiled meat. Jessie's muscles tensed. It was like the smell of death.

The old oak floor moaned softly under them as they crossed the room to the sink. Jessie looked at the meat. It was dark, almost black. The smell was very strong.

"Not good," Cobb said and slipped his pistol from its holster.

Jessie tugged the 9mm from her purse and released the safety.

They turned toward the doorway. It led into a dining room. The windows were open to let air circulate. A long table was in the middle of the room. It was littered with mail, brochures, forms, tax records, bills.

The dining room opened into a hallway—the front door on one side, a staircase leading to the second floor on the other.

They crossed the hallway to a living room. A huge fireplace dominated the far wall. Over it hung a poorly done oil painting of a country stream in autumn. A sofa faced the fireplace, a coffee table in front of it. Overstuffed chairs hugged the corners of the room. The furniture was sturdy, utilitarian. Hunting magazines on the coffee table and a coffee cup. Beyond the living room, behind the fireplace, was what looked like an added-on room. There was another sofa, a television set, and a cheap rack stereo set up in a corner. Bookshelves with very few books. Mostly hunting magazines and seed catalogues, and a gun rack filled with rifles and shotguns.

Cobb limped to the gun rack and nodded. "Interesting."

"What?"

"These shotguns " He pointed to the first one. "This is a Parker double barrel. VHE. Made before World War Two. A collector's shotgun." He pointed to the next one. "And this is a Parker replica made by Remington. Also a collector's gun. The Parker is worth four thousand or so, the Remington replica about twenty-five hundred." His eyes moved down the weapons. "Jesus . . ." he whispered.

"What?"

"A Winchester Model 21. Hand tooled. Made to order. They run from four to ten thousand dollars—"

"That's a lot of money for a shotgun."

Cobb nodded and glanced over the room. "Nothing else says money here." He pointed to the stereo and television. "Just what anybody would have. Normal folks. But the shotguns say money and a lot of it."

"And the ostrich skin boots Darlene told us about."

Cobb nodded. "Where's the money coming from?" He turned back through the door. "I'm going to go through the stuff on the dining-room table. You look around upstairs."

The hum of the attic fan increased as Jessie climbed the stairs to the second floor. The landing was in the middle of the hallway. To her left there were two doors, both closed. The window at the end of the hall was open. To her right, she could see that the doors into the hallway were open for circulation. Halfway down the hall was a small table with a lamp on it. A broom and dustpan leaned against the frame of the middle door. She walked through the open door of the first room. It was used for storage. Old clothes, a saddle, horse blanket, a toolbox. The second room was a large bathroom. Claw-footed bathtub with an added shower. Towels stuffed, rather than hung, on the racks. Plastic razors on the sink.

The next door led to a bedroom. Air rustled through the open windows in the characterless room. Plain. A bed, unmade. Nightstand. Dresser. A chair with clothes piled on it. No pictures, paintings, nothing personal. The next bedroom was the exact opposite. Skiing and surfing posters littered the walls. CD's were arranged in small boxes along the wall, and in a cabinet was an expensive stereo. A carousel compact disk player, top of the line. She crossed to the closet. Darlene was right. A lot of new shirts. Well cut. On the floor were the ostrich skin boots.

She turned to the dresser and pulled out the top drawer. Socks. The next one. Underwear. She pushed it back in and was about to pull the next one out when she heard something.

Faint, but there.

Like glass breaking downstairs someplace.

Lifting the pistol, she walked back out of the bedroom and down the hall. She came to the landing and paused.

"Cobb?"

No answer.

Panic exploded through her and she backed against the wall. "Cobb," she screamed. "Answer me—"

Her breath hammered through her and she waited.

But no answer came.

Thirty-five

Trembling, she pressed harder back into the wall.

She wanted to call out again, but she knew it would do no good. She knew they were down there.

Knew that Cobb was probably dead.

Hopelessness washed through her, strong and hot and draining. She closed her eyes for a moment, wanting to give up, just let it go.

Then she remembered the look on Swann's face when he tried to kill her.

No, you sonofabitch, she thought. No.

Bringing the 9mm up, she cocked the hammer and looked down the stairs. She could see a fragment of the hallway. Sunlight on the floor. The entrance to the living room. The corner of a chair.

Nothing moved. Cobb had been in the dining room, back to her right and out of her line of sight. That's probably where they were.

She raised her eyes to the second floor. There were windows at both ends of the hall. One would open out onto the back porch, the other out onto a side porch. She remembered trees around the house, close to the porch. That meant a way down. And a way up.

She looked back to the stairs, watching and listening.

Quiet razored through the old farmhouse. The only thing she could hear was her own breathing and the attic fan.

They were waiting. Waiting for her to move. To do something. To make a mistake.

She closed her eyes and hugged the pistol close to her. What would Cobb do?

She smiled suddenly. Probably something incredibly macho.

Cobb.

The smile disappeared into a sharp pain. And she shook her head. Don't think about that, she told herself. Don't let anything distract you. Paint. Focus.

With her eyes closed, she imagined drawing a line, a hand. *Her* hand. The thumb, forefinger . . .

What would Cobb do?

Don't let them rattle you. You rattle them. *Distract them.* Back at the shed in the woods, Cobb had told her to throw sticks to pull them out.

Opening her eyes, she looked down the stairs. Nothing moved. No sounds.

She drew in a deep breath, easing it through her. Then another.

She looked up and down the hallway. There was the table with a lamp on it. The broom propped against the first doorframe. The dustpan.

Her eyes went back to the broom.

Taking a breath, she took a step and crossed the landing of the stairs. The old floor moaned under her.

She pressed against the wall and looked down the stairs.

No movement.

She looked again to the broom. About six feet away.

Putting her purse down, she knelt and fished out the two extra clips, slipped them into her belt, and looped the strap of her purse over her head.

Pausing, she swallowed, then took a deep breath and stood up.

The old floor creaked as she rushed down the hallway. She didn't attempt to be quiet. She made it to the broom and dustpan, snatched them up, then ran back to the stairs.

Putting the dustpan down and shifting the pistol to her left hand, she picked up the broom, then hurled it like a spear at the window at the far end of the hallway.

It wobbled its way through the air, sinking fast, but the handle made it to the bottom pane of glass, shattering it. As it did, Jessie put the pistol back into her right hand and leaned around the corner of the landing and leveled the 9mm down the stairs.

A form flickered in the doorway to the living room, and she pulled the trigger — slowly, carefully pulled the trigger. The noise of the first shot startled her. Contained in the stairwell, it roared, piercing her eardrums, and she wished she'd thought to use something for earplugs. But now it was too late. She pulled the trigger again, putting five shots down the stairs, spraying the entry way. Somewhere in the roar of the shots, she thought she heard glass and wood shattering.

Then the blast of the shots whispered away into the humming of her eardrums.

Leaning down, she picked up the dustpan with her left hand and tossed it at the window at the opposite end of the hallway.

It tumbled through the air, but only made it about halfway down the hall, clattering against a wall, then dropping to the floor. She turned back to the stairwell.

And waited. Waited.

There was no movement.

She waited. Another beat.

Then she pulled the trigger, filling the air with shots until the gun was empty.

Pressing back against the wall, she released the clip, tugged another from her belt, shoved it home, released the safety nosing another shell into the chamber, then cocked the hammer. And remembered to breathe.

"Damn . . ." she whispered, closing her eyes. Keep going, she thought. Just keep going.

217

Opening her eyes, she turned down the hallway, running to the storage room.

Through the door. An old radio sat on the chair next to the door.

Picking it up, she flung it into the window, shattering it.

Then she turned back into the hallway and to the stairwell. Eased up to the corner and around it. Put two shots down it.

And eased back into the hallway and sat down.

"Do it," she whispered. "Just do it."

Laying the pistol down, she slipped her tennis shoes off and stuffed them into her purse; then she picked up the pistol and looked at the window at the end of the hallway.

A breeze fluttered the curtains.

"Shit," she sighed, and pushing herself up, she padded quietly down the hallway to the window. It was open far enough for her to slip through. Unhooking the screen, she pushed it out, looked back down the hallway, then stepped through the window. Dropping one foot, then the other onto the roof of the porch, she eased the screen back into the frame and pressed it shut.

Turning away from the front door to the back of the house, she padded to the corner and looked around it.

There were three oaks along the porch. The first two were smaller with branches reaching toward the roof, the closest about three feet. The third was the largest. Its limbs pushed up over the edge of the roof.

And, of course, it was the farthest away and closest to the kitchen door.

Of course.

Thirty-six

Pulling her purse around in front of her, she took the remaining clip out of her belt and pushed it down in next to her shoes and followed it with the pistol. Then she pushed the purse around until it hung on her back.

She looked around the corner again. At the far oak.

"Shit," she growled, and stepped around the corner.

Staying next to the wall, she ran on tiptoe until she was even with the tree, then, without stopping, she padded down to the limb.

The limb over the roof of the porch wasn't large enough for her to walk on, but it would hold her weight. The one next to it was only about a foot short of the porch, and smaller than the first.

Crouching onto her hands and knees, Jessie crawled a few inches out onto the first limb, then reached out and grasped the branches of the second and pulled it to her, then under her, until she was able to ease her weight over onto it; then she let go of the first branch and swung out on the second.

The limb bent down under her weight, lowering her toward the ground.

Then broke with a quick, loud POP!

Suddenly she was tumbling through the air, her feet

swinging out from under her, and she slammed into the ground on the point of her shoulder.

Her breath barked out in an involuntary scream as she rolled on the grass. For a moment blackness tinged the edges of her vision, and she fought to keep from passing out. Her face pushed into the grass, and the smell of it seemed to fill her. The darkness whispered around her, but she fought against it, working her feet, pushing across the grass until she felt the incline, then she rolled down the small hill.

Forcing air into her lungs, she looked up. The woods were about fifty yards away. She tried to get her legs under her, but they weren't working right, and she slumped down again. She had to move and keep moving. Please, she whispered to herself, struggling to get air into her lungs. Please. Her legs pumped under her and she inched across the grass. Toward the woods. Slowly, with the air, some strength came. Pausing, rocking up on her knees, she got her feet under her, then pushed up. Stood. And slumped back down. Then tried it again. This time she made it. She pulled more air into her lungs. God, breathing felt good. She staggered toward the trees.

The scattered edge of the woods began to finger around her. A small poplar. Brush. She slumped down again. And pushed up. Only a few more feet. Only a few —

She felt him there, just an instant before his fist hammered into her back. A dark presence. Then his fist hit her square in the middle of her back, driving her down to her knees. He took a step and hit her again with his open hand across her jaw, driving her down into the dirt and grass. His rough hands jerked her over onto her back, pawed her breasts, stomach, and back, searching, then he tore the purse from her.

She looked up, expecting to see Swann. But it wasn't Swann.

It was his partner.

He raked through the purse, then nodded and looked down at her.

"There it is," he said. "A Browning. Good gun." His jaw hardened. "You damn near shot me, you know that?" Leaning down, he slapped her again. "I can see why old Swann is pissed at you. And believe me, he's pissed. We need your boyfriend for a while, until we find out how far you've gotten. But not you." He smiled. "You're gonna beg him to die before it's over."

Reaching out, he dragged her to him, then stood up. She fell into him, her face in his crotch. Her hands fumbled over him.

He smiled. "Now I'd like that, too, nice quick blow job." He pushed her face in his crotch again.

And she knew she had one chance.

One. There was no time to think about it.

Concentrating all of her strength and will, she brought her hands together, clasping them, then as he lifted her up, she used the momentum to bring her fists up, slamming them into his crotch, crushing his testicles.

He coughed and made a squeaking sound, stumbled backwards, dropped the purse, took another step, and sank to his knees. His hands held his crotch, his face had blanched absolutely white and the muscles in his face and throat corded as if they were struggling to break free of the sweat-glistening skin. His eyes rolled, unfocused, then he looked at her and his mouth slackened open and he moaned again. Slowly, in nightmare time, his right hand released his crotch and dragged across his dark slacks upwards toward his belt.

Toward the gun in the holster.

Still dazed, Jessie blinked. His hand kept moving.

She reached out for him, but she had no strength. Her fingers fumbled weakly onto his hand, trying to grasp it. His hand slipped away from her fingers and curled around the butt of his pistol.

Gathering all the strength she had, she lunged into him. Both of them slumped over onto the grass.

But his hand closed around the butt of the pistol and dragged it from the holster.

She crawled to him and, reaching out, she managed to get her hand on the pistol.

His thumb rested on the hammer. Pressed it back. The click of metal snapped in her ears.

Pushing into him again, she tried to get her fingers around the weapon, but he kept raising it toward her.

Mustering her strength once more, she shoved her hand into the pistol, fighting to get her fingers around it, but pushed it into his stomach instead.

The explosion of the pistol roared through her.

The man blinked, stared at her, then slumped back into the grass still staring at her.

She looked down and saw the blood spreading across his shirt.

Unbelieving, she touched it, then looked at his eyes again.

They stared at her. Fixed.

A flicker of movement tugged her eyes up and she saw Swann come around the house. He paused, his gaze sweeping the hill.

Then it found her.

Reaching down, she grasped her purse, and had to think to get her arms and legs to work. To move. But she did.

Stumbling, crawling, she felt the leaves brush her face, and the limbs blocked out the sky.

Behind her, she knew Swann was coming.

Thirty-seven

She pushed deeper into the woods. Dark, cool shade closed around her, and when she was sure she was covered, she stood up, and stumbling, she ran.

Motion seemed to breed motion. The more she moved, the stronger she got.

The ground dropped away sharply into a creek, and she ran to it, then along the bank. Rounding a huge oak, her bare foot caught one of the roots; stumbling, she went down, crashing into the leaves.

Her foot throbbing, she sat up and looked back. The crest of the hill was outlined clearly against a thin spot in the tree cover.

Anybody coming over the hill would be in plain sight. A perfect target.

Reaching into her purse, she found the pistol and tugged it free, crawling behind the trunk of the oak. Stretching out, she faced the hill.

Her foot pulsed with pain and with it came anger.

She wasn't running any more.

She cocked the hammer back. "Come on, you sonofabitch," she whispered. "Come on."

She raised the pistol and resting it on the root, she leveled it on the hill.

And waited.

Listening.

A breeze rustled the treetops. Birds and insects.

No footfalls.

She kept the pistol on the crest of the hill, and waited.

Swann dragged Hanks into the brush, until he was well out of sight, then rolled him into some leaves.

He would send a cleanup team after him later.

Standing up straight, Swann stared into the shifting of trees, sunlight, and bushes.

His jaw hardened.

He would never have believed a woman, a cunt, could have been this much trouble.

But her luck would run out.

And when it did, he would be there.

He looked back toward the farmhouse. But that was for later.

Right now, he had Cobb to deal with.

He walked out of the woods and toward the house.

Cobb awoke into dull, pulsing pain. His eyes fluttered open into a blur. He remembered hearing something in the kitchen. He had pulled his gun and gone into the kitchen, and they hit him from both sides.

He frowned. If he'd just been able to move. But he hadn't. His foot slowed him too much.

His vision cleared. A ceiling stretched above him. He moved his head and could see a stove next to him. He was in the kitchen. On the floor. Alone. And alive.

He blinked. He was still alive.

Why?

Think about that later, he told himself. He jerked upward, and tried to sit up, but something held him down. Something around his wrist.

A handcuff.

His eyes followed the chain to the other cuff around the gas pipe for the stove.

Getting up onto his knees, he grasped the chain with his free hand and tried to pull the pipe free.

No luck.

He tried again, but it was no good. The pipe was anchored like lead.

He pushed around, placing his shoulder against the stove, then tried to rock it backwards. It didn't budge.

Sweat popped out on his face and back. He tried again. Nothing.

He leaned into it again. Pushing. Pushing—

"You know," a voice said behind him, "I've seen guys do a lot of things to get out of a handcuff."

Cobb eased back down, and slumping into the stove, he turned around.

Swann stood at the back door. A heavy .44 Magnum in his hand, the hammer back.

"I knew a guy once that broke his own hand, crushed it with a tire jack so he could pull it free."

Shaking his head, he walked forward. "Another guy one time used an axe. Bled to death. Kind of like wolves or coyotes in a trap, chewing their own paws off to get free."

Staying well away from Cobb, he pulled a kitchen chair out, turned it around, then sat down and leaned on the back. "Just shows you, we're all animals way down deep."

Cobb wiped the sweat from his face.

Swann smiled. "Aren't you going to say something? Haven't you been through the FBI training course, Cobb? You're supposed to establish rapport with me. Find common ground. Make me think of you as a person."

"Wouldn't work.

"Why?"

"In order to relate, you'd have to *be* a person."

The smile faded. "That's not very smart, Cobb. Hostility. Trying to make me angry."

"I flunked the course."

"We're having a refresher."

"Sure."

Swann shook his head. "You're not doing this right."

"You mean I'm not doing it the way you want me to."

"I'm the one with the gun."

Cobb smiled. "Do you know how clichéd that is?"

"Clichés come out of truth."

"Profound."

Swann's lips pressed into a hard line. "You're still not getting this, are you? I'm—"

"You're going to kill me, Swann. I'm dead. But so are you. The difference is, I know it."

Swann stared at him for a long moment. "Aren't you even going to ask me about the woman?"

"I don't ask fags about women."

Swann blinked. "What did you call me?"

"A fag. Queer—"

Swann's face reddened.

"—that's what I've found out. About you and Jerry. Doing a little dick-kissing—"

Swann bolted out of the chair, knocking it over, rushing into Cobb, kicking him in the side of the head, driving him back into the stove and darkness.

Time dragged by for Jessie. The sun shifted through the leaves. Five minutes passed. Then another five.

She frowned. He wasn't coming. Sighing, she lowered the pistol and sat up against the oak. Of course not. He knew she had the gun, and he wouldn't take the chance. She knew that about Swann now.

He didn't take chances. He made his moves very carefully. Like taking Cobb—

Cobb.

Pain and relief filled her chest. Cobb was alive. What was it Swann's partner had said? *We need your boyfriend for a while, until we find out how far you've gotten.*

226

"Cobb," she whispered, then reached down and pulled her tennis shoes from the purse and put them on, and as she did, she remembered what else he'd said. *You're gonna beg him to die before it's over.*"

Trembling, she stood up, the words echoing through her. *You're gonna beg him to die . . .*

Then she slipped the pistol from her purse and started back toward the farmhouse.

Staying low and keeping to the brush, she made her way back the way she'd come. As the trees began to thin toward the open ground, she saw the form in the leaves. A body.

Swann's partner.

Swann had moved him out of sight.

She thumbed the hammer back on the pistol and kept moving. Circling the house.

A car engine revved and coming around where she could see the back porch and the barn, she saw the white Buick parked beside the Bronco. Swann got out, opened the trunk, then went inside.

She weaved through the brush until she could get a better line on the back door. She was still moving when Cobb staggered through it, his hands behind his back. Swann followed him onto the porch.

It was over a hundred yards to the porch, but Jessie raised the pistol.

Swann pushed Cobb across the porch and down the steps.

Jessie tried to get a bead on Swann, but at that distance the pistol wavered between Swann and Cobb.

Swann shoved Cobb into the trunk and closed it, then turned to the driver's door.

She followed him, then he was gone. In the car.

She kept the 9mm on the car, thinking about just opening up, emptying the gun, taking a chance of hitting him.

Then she lowered the gun.

It was no good.

She might hit Cobb.

If she could even hit the car. It was too far away, and she wasn't that good a shot.

The Buick nosed around and drove away down the drive, then turned, sped down the road and was gone.

Scrambling to her feet, she ran across the open ground, past the barn to the house and the Bronco.

Climbing in, she put the pistol on the passenger seat, started the car, roared back down the driveway, then skidded onto the road.

She pushed the Bronco to sixty and reaching the corner, she swept around it, then gunned the engine up until she was doing eighty.

But the road was clear.

She kept going. Up a long straightaway into a curve, then into another straightaway.

The road was empty.

She slowed the Bronco to a stop; sitting, staring at the road, the realization that Cobb was gone swept over her and she began to cry.

A helplessness ached through her. He was gone.

But not dead.

She wiped the tears away.

Not dead, she thought, then remembered again what Swann's partner had said. *"We need your boyfriend for a while, until we find out how far you've gotten."*

She dried her eyes. *"Until we find out how far you've gotten . . ."*

Until.

She had time. Probably not much, but she had some time. She had to move. Now.

Pulling the Bronco into gear, she gunned it out and down the road.

Thirty-eight

Back at the motel, she started through Early's files again, her eyes moving over them for any mention of Carl or Larry Atherton.

At first she stayed only to the later cases, but finding nothing, she went deeper and deeper into the files. The more she read and searched, the more her desperation grew. All she could think of was that she was running out of time.

No, *Cobb was running out of time.*

She hurried on, then realized she wasn't really reading anything, just letting her eyes comb over the words.

Dropping the papers, she stood up and walked into the bathroom and washed her face with cool water, and that brought a wisp of calm.

She looked at herself in the mirror. "You're panicking, Jess," she whispered. "Easy, just take it easy." She splashed cold water over her face again. "And stop talking to yourself."

She patted her face dry and walked back into the files scattered over the floor and bed.

Frowning, she turned to the telephone. First she dialed information, then Russ MacDonald's office phone.

"Mac," she said, "This is Lynn Monroe. I talked to you Saturday."

"I remember. Looking for Joe's old files."

"I found them, but they're not doing me any good. Did he ever mention Carl or Larry Atherton? They live near Rappahannock."

"Atherton," he repeated. "Carl or Larry. Brothers?"

"Father and son. They have a farm."

It was quiet for a moment. She heard him puff on his cigar, then sigh. "No, sorry. Doesn't ring any bells. But I'll look back through my files."

"That would help."

He puffed the cigar. "You sound like you're in trouble."

"I am. And I need it fast."

"I'm on it."

"Call me back in a couple of hours."

She hung up and turned back to the files and frowned. She was burned out on that. Take a different tack.

Sitting down at the desk, she opened the telephone directory.

She found Grant Yearwood's number and dialed it.

Darlene answered.

"This is Lynn Monroe," Jessie said. "We talked earlier today."

"Oh, sure. Did you find Carl and Larry?"

"No, not yet. Darlene, you said that Larry went out with a couple of girls locally."

"Yeah, Trish Forman in Rappahannock. And Carrie Rush from Urbana."

Jessie wrote the names down. "Are they in the book?"

"Well, Trish would be. She's got an apartment there. But Carrie still lives at home. Her daddy's name is Miles."

"Do you know where they work?"

"Trish is a waitress at the Busy Bee on the highway. And Carrie, now let me think. She was at the Marina for a while, but I think she works at Bloodworth's Hardware there in Urbana now."

"Thanks, Darlene. You've been a big help."

"Oh, I'm glad to do it. Helping the police and all."

Hanging up, Jessie looked up the addresses and telephone numbers of Trish Forman, Miles Rush, the Busy Bee, and Bloodworth's Hardware.

She called and found Trish Forman at home.

"Sheriff's office?" she said, her voice nervous. "I haven't done anything—"

Jessie made her voice businesslike. "It has nothing to do with you, Miss Forman. I'm trying to locate Larry Atherton."

"Larry? I haven't seen Larry in a month or so."

"I'd like to drop by," Jessie said. "These things are done easier in person. Would a half an hour be all right?"

"Well, I . . . sure, I guess, but I haven't seen him."

"I'll see you in a half an hour."

Next she called the Rush home. Mrs. Rush answered and told Jessie that Carrie was still at work. The hardware stayed open until eight o'clock.

She called Bloodworth's and a man answered, then put Carrie on. Her reaction was a carbon copy of Trish Forman's.

"I paid that speeding ticket," she said. "If you look, I know that—"

"This is not about a speeding ticket, Miss Rush."

"It's not?"

"No, it really doesn't have anything to do with you. I'm trying to locate Larry Atherton."

A long pause. "Is he in trouble?"

"No. We're investigating a traffic accident, and Larry was a witness. I just need to interview him."

"A traffic accident. He didn't say anything about a traffic accident."

"When did you see him last?"

"Ahh . . . a week ago last Friday."

"But not since?"

"No. He stood me up. I'm really mad at him."

"When were you supposed to see him?"

231

"At the fish fry at the Fire Department. He was going to pick me up. But he didn't. Didn't call or anything."

Jessie looked at her watch. "Miss Rush, I have an appointment in a few minutes. What time do you get off?"

"Eight, or a little after."

"Can you meet me at eight-fifteen?"

"I . . . guess. Where?"

"You name the place."

"Well, there's a coffee shop next door to here."

"That'll be fine. I'll see you at eight-fifteen."

Cobb hovered in a shadowland, not conscious but not quite out either. A place of half-light, wandering sound, fragments of things not connected.

When he drifted on the edge of consciousness and the wisps began to stitch together, he knew to go back. To stay where it was safe.

Then finally he drifted into dark consciousness and the heavy smells of hay and cow manure and dust.

His eyes fluttered open to more shadows. Then a blinding light. He tried to raise his hands to cover his face, but they were restricted, bound. He remembered the handcuffs.

Something shuffled, stepping into him, then slapping his hands down.

"Welcome back," Swann said.

His hands were jerked up and he was lifted back into something — a hay bale, and he could make out a form in the bright light. Swann. As he moved, Cobb realized there was a bulb dangling from the ceiling behind Swann. Wood scraped on wood and Swann sat down in a chair, the gun in his hand.

"Well, here we are again." Conversational. Just a couple of guys shooting the shit.

Cobb closed his eyes and Swann slapped him.

"Gotta keep 'em open," he said. "You sleep too much."

"It's the company."

"Ah, that's the old Cobb. Pretty smart, getting me mad. The longer you're out, the longer you have to keep from talking. And maybe let the woman get clear."

"Brilliant. Now I can see why you went into police work. You might even be able to catch yourself. And I'll bet you do all the time. Your dick with your hand."

Swann's hand tightened on the pistol grip, and Cobb could see the sweat glisten in the bright light.

"Trying to piss me off again?"

"I'm beginning to think you're too stupid to piss off."

The .44 Magnum nosed up, almost like it had a life of its own. "You know, you just might talk me into it."

Cobb shook his head. "I don't think so."

"Oh?"

"No. You need me."

"You think so?"

"Yeah. Or I'd be dead by now."

Swann's voice tightened. "Maybe I just want to see how far you can go."

Cobb sighed. "Bullshit. You need to find the string."

Swann stared at him for a moment, then lowered the pistol. "Okay, tell me about it."

Cobb shook his head again. "Look, why don't we do this the easy way.

"What's that?"

"Put me on the payroll."

Swann laughed. "Man, that's good, Cobb. Put you on the payroll."

"It makes sense. You compromise me, have something on me, and I'm not going to be able to turn. I get what I want, and you get what you want."

"And what does this buy?"

"The whole thing.

"The whole thing? You haven't got the whole thing."

"Early did."

The laughter sighed away. "You're bluffing."

"Am I? You think he went back out to the farm without putting something down? You're supposed to be a cop, Swann. You know you always keep some kind of a record."

Swann stood up. "You've got balls, Cobb, I'll give you that."

"Early wrote it all down. In a letter."

Swann paused, rubbing his chin with the barrel of the pistol.

"What about the woman?"

"She's in."

Swann turned slowly and walked across the floor, the old wooden planks moaning beneath him.

Then he looked back to Cobb.

Reaching into his pocket, he tugged something out and tossed it to Cobb. It was the handcuff key.

Cobb picked it up and unlocked one cuff. As he turned to the other, Swann shook his head.

"No," he said. "Throw it back."

Cobb did.

"Now," Swann said. "Over there." He gestured into the shadows to an old rusty harrow.

Cobb started to get to his feet and Swann shook his head again. "Huh-uh," he said. "Crawl."

Cobb crawled to the harrow.

"On the cross bar."

Cobb closed the cuff over the crossbar, between two iron ribs. Now there was no way off the crossbar.

Swann looked down at him.

"Tell you what I'm goin' to do, Cobb. I'm goin' to go get your girlfriend. Bring her back here. Then I can do her real fast, quick. Or slow." He smiled. "I may not be able to get to you. But I can get to her."

"If you can find her."

The grin widened. "Oh, I can find her. That's easy."

Cobb's jaw tightened and Swann nodded. "That's right. I put another bug on the Bronco. Finding her will be easy."

234

Thirty-nine

Trish Forman's address was a garage apartment next to a huge white frame house in an old and well-to-do neighborhood. The four-car garage was set back from the street under two vast oak trees. Three cars were parked in front of the garage — a Lincoln, a Cadillac, and a Ford Escort. The little Ford looked like a toy next to the others.

Evening began to darken the air as Jessie walked up the stairs on the side of the garage.

The door was open, and she knocked on the screen door.

A tall, pretty girl with permed, dyed blond hair came to the door. She was heavily made up and wore cut-off jeans, high heels, and a yellow halter top over ample breasts.

"Hi," she said tentatively and opened the door. "Come on in."

Jessie stepped inside and Trish led her through a small hallway to a medium-sized living room overlooking the drive. Jessie couldn't help noticing her jewelry, mainly because there was so much of it. Rings on several fingers, three bracelets, and huge, sparkling earrings. None of it by itself was bad; as a matter of fact, it was good jewelry, but there was just too much of it. The living room was the opposite. The furniture was cheap, functional, but clean. All of Trish's money went into her wardrobe.

As they sat down, Trish eyed Jessie's khaki shirt.

"That's nice," she said. "Where did you get that?"

"At the Marina. Kind of a general store down there —"

She nodded. "Oh, yeah. I know the place. Expensive." Her eyes narrowed. "I wonder if somethin' like that would look good on me."

"Probably. You've got a good figure — you could wear almost anything."

She looked down at herself. "Yeah, well, it's all I've got, you know, so I like to really dress right. I work two jobs."

"I'd like to ask you about Larry Atherton."

Her eyes darkened. "Like I said, I haven't seen him in over a month. We broke up."

"Why?"

Trish's gaze settled on her, and Jessie could tell she was weighing something. Trish reached to the coffee table and took a cigarette from a pack, her movements slightly self-conscious, showy. She slowly placed the cigarette in her lips and teeth, biting down on the filter, holding it almost sensually, then lit it and settled back on the sofa. "My mama says smoking makes a girl look cheap. You think that's true?"

"I think it depends on the girl."

"I started because I thought it looked sexy." She puffed the cigarette, then looked at it. "Larry thought it looked sexy, too. He liked for me to smoke."

"Why did you break up?"

She frowned. "Can I ask you somethin'?"

"Sure."

"This isn't about any accident, is it? Larry's in trouble, isn't he?"

"Why do you say that?"

Trish slipped her shoes off and pulled a foot under her uncomfortably, and studied her cigarette.

"If I thought something was going on . . . could I get in trouble?"

"You can't get in trouble unless you've broken the law, Trish. Now tell me what's bothering you."

"I don't want to get Larry in trouble, you know . . ."

Jessie leaned forward. "You're right, Trish, this hasn't anything to do with an accident. But I'm not after Larry. This has to do with something else — I can't tell you what. All I can tell you is the more I look into this, the more I think Larry may be in danger. You can only help him by telling me what you know or suspect."

She drew on the cigarette and sighed smoke into the air.

"I think he was doin' something illegal."

"Why?"

She pulled the other foot under her, sitting yoga style. "Well, when I met him, I thought he was real good looking and all that. Dark, curly hair, nice body, and he dressed real nice. I mean real nice. Good boots, shirts, ironed jeans. I love a man in ironed jeans. That just looks real classy to me." She shrugged. "I mean, to be truthful about it, he looked like he had money. I mean looks and money. The only way I'm ever gonna do better is marry right. What's that old sayin', 'It's just as easy to marry a rich man as a poor man.' Somethin' like that. And I've had enough of bein' poor." She took a long draw on the cigarette and the smoke blurred up around her. "My mother is thirty-five years old. And she looks fifty. And never had anything except two husbands that went off and left her with five kids. Raised us in a double-wide trailer. She worked three jobs to keep us going. Never any welfare. Three jobs and a garden out back that she made all of us work." She shifted uncomfortably on the sofa. "I know I must sound like a gold digger, but I'm never gonna live like that. Never. I got my looks

237

and that's all. And I work real hard to look good. Did I tell you I work two jobs—"

"Yes."

"—And I spend most of it on clothes and jewelry. I got one thing goin' for me and that's my looks. Men marry looks."

"And you thought Larry was a good prospect?"

She nodded. "Yeah, I did. I mean, he treated me real good. We went out a few times; then, after a while, we started going down to Virginia Beach and it got even better."

"How?"

"A beach house, and a 'Vette."

"A Corvette?"

"A new one, not a used one."

"But he kept it down there?"

"Yeah, and he asked me not to say anything about it to folks up here."

"Why?"

"He just said, 'What the IRS doesn't know can't hurt me.' Another time when I asked him about it, he said that he and his dad were using the money down here, but counting it off as expenses against the farm."

"What was the house like?"

"Expensive. Big. Two stories. Deck, a little dock. Everything. It was wonderful. When we went down there, I felt like I lived in a different world."

"You went down there often?"

"Quite a bit." She stubbed out the cigarette and lit another.

"Did he rent or own the house?"

"Rented it, I think, but that's still a lot of money. And we always went to the best places."

"Why do you think he was doing something illegal?"

"Because there's no way he could be getting that kind of money out of the farm."

"Was that all?"

"No, ever' once in a while, he would get real jumpy, you know. Nervous. Bad tempered." She drew on the cigarette. "Like he was afraid."

"Every once in a while?"

"Yeah. Then it would kind of go away. Then come back."

"Any kind of regularity to it?"

"Regularity?"

"Did it happen at the same time? Every week or every month?"

"You mean like a period?" She smiled and shook her head. "No, I mean, not that I noticed. I don't think so."

"Did something happen that caused it? Like a phone call or somebody showing up?"

She puffed the cigarette. "No, I mean, I don't know. I wasn't really paying that much attention. It would just happen, and he would get all jumpy. And I mean real jumpy. His hands would shake and he'd get the sweats and then start drinking. If we were at the beach house, he would go out on the deck and sometimes stay out there all night."

"Did he talk about it?"

"Well, one time he was drunk. We were out on the deck, looking at the ocean, and he just kept drinking, pouring it down, saying something like, 'Fucking snob sonofabitch, I'll show him who's a fucking aristocrat.' And when I sat down and asked him what he was talking about, he kind of blinked like he suddenly realized what he was saying, and shut up, and stared at me and told me to go back into the house. One of these days it was going to catch up with him. When I asked him what the hell he was talking about, he just stared at me and told me to go back into the house. That scared me, but another time, he scared me worse."

"How?"

"He was out on the deck, drinking, doin' his thing. I went out there. He was sitting in a chair and there was a gun in his hand. I said, 'What the hell is that for?' and he said something like, 'It's a sleeping pill.' And I said, 'A sleeping pill?' And he said, 'Yeah, this is gonna help me sleep tonight.' That's when I decided to give it up. I mean I can do a lot of things, but guns, no way." A sad smile pouted her lips. "Funny thing is, he said he didn't really blame me."

"Who was this snob he was talking about?"

She shook her head. "I don't know, that was the only time he said it."

"But no name?"

"No."

"Could Larry be growing marijuana or smuggling drugs?"

"I don't know. Maybe." She drew on the cigarette. "I kind of miss him, you know. We had some real good times."

"Did you know any of his friends?"

"Oh, we sort of hung out with the same crowd."

"How about friends not from around here? Did anybody come to the house in Virginia Beach?"

"No, it was always just us."

"How about his father?"

She laughed. "Carl? All he ever did was clean his guns or hunt."

"Did he travel much?"

"Some. Once or twice a month."

"Did you ever go with him?"

She shook her head. "No."

"Do you know where he went?"

The hand with the cigarette came up and paused. "Around. Philadelphia. D.C. Like that."

"Did he ever talk about the trips?"

She puffed the cigarette and shook her head in a cloud of smoke. "No. Not really. I'd ask him how it went and he'd say fine, the usual. Hotel food and hotel rooms."

"Do you remember the address of the house in Virginia Beach?"

"The address, no. It's just off Atlantic. I can write down the directions for you—"

"That would help."

Trish got up and went into the next room and came back out with a yellow pad and pencil. She returned to the sofa and wrote for a few minutes, then tore off the sheet and handed it to Jessie. "There's a map on there, too," she said and lit another cigarette.

Jessie folded it and slipped it into her purse, then they walked to the door.

"I hope I'm doin' the right thing," Trish said. "I mean, I hope I'm not gettin' him in any trouble."

Jessie shook her head. "You're not. You might just have done him some good."

Trish nodded. "I hope so, you know," she stammered and took a drag from the cigarette as Jessie walked outside. Starting down the steps, she glanced in the window. Trish stopped at the mirror and with the cigarette in her mouth was adjusting her hair.

Forty

Stepping into the small coffee shop next to Bloodworth's Hardware, Jessie recognized Carrie Rush immediately. Her answer on the telephone had been almost the same as Trish Forman's and so was her look. Dyed blond hair. Tall, lean body with large breasts. A little too much makeup. And she smoked. But there were differences. There was no sensuality to her smoking, only need. And she dressed conservatively. Plain gray skirt, white blouse. Flats. And where Trish was brassy, up front, Carrie seemed shy and a little vulnerable. She sat at the table in the rear with her head down and her shoulders slumped. She jerked slightly when Jessie closed the door and when her eyes came around, fear darkened them.

"Are you the policewoman?"

"I called you, yes. Lynn Monroe."

"Miss Monroe. Or is it officer?"

Jessie smiled. "Miss Monroe will do. And there's no need to be nervous, Carrie. You haven't done anything wrong.

She drew on the cigarette. "Well, my daddy would sure disagree with you."

"Your father? Why?"

She shrugged. "Oh, lots of reasons. I never was a

good girl like my sister." She looked at the cigarette, then stabbed it out in the ash tray. "Like smoking. He'd kill me if he knew I smoked. And the makeup. I have to wash it off when I go home."

"He's strict with you."

She blew out a little sigh of air. "Boy, I'll say. Strict, yeah. Him and Jesus."

"Jesus?"

"Yeah. When I was a little girl, to hear Daddy tell it, Jesus was this mean guy who went around blasting people with lightning bolts. That if you said bad words or had bad thoughts, Jesus would jump out from behind a bush and blast you. Which always sounded like what he said about the Devil, too, and that confused me. And, of course, I always had trouble bein' good and I thought Jesus was goin' to jump out at me at any minute. But he never did. Then a little girl down the road, Bonnie Rose, was killed when the school bus driver lost control of the bus—a deer jumped out of the woods and he swerved—and he glanced off a tree. Just scraped it. Nobody was hurt but Bonnie Rose. Broke her neck." She smiled grimly. "And she was the most perfect person I ever knew. Went to Sunday School. Was sweet and nice. And I don't mean put-on, she really was. And she was killed. Right then I kind of figured out that my daddy didn't know anything about Jesus. All he knew about was fear." She looked at Jessie. "I kind of think Jesus loves everybody no matter what, don't you?"

"I'd like to think so, yes."

Carrie blinked suddenly, and smiled shyly. "I'm sorry, I'm just rattling on, tellin' you my life's story."

Jessie smiled. "Sometimes people feel safer when they talk to strangers. And sometimes talking about things helps."

"I guess." She hurriedly lit another cigarette. "Daddy smells the smoke in my hair and on my clothes, and I tell him it's the customers in the store."

"Why don't you move out?"

She nodded. "I'm savin' to, believe you me. Maybe another month or so." She took a long drag on the cigarette. "I thought Larry was goin' to . . ." She shrugged. "You know . . ."

"Marry you?"

She frowned. "Yeah. Guess Daddy was right about him after all."

"How so?"

"He said all Larry was after was, well, you know—"

"Sex?"

She blushed. "Yeah." She pursed her lips into a mocking pose. " 'Why buy a cow, when you can get the milk free,' he said all the time." She shook her head. "God, I'm tired of hearin' that one. Like I'm a cow for sale. Like love was buyin' somethin' . . . you think love is like buyin' somethin'?"

"No."

"Neither do I," she said, then sighed with frustration. "Sorry, I'm doin' it again."

"It's okay."

"Thanks."

"But you went out with Larry even though your father disapproved."

She nodded. "He was real nice to me. And he's good looking."

"And he had money."

Carrie's eyes came up tinged with guilt. "Yeah, but that didn't matter. It was him I liked, not his money." The words came a little too forcefully, as if she was trying to convince herself. "If you think that's why—"

"No, I didn't mean that. I'm sorry. I think you're in love with him."

Tears glistened in the girl's eyes. "I . . ." She

brought the cigarette up, then changed her mind and stabbed it out. "I just don't understand why he hasn't called me." She shook her head. "He stood me up, then didn't even call."

"But you've called him."

She nodded. "But there's nobody home. Not even Carl." She shrugged. "I guess they went on one of those business trips, and he didn't have time to call me. That's all I can figure out."

"Has he done this before?"

"He never stood me up before. If he was goin' out of town, he always called me. And he's never stayed gone this long. I kind of wonder if he was killed in a car wreck or somethin'."

"Did you ever go to Virginia Beach with him?"

Her eyes jerked up, widening. "How did you know about that?"

"I know about the house in Virginia Beach." Reaching out, she touched Carrie's hand. "It's all right, I'm not going to tell anyone. Everything you say is just between you and me."

"You mean like between me and the pastor?"

"Yes."

Carrie nodded reluctantly. "We went to Virginia Beach. To the house. It was so beautiful. So big. A deck and boat dock, and the Corvette. It was like a dream. I'd never done anything like that. Been anyplace like that." She ran her fingers through her hair. "It took a lot to get down there too. I had to get my girl friend, Sandy, to lie and say I was with her. All of that. But it was wonderful. I never felt guilty for a minute."

"How many times did you go?"

"Just the one time," she answered and the disappointment was heavy in her voice. "It was real hard setting it up. We were going to go again in a couple of weeks."

"Did Larry ever get nervous or on edge?"

245

Her eyes darkened. "Sometimes. He slept with a gun beside the bed. That was kind of weird."

"Weird?"

"Well," Carrie's face reddened. "I don't know if I should tell you, I mean . . ."

"I told you, anything you say to me is in confidence."

"Well," she shrugged. "I guess so. Sandy knows about it. Larry and I had a lot of champagne to drink and we were, you know, kissing, and getting kind of . . ." she cleared her throat.

"I know what you mean, Carrie."

"Anyway, we were . . . well, I mean I was ready, and Larry was too, we were on the bed, and then all of a sudden, he jumps up and runs; goes over to his suitcase and takes this gun out and puts it on the table beside the bed." She looked at Jessie, the exasperation in her eyes. "I mean, that's weird, you know."

"Did he say why?"

"No. Well, yeah, come to think about it, he did. It was kind of odd. I asked him what was wrong. He said it was in case Raymond dropped by. And I said, 'Who's Raymond,' and he just looked at me kind of funny and said, 'Forget it, and I mean forget it.' That kind of scared me, so I didn't say anything about it."

"Did he ever mention Raymond before?"

"No. Or after. Just that one time. But whoever this guy was, Larry was scared of him."

"Do you know a Raymond?"

She giggled. "Just Raymond Bloodworth, the guy that owns the hardware store, and believe you me, he's nobody to be scared of."

"Did you ever go any where else with Larry?"

"No. Just that one time to the beach, honest." She looked at her watch. "Oh, gosh, it's nearly nine-thirty. Can I go now, my daddy—"

"It's all right."

"It's just that I've got to get this makeup off and brush my hair out and pin it up, and that takes time—"

"You do that every night?"

"Yeah. But not for much longer," she said and getting up, she hurried to the restroom.

At first Cobb had thought about trying to escape. That lasted about fifteen minutes.

The cross bar of the harrow was iron. There was no way of moving or altering either the harrow or the handcuff. Then he examined how close Swann had closed the handcuff around his wrist. Wondered whether he could squeeze his hand small enough to get it through. He tried. No way. Then he thought about what Swann had said, about guys cutting off their hands. He understood that desperation.

Sighing, he leaned into the iron hoops and thought about the other thing Swann had said. About Jessie. About what they would do to her. Which was exactly what Swann wanted. He tried not to think about her. He settled his mind on something else. He decided to take inventory of the room.

His eyes moved through the darkness. Harrow. Anvil. Hay bales. Then he noticed that the hay bales weren't stacked, but lined up against the wall. One against the other. Like a bench. At the far end was a water faucet. And a bucket. Other than that, the room was empty. A large storage room almost empty.

His eyes went back to the hay bales.

At the far end, in shadows, he saw something else. He squinted, not quite able to make it out.

Almost three feet high. Uncertain edge. Wavy. Soft?

His jaw tightened. He looked into the darkest

parts of the room, trying to let his eyes adjust to that lesser light. Then back to the form.

The edge became clearer. There was more than one edge. More than one thing there. The top side was wavy, uncertain, too. But different.

Sighing, he closed his eyes for a full minute, then opened them again, concentrating.

Top. Sides. More than one. Slowly, the detail came into focus.

Blankets. A lot of them.

His eyes went over the room. Then the hay bales, and the faucet and the bucket. Easing back to the harrow, he smiled. "I'll be damned," he whispered.

Forty-one

On Highway 17, Jessie stopped at a convenience store and called Russ MacDonald.

"Sorry," he said with a sigh. "Nothing on either Carl or Larry Atherton."

"How about a Raymond? Do you remember that name from any of your cases?"

"Raymond?"

"Yes."

"First name or last?"

"I don't know. That's the only name I have."

Mac paused, thinking. "Raymond," he mulled. "The first one that comes to mind is Herb or Harry, something like that, Raymond. Makes porno films. We put a mike on him because we thought he was doing kiddie stuff. This was about a year and a half ago. Never could get anything on him, though, and finally had to stop the surveillance."

"What kind of person is he?"

"He's a puke. He makes kiddie porn, even if we can't prove it."

"No, I mean is he violent?"

"Violent?" he laughed. "Shit, no. He's usually got his hands occupied, if you know what I mean."

"I know what you mean. Anybody else?"

"Anybody else . . ." He thought for a moment. "Well, maybe Ray Burke. Running drugs from Bermuda. Now this was a violent guy, but I don't think it was him."

"Why?"

"We put him away. Got him cold."

"Could he be out?"

Mac laughed grimly. "With the way they do sentencing, he could be, yeah."

"Can you check that for me? And anybody else named Raymond in your files."

"Okay." He paused. "You all right?"

"Yeah, why?"

"You sound like you're in trouble."

"No more than usual."

"Look, I'm busy, but you want to let me in?"

She leaned against the wall. She wanted to. She wanted all the help she could get, but she was even worse off than she was when she started. A policeman was dead and now they had Cobb. And she had no proof to back up her story. Not even Swann.

And if they arrested her, Cobb would still be out there.

She had no room for mistakes.

And Mac was a cop. An ex-cop, but still a cop. He might help her; then again, he might take her in.

It was a toss-up, and she couldn't afford to gamble. Not now. She had to stay free.

"I'd like to, but I can't, Mac."

"Okay. I'll check for you.

"I'll call you in an hour or so."

With the traffic, it took her a little over two hours to reach Virginia Beach.

Following Trish's directions, she found the house just off Shore Drive.

250

It was on a short private road, set deep in pines. It loomed in front of the water. Two stories. Decks. Floor to ceiling windows.

There were no cars in the drive and no lights in the windows.

Parking in the drive, she found the 9mm in her purse, tugged it free, then stepped out of the Bronco.

She hurried up a walk that led to the steps to a deck. She went up them, crossed to the door, and tried it. It was locked.

Turning, she walked around the deck and tried the back door.

There, next to the garage, she thought she smelled something, but the wind off the water was brisk and she couldn't quite be sure. There was a sound, too, like a low hum. Again, she couldn't quite place it.

She went on to the sliding doors. All locked. A stairwell led to the upper deck; she went up it, and tried all the sliding doors. All locked. She walked around them again, peering through the glass. Three bedrooms. A family room.

Clouds drifted across the moon, and a breeze came off the water.

She went around back, and facing the door to the bedroom, she drew in her breath, prayed that there was no alarm, and swung the barrel of the 9mm into the glass. It made a rapping sound, and the glass splintered, but didn't break.

"Dammit," she whispered. If that didn't wake up this end of Virginia Beach, nothing would.

She quickly swung the pistol again. This time the glass shattered, crumbling away from the handle and the lock.

Reaching through the hole, she tripped the lock and eased the door open.

Stepping inside, she smelled something immedi-

251

ately—the same odor she'd smelled next to the garage.

Faint, but there.

Like the smell in the farmhouse. Trapped air. Tainted meat.

She walked out into the hallway and the smell was stronger. The hallway opened onto a balcony that overlooked a huge living room. She walked down the stairs, and the smell gained intensity.

Thick. Smothering.

Rotted meat.

Off the living room was a spacious kitchen. The windows held a view of the water. There was a door that she assumed led to the garage. She walked to it, and as she reached for the knob, she almost knew what she was going to find.

She opened the door, and the smell washed over her, thick with death, and a roaring hum. She vomited into the garage.

Pivoting out of the doorway, she staggered to the sink, found a dish towel, wet it, and held it up to her nose. Breathing through it, she went back to the garage.

Her hand fumbled over the wall, found the switch, flipped it, and the garage was jerked from darkness.

The first thing she saw were the millions of flies.

Then the red Corvette.

At the wheel was a man, his head slumped back, flies covering him in a quivering blanket, his mouth open, his flesh beginning to slough away.

On the floor, between the car and the garage door, was the second one.

Forty-two

Jessie turned the light off, slammed the door, staggered to the sink, and vomited again.

A long, moaning sound came from her throat and she sobbed for a moment. "God," she whispered. "Oh my God . . ."

Still crying, she rinsed her mouth out with cold water, but the smell was still there and she was sure she would throw up again.

She wiped her eyes. No, she thought. Holding her breath, she opened the cupboard under the sink. There was a plastic bottle of lemon dish soap there. She dowsed some onto the towel, then reversed it and held it close to her nose. Lemon overwhelmed her. It was almost as bad as the death smell. But not quite.

She looked back toward the garage. The man in the car would be Larry Atherton. Before she'd closed the door, she had glimpsed the dark, curly hair Carrie and Trish had talked about. From the position of his body, she guessed it was supposed to look like he'd committed suicide. Then the other man had come out to try and save him and been overcome by the fumes. The man on the floor would be Carl Atherton. A father trying to save his son.

That's the way it looked.

She swallowed. It had all been arranged. Placed. All nice and wrapped up. A perfect scenario. A tragic suicide and accidental death.

Except that Carl had never come here.

She turned toward the bedrooms upstairs. As she staggered to the top of the stairs, she tried lowering the towel.

The smell was fainter, but her stomach still lurched and she pulled the towel back to her nose.

She went into the master bedroom first. It was furnished sparsely. Bed, nightstand, a dresser with a mirror, a modern frame chair. She rushed to the closet and glided the door open. The closet was full of jeans, cowboy shirts, and boots.

She moved to the nightstand, pulled the drawer out, and put it on the bed. A paperback western. An old wristwatch. Telephone book. Note pad, blank. She opened the telephone book to the back. A few numbers jotted down. Tearing the back off, she shoved it into her purse. She leafed through the book. There were no more handwritten numbers.

She rummaged through the dresser next, but found nothing but clothing.

Still breathing through the towel, she went into the next bedroom, searched it, and found nothing, Then the family room. She found nothing there but old television guides and a few cigarette butts.

She went back to the door she'd come in and stepped back out into the night. Lowering the towel, she could still smell the garage. Trembling, she leaned against the wall and wondered if she always would, wondered irrationally if the smell and the image of Larry and Carl Atherton covered with flies would stay with her forever.

Then, strangely, she thought of Donna Hooker and the motion she'd made wiping the tears from her

254

eyes; something rustled on the edge of her consciousness. Only a hint, a glimpse.

But what?

The interior of the garage seemed to fill her. The Corvette. Larry Atherton sitting in it. The flies. The smell.

Something. Something about the garage.

She turned back to the door. She had to look again, longer this time.

Holding the towel to her face, she forced herself to go back into the house. Across the room. Down the stairs. Through the kitchen to the door.

The drone of the flies coursed through her like dark electricity. The smell gagged her even through the towel.

She opened the door.

Turned on the light.

He was still there. In the car. His beautiful red Corvette—the one Trish and Carrie had cooed about. And his father on the floor.

The flies moved over them. But her eyes went to Larry. The only thing still human was his hair. The dark, curly hair. And she thought of Donna wiping her tears again.

Why?

Jessie had to force herself to pull her eyes away. To look someplace else. Her eyes moved over the garage. Lawn tools. Fishing poles. Gas can.

She thought about going into the garage, but knew she couldn't.

What was there? What was she seeing, but not seeing? And what did it have to do with Donna Hooker?

Switching off the light, she turned back out of the doorway and ran back upstairs and out onto the deck.

She walked to the railing and dragged fresh air

into her lungs. But could still smell the garage.

Dropping the towel, she ran down the stairs, then down along the walk to the beach and the water.

A hard, fresh breeze blew over her, rustling her hair, and she pulled in deep, desperate gulps. It tasted wonderful. Alive.

She slumped down into the sand, just breathing. Then she looked back at the house. What had she seen back there? It was right there, close . . . but she couldn't quite grasp it.

Sighing, she shook her head. It was no good. The harder she tried, the more it ebbed away.

Standing up, she saw the light from the next house down the beach.

She turned toward it.

Forty-three

Jessie knocked on the door of the neighboring house. It was much smaller than the house Larry Atherton had rented, a one-story cottage.

Jessie knocked again and the door was opened by a handsome, sandy-haired man in his late thirties. Barefoot, he wore cut-off jeans and was pulling on a flowered shirt over a barrel chest and flat stomach.

He smiled when he saw Jessie. It was a good smile, genuine. He looked at her eyes instead of her breasts.

"Hello," he said.

"Hello. Sorry to interrupt you, but—"

He shook his head. "You couldn't interrupt me. I haven't been doing anything for a couple of months except stare at the water." He stood aside. "Please come in out of the snow and rain—"

She smiled as she stepped into the small living room. "It's not quite *that* bad out."

"It could get that way, though."

The room was larger than she would have thought. High ceilings, wide windows opening onto the water. Wicker furniture, old and worn but comfortable. A small kitchen off to one side.

"May I offer you something? A beer?"

"Have you got anything stronger?"

"Brandy?"

"Brandy would be terrific."

He walked around the breakfast bar separating the two rooms and opened the cupboard. He took out a glass and a bottle of brandy, poured a healthy slosh, and handed it to her.

"Thanks." She downed the brandy in one gulp, and put the glass back on the bar. "Again. Please."

He cocked his head, smiled, and poured her another.

This one she sipped. "Really, thanks."

"You must have had a long day."

"You could say that."

He reached across the bar. "Ben Perry."

She took his hand. "Jessie Marsh," she said without thinking.

Opening the refrigerator, he took out a bottle of Dos Equis, opened it and came back into the living room. They sat down, Jessie on the sofa, the man in a chair across from her.

"So why are you out on this terrible night?"

She smiled. "I'm trying to locate your neighbor," she said. "Larry Atherton."

He tasted his beer and studied her for a moment. "Larry?"

"Yeah."

"You'll pardon me for saying so, but you don't look like the kind of girl Larry usually hangs out with."

"I'm a blonde."

"That's about as far as it goes."

"Have you seen him?"

"Not lately. Not in about . . . yeah, just about two weeks ago." He nodded. "He came up on the sixth and left on the tenth."

She smiled. "You've got a good memory for dates."

His mouth soured. "Some habits are hard to break. I've been trying to be on a sabbatical."

"You're a teacher?"

"A lawyer," he said. "Why are you looking for Larry?"

"It's a business matter."

"Larry? Business?" He shook his head. "Again, this doesn't compute."

"Why?"

He shrugged. "Well, mostly, because Larry is the kind of lad who does everything he can not to work."

"You know him pretty well, then?"

He shook his head. "Not really. He's come wandering over a couple of times and had a beer, and we sat and shot the bull."

"What did you talk about?"

He sipped the beer, then looked directly into her eyes. "Look, in order to give you an honest answer, I'm going to assume that you're not, ah, what's the word—close."

"You assume correctly. I've never met him, but I'm thinking about doing business with him and his father. I need to know everything I can about him."

"A background check."

"Yes."

"Good, then I can be brutally honest. He was a bum. Shallow, thoughtless, maybe even a little mean."

"Why do you say that? The part about being mean?"

He shook his head. "I'm not sure. Just a feeling I have."

"You didn't like him?"

"I don't know him well enough to like or dislike him, but every time he comes over, I can't wait for him to leave. He's one of those people who only talks about himself, and yet never says anything. His 'Vette. His girlfriends. Lectures on how he has everything figured out. A lot of macho posing." He smiled. "Pretending. I guess to tell you about him, I'm going to have to tell you a little about me. Six months ago, I turned thirty-nine—"

Jessie smiled suddenly and nodded. "I believe the phrase is 'Ah, ha.' "

"Exactly. The old mid-life crisis bit. Anyway, I took a year off from my practice to kind of reevaluate things, take a look at my life. But Larry saw it as just doing what I wanted and telling the world to go to hell. He thought that was just great. Do nothing all day but fish and get into shape and drink. One day out on the deck we were both having a beer, looking at the sunset, and he started going on about all this and I guess I got a little fed up; I told him I was here because I got scared and because I had read too many books. He had no idea what I was talking about so I tried to explain. I told him I had turned thirty-nine and it frightened me. I think up until then we have a sort of built-in protection device that says you're never going to die. Then somewhere near forty, you realize you are, and that maybe you haven't done all you wanted to do. I told him I was just another scared guy who was trying to figure out how to make his life count for something. He gave me a long, blank stare. Probably the same stare I would have given some crazy bastard if he'd tried to tell me the same thing at his age. Then he said something like, 'Nothing scares me, nothing.' Typical macho pose."

"You sound angry."

He looked at her. "I do, don't I? Maybe Larry taught me more than I'd like to admit." He stood up and went into the kitchen. Setting his bottle down, he opened the refrigerator. "Maybe finding yourself isn't all it's cracked up to be." He took out another beer and paused. "Or maybe what I found was Larry." He opened the beer. "Now there's a scary goddamn thought," he said as he returned to his chair.

"Has he done that often, this thing about not being scared? Doing the macho thing?"

"He's doing the macho thing all the time."

"No, I mean did he—does he seem frightened at times? Jumpy?"

Perry rubbed the end of the bottleneck on his chin. "Now that you mention it, yeah. Sometimes he's absolutely hyper. Mostly when he's over there without one of his blondes."

"He doesn't like being alone?"

"No, I guess not. But then who does?"

"Did he ever mention a man named Raymond?"

"Raymond? No."

"Did you ever notice anyone over there, other than the blondes?"

He shook his head slowly. "No, not that I remember." Then his eyes narrowed. "This sounds like a little more than a background check."

"Let's just say I do a complete job."

His eyes widened with realization. "You're a Police Investigator."

She used the best coy smile she could come up with. "Let's just say, I do a complete job."

"No kidding. You know, all my years in practice, I never met a P.I. And I'm a lawyer. But I do tax and corporate law. Who are you with?"

"Let's just say—"

He held up his hands. "Okay, okay. Never mind. Ask your questions."

She shrugged. "Visitors. Unusual activity. Anything like that?"

He sipped the beer. "No. Except now that we put

261

it in that context, he really didn't seem to know how to handle money. In other words, he wasn't born to it. He came into it and probably suddenly."

"Why do you say that, the car and the house?"

He nodded. "And the clothes. He was a little like Elizabeth Taylor; he never wore the same thing twice, and what he wore was expensive, the best." He looked at her. "Drugs maybe?"

"Maybe. I don't have any proof of that. Did he use any that you know of?"

"That I know of . . . no. Not really. Mostly it was beer. Wine. Champagne. The best champagne."

Jessie finished her brandy. "Thanks for the drink."

"Another?"

She shook her head. "No. I need to be going."

Disappointment darkened his eyes. "You're sure?"

She stood up. "Yes."

He pushed up to his feet. "It's just that you're the first interesting person in a while. A beautiful P.I. out of the night."

"You're romanticizing a bit."

"Maybe that's what guys who are finding themselves do."

She laughed. "Could be."

"Listen, could I . . . could I call you sometime? Tomorrow?"

"There was a time I would have said yes."

"But you're involved."

"But I'm involved." She held out her hand. "Good night," she said. "And thanks."

"Anytime," he said. "And I mean anytime. I'll be right here. I've got another ten months to go on my sentence."

Forty-four

Jessie drove to a small restaurant, found a telephone just inside the bar, and called Mac's number. It was busy. Her jaw tightened. Of course it was busy.

Slamming the phone back into its cradle, she walked to the bar, ordered a brandy, carried it to a corner table, and sat down. There was a deck with tables overlooking the water. Moonlight and fresh air. She didn't want moonlight and fresh air. She wanted someplace dark and private. Someplace to hide.

She gulped half of the brandy down, then sat and stared at the remainder. Was it half gone, or half to go? Who gave a damn? She wanted to get drunk. She downed the rest, and with what Perry had given her, it was doing a pretty good job. Her head seemed to shrink and expand at the same time.

A waitress that looked a lot like Trish and Carrie came by and asked if she wanted another. Silly girl. Of course she wanted another. It came. She sipped it. And closed her eyes.

The image and smell of Carl and Larry Atherton rushed into her.

Carl on the floor. Larry sitting there with his curly

hair and flies. That's when she almost lost all of that perfectly good brandy. The world tilted slightly, then did a nifty back-flip. She almost closed her eyes again, but didn't. She was wise to that trick. Instead, she moaned. That worked out pretty well because it brought the waitress who looked like Trish and Carrie. She asked if she was all right. Silly girl. Of course, she wasn't all right. "Ice," she managed to say. "A lot of ice." The waitress brought it wrapped in a towel. That was good. She buried her face in it and the world, or at least the part of it confined to this end of the bar, began to right itself. After about five minutes, she pulled her face out of the towel. Putting it down, she picked out a piece of ice and rubbed it over her face until it melted. Then another. Then she put a piece in her mouth and felt the slow, spiky pain of it melting. That was good, too. Her eyes fell on the brandy. That wasn't good. She pushed it away and kept nursing the ice. Good stuff, that ice. There was a fortune to be made there. Then it all came back again.

Larry Atherton.

Joe Early.

Cobb.

Swann.

Raymond.

Donna Hooker wiping the tears from her face.

She pushed her fingers through her hair. Donna again.

What was the connection?

The waitress came back over, a worried look squeezing her face. "You okay? I mean you're not gonna be sick, are you?"

"No, I don't think so. But I could use some coffee."

"Cream and sugar?"

"No, that really would make me sick."

"Right. No cream and sugar. Just coffee."

The waitress hurried off, then came back with the coffee. The service was great, she thought as she sipped the coffee, then grimaced. Well, you couldn't have everything.

She drank one cup, then another, and kept using the ice. After a while she made an effort to stand up.

Success. Finally. What a great night it was turning out to be. After that, walking was easy. She made her way back to the telephone and dialed Mac's number.

This time he answered.

"Any luck with Raymond?"

"No. Sorry. Just a dead man. The only ones I can come up with are Harry Raymond and Ray Burke. Burke is in jail, and it turns out that Harry has found Jesus."

"I'm sorry, did you say —"

"Yeah, you heard me right. Harry Raymond has found Jesus. He's preaching even as we speak — over in Martinsville. Has been for a week. Telling folks how Jesus has forgiven him for buggering little boys."

She sighed. "That sort of leaves him out, doesn't it?"

"Probably until he finds another little boy."

"Thanks, Mac."

"You okay?"

"Yeah. I'm fine. Peachy."

"You don't sound peachy."

"Too much brandy."

"I . . . She heard a voice in the background call Mac's name. "Sorry," he said, "gotta go." Then he hung up.

She stood staring at the receiver, and suddenly felt absolutely alone. Even more than when Cobb had been taken. Maybe it was a delayed reaction or the abruptness of the hangup, she didn't know, but standing there, with the receiver in her hand, she couldn't think straight. Leaning her head against the wall, she seemed welded to it for a moment. An oldie wailed from the jukebox. "It's My Party And I'll Cry If I Want To." Heavy smoke thickened the air, mixing with the voices of the drinkers. ". . . And I told him, by God, he wasn't goin' to pull that shit on me . . ." ". . . I know what I'm talkin' about . . ."

The phone started beeping. Jerking from her reverie, she fumbled it back into its hook, then turned back toward her table, and saw other tables on the deck. *Now* she wanted moonlight and fresh air. Ordering another cup of coffee, she walked outside and sat down.

The waitress brought her coffee and Jessie paid her; sitting with its aroma mixing with the salt air, she stared at the water.

And thought of Donna Hooker again.

Pushing the coffee away, she stood up and hurried to the Bronco.

Donna Hooker opened the door and sighed. "I thought you said you were through with me." She shook her head with frustration. "You can't keep—"

"I just need a few minutes of your time," Jessie said and stepped inside without being invited.

Donna backed away from her, surprise and a little fear seeping into her eyes. "What do you want?"

There were books open on the desk and papers littered around it.

"Studying?"

"Yes. What do you want?"

"Two weeks ago Wednesday, where did you say you went after school?"

"To The Harbor. I had a couple of drinks with Cindy and Lou Anne."

"You didn't go anywhere else?"

"No. What does this have to do with—"

"You didn't go to The Mainsail later on?"

She blinked. "The Mainsail? No. I—"

"How long have you been seeing Larry Atherton?"

She blinked again. "Who?"

"Larry Atherton."

She shook her head. "I don't know any . . ." She paused. "Larry Atherton," she said. "Do you mean the guy who has a farm out north of town?"

"Yes. How long have you been seeing him?"

Bewilderment narrowed her eyes. "I don't know . . ." she stammered. "Larry Atherton was a couple of years ahead of me in high school. No, three. He was a senior when I was a freshman. That Larry Atherton?"

"Yes."

She shook her head. "I only knew him to see him in the halls. I never even had a class with him, much less went out with him. He was a senior, a big shot. Why would he go out with a skinny freshman? Besides, he liked blondes."

"I don't mean then. I mean now."

"Now? You think . . ." She shook her head again. "Look, I don't know who told you that, but either they're lying or they're thinking about somebody else."

"What about Raymond?"

"Raymond? Raymond who?"

"He works with Larry."

"On the farm?"

Jessie stared at her for a moment, then sighed. "You really don't know, do you?"

Donna trembled, her eyes widening, and Jessie re-

alized she was frightened. Of her. She had no idea
what Jessie was talking about.

Jessie sighed. "I'm sorry, Donna. Forget I was
here. I had to ask you these questions."

"But what's going on? Why are you asking me
about all this?"

Jessie sighed. "To tell you the truth, I really don't
know."

Turning, she opened the door and walked back out
into the chill air.

It seemed to take her a long time to reach the
Bronco, and with each step, she felt a little more en-
ergy drift out of her, as if it were wafting away on
the wind.

She opened the door and climbed in and realized
she had absolutely no idea where to go. She felt lost.

And the strange thing was that the connection between Donna and Larry Atherton was still there.

But she believed Donna. She really didn't know
what was going on.

So where did that leave Jessie?

She frowned. Out in the cold, that's where.

She pushed her fingers through her thick blond
hair and leaned forward on the steering wheel. She
had to do something.

The weak, tired feeling trembled through her, gaining intensity, and she realized she hadn't eaten since
breakfast.

She started the Bronco and drove to The Mainsail
where she ordered soft-shell crabs and a cup of coffee. She ate only half of her meal, then pushed the
plate away and sipped her coffee, staring out of the
plateglass window at the street. Her eyes rested on
the Bronco parked at the curb, and the thought that
had been rustling at the back of her mind finally
stirred to more than a whisper. She wanted to get the
hell out of there. Away. It had always been there, of

268

course. Self-preservation. Fuck everybody else on this burning boat and swim for it. And it was odd because once the thought was allowed room, it pushed forward full-blown. She could make it away easily. Get back to D.C. Take her money out of the bank. Find a small town someplace. Work out something with Kay Haug at the gallery, have her sell her paintings then send money under another name. Sitting there, staring out at the Bronco, Jessie was amazed at how complete the plan was. They would never be able to trace her. Not once she left this area. That was how they were finding her. By knowing where she was going. And the directional bugs. But Cobb had checked the Bronco after the incident in the woods near the shack and—

The cup of coffee drifted toward the saucer.

She stared at the Bronco.

Cobb had checked it after the shed.

But Swann had been close to the Bronco at the farm. After he had taken Cobb.

She dropped the cup into the saucer. He knows, she thought. He knows where I am.

She paid her bill and almost ran outside to the Bronco. Her breath pounded through her and her mind reeled with panic.

She opened the door and threw her purse in, then found the flashlight in the console. She would check the wheel wells first, then—

She paused.

No. He might see her. He would—

She eased over in the seat and sat down, holding the flashlight.

No, she thought. There was another way of doing this. Reaching out, she grasped the door handle and pulled it shut, then started the Bronco and started driving.

Forty-five

Jessie rounded the curve and saw the farmhouse at the top of the hill, stark against the night sky. Dark windows. The pickup still parked in front.

Without hesitation, she turned into the driveway and drove up it. There had been no hesitation since she started from Rappahannock. She knew what had to be done. The only thing that could be done. It frightened her, frightened her deep into her marrow, but she hadn't thought about not doing it. Thoughts about running were completely gone now. Instead, as she drove, her hands on the steering wheel, a kind of coldness seeped through her, numbing her, and she planned it very carefully. She tasted that word and her mouth soured. Carefully. There was nothing careful about it.

She worked out most of it in her mind as she drove, and by the time she parked in back of the pickup, she knew exactly what she was going to do.

Carrying her purse, she walked up on the porch to the back door. It was still unlocked. Opening it, she stepped into the dark kitchen. The stench of the spoiled meat clung to the air, and her stomach twisted. Hurrying to the sink, she snatched up a towel, picked up the meat and package with it, then rushed back to the door. Putting the meat in the garbage can at the end of the porch, she returned to the kitchen. The smell was still there. It was like a refrain. The beach house and here. And she remembered Larry Atherton sitting in the Corvette, and his father stretched on the floor.

Forcing the image from her mind, she crossed to the table. Setting her purse down, she took the 9mm and the extra clip from it, then walked to the corner of the kitchen diagonally across from the back door and sat down.

She let her eyes roam over the kitchen. The table was in the middle of the room, between her and the back door. There was a pantry beside her, between her and the door into the dining room. The only windows were the one over the sink and the one beside her. Both were locked, but the shades were up. When she sat in this corner, the pantry partially blocked the view of her from the window over the sink. From the window beside her, she couldn't be seen at all. From the dining room door, she was also partially blocked from view by the pantry. From the back door, the table blocked the view slightly. In order to see her, he would have to step into the room. The same was true of the dining room door. But if he had a clear view of her, she would have one of him. And that's what she wanted. The darkness would protect her for a few moments. She had that and the element of surprise. And Swann's attitude toward women. He hated women—thought they were stupid, weak little bitches who got what they wanted by manipulation. He would never expect this from her. At least she hoped not. She was betting her life—and Cobb's—on it.

Resting the pistol in her lap, she closed her eyes and shook her head.

"Damn," she sighed. A lot of variables in there.

So much for her careful planning.

She smiled grimly. Welcome to a parallel universe.

She opened her eyes to the darkness. The quiet drifted over her. The air was cool but still soiled with the odor of the meat.

She wondered if she would ever get that smell and the image of the Athertons out of her mind.

Outside, she could hear the rustling oaks, and she listened. Listened for something other than the trees.

Time seemed to hover someplace in the wind, and the quiet ebbed through her, and her mind wandered. Fragments of memories lingered for a moment, then brushed each other, shifting, blending in a blurred collage. Larry in the garage. The red of the Corvette. His hair. The only thing left was his dark, curly hair. And Donna Hooker wiping tears from her eyes. Then Joe was there. Riding in his trunk. Smiling. "You should have been the spook," he said. Trish drawing on the cigarette. ". . . That dark, curly hair, and the Corvette. I mean, looks and money, too." Ben Perry sipping his beer. "He came down on the sixth and left on the tenth . . . he was a bum. Shallow, thoughtless, maybe even a little mean." Riding over the farm roads with Joe Early. "You should have been . . ." Stopping at the farmhouse. The two men walking up from the barn, looking up as they drove in. The older man, lean and wiry. Blue jeans. Work shirt, blue baseball cap. The younger one almost exactly the same, except his baseball cap was red. Joe asking questions. The two men nodding. The older one pointing while the younger took off his cap, rubbing his chin. *Donna Hooker wiping the tears from her cheeks . . . her shoulder shifting up* . . . Joe turning and walking down the drive. The newspaper on the coffee table at Joe's. The picture of Carl and Larry. Ben Perry sipping his beer. "He came up on the sixth and left on the tenth—"

She sat up.

He came on the sixth and left on the tenth. The sixth was a Monday. The tenth a Friday. Two weeks ago. Two weeks ago Wednesday, she and Early stopped at the farm. And saw Larry here. But Perry had said he stayed the sixth through the tenth. Sunday through Friday.

She closed her eyes again, trying to regain the image.

The two men walked up from the barn. Saw Joe. Stopped. The older man talked. The younger one stood. Took off his baseball cap. *Donna Hooker wiped the tears from her cheek with an awkward motion. By rolling her shoulder up.* Jessie's breath caught. The man with Carl Atherton had done the same thing. *Had rolled his shoulder up to wipe the sweat from his cheek.* That's why she had associated Donna with Larry Atherton. He had rolled his shoulder up to wipe the sweat off his face, then ran his fingers through his hair.

His hair.

Jessie opened her eyes. His hair had been dark. But straight. Almost spiky. Not curly. Not the curly hair Trish and Carrie loved. Not the curly hair of the man in the Corvette at the beach house.

Larry Atherton hadn't been here that day.

Jessie pushed her legs under her to get up, then heard the footfalls on the back porch.

Forty-six

Startled, Jessie almost dropped the 9mm. She pressed back into the corner and fixed her eyes on the door.

Outside the wind rustled the oaks. The attic fan droned above her.

Her fingers slipped over the cold metal of the pistol—the roughness of the grip against her palm, the edge of the trigger against her forefinger.

She could see the door clearly. The pane of glass. The doorknob.

She pressed into the pantry. Listening. She knew she had heard it. Knew he was—

A board moaned slightly, almost lost in the wind and the hum of the fan.

Then the knob pulsed. Just a tick. And began to turn.

She raised the pistol, leveling it at the door, just below the knob.

Her throat tightened and her heart hammered in her chest.

At this range, about ten feet, it was an easy shot—even in the darkness, because her eyes had adjusted. What was going to be hard was doing it.

Just doing it.

Even Swann. Even this bastard.

The knob completed its turn. The door began to ease open.

She looked at the windowpane. There was nothing there.

He was below the pane. Crouched down.

She trembled. If he comes in that way, I won't be able to see his legs clearly.

The door swung open and stopped.

It was clear. Just the porch and the night beyond.

She pulled her breath in. It was a stupid plan. It always had been a stupid plan.

Her jaw tightened. It was too late for that. Too goddamn late. Paint, she told herself. Focus.

Pushing everything else out of her mind, she kept the 9mm on the door.

Her eyes sighted down the metal of the pistol. Its long, clean, cold lines. Her breath thickened like glue in her lungs, and for a moment, she was afraid she was going to moan.

Then he moved. Quickly. Gliding in from the right, crouched, the moonlight whispered off the steel of his pistol as it swept into the room. He kept moving, his body compressed, so fast she couldn't pick out detail. It was all bulk, all one thing.

He pressed into the kitchen. Then the shadow changed shape, pistol extended. She could see his arm, his foot, then the leg stretched outward—

Leveling the pistol on it, she squeezed the trigger.

The roar of the shot startled her, deafened her, but even through it, she heard him scream as he twisted through the darkness, slamming into the table.

Vaulting up, she scrambled toward him. His pistol was on the floor as he writhed, knocking over one of the chairs. Skirting him, she made it to his pistol and picked it up and threw it out the door. On the floor,

275

Swann groaned, reached out, knocked over another chair, then lay still, his breathing deep and heavy.

Jessie crossed to the door and turned on the light. The light jerked the room into sharp relief, and for a moment, she wished she hadn't turned it on.

A dark spray of blood patterned the floor, and Swann slumped over onto his back holding his shattered right hand. She had hit him in the hand, not the leg.

He looked at the hand, then his eyes came around to her, glinting with pain and a wrath so pure it was almost physical in intensity.

Even down and wounded, she was afraid of him.

Trembling, she lifted the 9mm and leveled it on him.

He stared back at her unblinking.

"Go ahead, you cunt."

She shook her head. "I got the idea from you," she said. "I don't want to kill you. I just want Cobb."

"Fuck you."

Sucking her breath in, she set her jaw. "Like I said, I got the idea from you. I'll put another one through your knee and leave you here. Now tell me where Cobb is."

He stared at her, then reaching out with his good hand, he pulled a chair to him. "You're out of your league, bitch." Using his good hand, he began lifting himself up, slowly at first; then the motion became quick, sudden, and with his feet under him, he pivoted, rushing into her. She tried to sidestep and fire at the same time, but in moving, she threw the pistol off.

He slammed into her just as she pulled the trigger. The 9mm went off next to the point of his shoulder, blowing the padding of his coat into a shower of white. His hand swooped down, knocking the 9mm from her grip, sending it rattling across the floor.

The hand closed on her throat. His strength

276

amazed her. Even wounded, his fingers were like bands of steel clawing into her throat. And looking into his eyes, she saw again where it came from.

He enjoyed this. Loved it.

She twisted, trying to break his grip, but he held on. Smiling. She backed into the sink, then sitting up on it, she brought both of her legs up, and placing her feet squarely into his chest, she shoved.

He staggered back, but incredibly, he held on. Focusing all of her strength, she pushed again, this time straightening her legs, sending him reeling into the refrigerator.

Blood splattered on the floor and counter. He paused, but only for a second, then turned toward her.

Dropping off the sink, she picked up a heavy stoneware plate from the dish rack and swung it into the side of his head. It slammed into him with a meaty clunk and shattered.

Dazed, he blinked, then screaming, he grasped her shirt. Flinging her around like a rag doll, he hurled her across the room and crashing into the pantry. The cabinet rocked back, and she tumbled to the floor as the twin doors opened and dumped cans and bottles down around her.

Still screaming, Swann bulled toward her. Trying to roll and get away from him, she scrambled over the cans and bottles. Reaching down, he grasped her by the back of her shirt and jerked her upright and threw her into the wall next to the pantry. Her head smacked into the wall—then his hand was on her shoulder, wrenching her around. His hand closed over her breast like a vise, crushing it. She screamed and flailed against him, and his rage seemed to come into her, filling her, exploding through her. He rammed her back into the wall, and stumbling over the cans, her feet went out from under her. She kept screaming, knowing in a way that it was what he wanted. He held her breast. Half on her knees and pushed against the wall, her hand went down to the floor to keep her from falling any more. It closed over one of the cans. Still screaming and without thinking, she brought the can up, catching him on the point of the chin with it, staggering him back into the table. His eyes glazed, filling with astonishment. She swung hard, driving the edge of the can into his face again and again, hammering and screaming at the same time. Suddenly, he shuddered as if someone had pulled his bones out of him. He went down heavily, sagging into the table, then off the edge to the floor. Jessie went down with him, lying on his chest. Sobbing, pushing herself up and away from him, she saw his face was a mask of blood.

She backed away staring at him, but he didn't move.

She looked at the can. There was blood and hair and tissue on it.

Dropping it, her eyes combed over the litter on the floor. The 9mm was under a pile of beans and catsup. She gathered it up and brought it around to Swann.

He still didn't move.

Cocking the hammer, she knelt down and placed the gun against his head, then felt his throat for a pulse. There was none.

The gun drifted down, and she sat in the chair, staring at him.

He was dead.

And so was any chance of finding Cobb.

Forty-seven

Jessie drove.

The night wandered around her in fragments of trees, farms, fields, bait stands, empty stores.

Nothing seemed to be connected or coherent. Just fragments, pieces of things.

She found herself back at the motel. She went inside, locked the door, stripped off her clothes as she walked into the bathroom, then sat in the tub as it filled with steaming hot water. It glided up around her slowly, soothingly, and she welcomed it. She wished she had some brandy, anything that would dull her senses and bring with it the blessing of amnesia. Anything to take the dead men away. Swann's partner. Larry Atherton. Carl. Swann.

The water reached near the top of the tub and she turned it off.

Swann was dead.

She was safe.

For a while.

But only a while. They would send another one.

They. He. Raymond. If her pursuer was Raymond. If.

If she hadn't killed Swann, she would have had a chance. A chance of finding out what all this was about.

A chance of finding Cobb.

Cobb.

She closed her eyes. Did I kill you, too, she wondered.

She eased back against the smooth plastic of the tub and tried to make some sense of it. Put it in some kind of order. Again.

Larry Atherton had not been at the farm that day, but at the beach house. She and Joe stopped at the farm and asked directions and somebody else had been there. Somebody who had introduced himself as Larry.

Somebody Joe knew.

She frowned. No. If he had known the man, recognized him from an old case, he would have done something then or gone back to town and reported it to the police. Or called Mac.

But he didn't. Instead, he had become preoccupied. Then he saw the newspaper. The picture was not clear, detailed, but it had jogged his memory. Connected the vague feeling he had to something. But hadn't completed it. So he went back to make sure. Probably to the farm.

And—

Sighing, she shook her head.

If Joe knew him, why didn't he recognize him? What was the connection? What was it that triggered his memory, preoccupied him?

"What, Joe?" she whispered. "What the hell was it?"

Closing her eyes, she wanted to slink back into the water. Dissolve. But she wouldn't. Instead, the water would just get cold. She smiled grimly and nodded. "Okay," she said, and pushing herself up, she got out of the tub, scrubbed herself dry with both of the tiny towels, went back into the room, dressed in a fresh shirt and a pair of blue jeans, pulled her hair back into a ponytail, and turned to the files. "Joe," she said, "I hate paperwork almost as much as you do. Did."

Then she went to work.

Gathering the cases that were connected to the Rappahannock, she sat down at the desk and went through them again. Norris, murder. McClure/Rodriguez, smuggling. Miller/Sullivan, smuggling. Glebov, burglary, transporting stolen goods.

All closed. All resolved.

She read through them again. Pushing through Joe's terse, clipped style. Sometime past midnight, she went out to the convenience store, bought an extra-large coffee and a packaged sandwich that claimed to be turkey, and walked back to the room. Eating the sandwich and sipping the coffee, she started through the cases again. Read them. Nothing there.

She drank more coffee, then looked at the stack of files. Okay, anything in the past year. The past-year file was on the coffee table. On top was the White file—the man who had killed the twelve people in the van. Picking it up, she went through it again, and remembered this was the case that had brought Joe to the Rappahannock, even though there was no real connection. What had it been . . . she looked to the backside. Gas ticket. White had bought gas here. Ed's Quik Stop.

She sat down with the file, reading through it again. "Seven Hispanic males, one white male Caucasian, four Hispanic females were shot at close range. Approximately thirty rounds of ammunition were discharged." Then at the end, a notation in pen, "Got the bastard." She remembered Mac telling her that White had been killed in D.C.

She was about to put the report down when she noticed White's name at the top. Martin Raymond White.

The only problem was, he was dead.

Closing the file, she put it down and drank the rest of the coffee. Then she found a clean sheet of paper in the desk and wrote *Raymond* at the top of it. Then, *Ray Burke, drug running. Harry Raymond, porn. Martin Raymond White, murder.* Burke was in prison. Martin Raymond White was dead. Harry Raymond was the only one still around and on the street. But he had found Jesus.

Still, she pulled his file with the others and went through them carefully. No connection to Rappahannock. Except for the gas ticket Martin Raymond White had left behind in the van.

Easing back in her chair, she stretched, then placed the files into two piles. The Rappahannock pile and the Raymond pile. Only one could go in either pile. White's. And that was marginal. She wasn't sure a gas ticket qualified. He was probably just passing through and bought gas. And he was dead.

She put it in the Raymond pile. If there even should be a Raymond pile. A name mentioned in passing. Skinny stuff.

She looked at both piles. Essentially all of them were closed.

All right, then possible exceptions.

Harry Raymond. He was never convicted. And Elliot Norris. He said he didn't kill his wife, that his girlfriend Donna Hooker had done it and framed him. She shook her head. Donna didn't know anything about this, Jessie was sure of that.

And there was no mention of a Raymond in her file.

Sighing, she looked at her watch. Four-thirty. In

the morning. Of course. A heavy weariness suffused her.

She looked at the files again. "Where is it, Joe?" she whispered. "Where the hell is it?"

Shaking her head, she pushed away from the desk and went to the bed and lay down. That was a mistake. The weariness turned to lead, overwhelming her, and she sank into sleep almost immediately.

She awoke slowly, struggling through what seemed like a thick membrane.

Then eased back again.

She didn't want to be awake.

She wanted to stay there.

Then she remembered Cobb.

"Okay," she said and forcing her eyes open, she sat up. Shook her hair out. Craved coffee. She looked at her watch. Eight-fifty. She had slept four hours.

She gathered her purse up, went outside, and was torn for a moment. What she wanted was a full breakfast — bacon, eggs, toast, hash browns, gravy and grease.

She looked at the convenience store. But this was easier. Quicker. A habit now.

She turned toward the convenience store. Do what's easiest and quickest.

Crossing the two parking lots, she went inside, bought an extra-large coffee and two breakfast biscuits with egg and cheese, then carried them back to the room and wolfed them down. They weren't bad. Okay, they were bad, but she didn't care. Sipping the coffee, she turned to the files. How many times could she go through them? Pausing, she turned to the telephone.

Mac answered. "You're up early."

"You'll never know. Do you still have the tapes and videos of Joe's old cases?"

"Sure. Well, someplace. What do you need?"

She sighed. "I don't know. Norris. Glebov. McClure/Rodriguez, Miller/Sullivan. White. And Kelly."

"I can find them for you. But they're all closed."

"I know, but I'd still like to see them and hear them. I've gone through all the transcripts. Maybe there's something on the tapes themselves."

"I'll be ready when you get here."

Mac set her up in a small room with a VCR, TV, and a cassette machine.

"A complete home entertainment center," Mac said as he finished hooking up the VCR to the TV. "Depending on what you call entertainment."

As he turned to go back to work, he looked at her. "Some of this is pretty rough stuff . . ."

She nodded. "I know."

Shrugging, he walked out, and she slipped the first video in and using the remote, started the VCR.

This was McClure/Rodriguez. Smuggling. Black and white shadows blurred across the screen, and she was amazed at the distortion of the wide-angle lens. Two men seemed to swim across a fishbowl of a room, talking about tides and times and shipments of medical supplies.

The next tape was of Martin Raymond White. It too was in black and white and was warped. Again the wide angle lens was used. The outer edges of the picture bowed into the middle, but it made the entire interior of the van visible. Again, there was an unreal quality, as if the people were swimming around in a fishbowl. White numbers rolled at the bottom.

The illegals were herded into the back and the two runners, White and Paulson, walked up through the middle. Both were tall and wore blue jeans. One wore a baseball cap and a flowered shirt. The other was bareheaded and wore a pullover golf shirt and a windbreaker. She didn't recognize either of them.

The one with the baseball cap walked through, checking the aliens. Then at the front he turned and faced the camera.

She pressed the pause button on the remote and Martin Raymond White was suspended in time, caught in the motion of standing up, his face slightly blurred but clear enough to see. She didn't recognize him.

She released the pause button and White and Paulson continued through their blurred world. On the floor, one of the children began crying, and another wiped sweat from his face. Even with the poor quality of the picture, she could see sweat on all of them. Dampening their clothes.

"Need to get the AC going," said Paulson.

"Yeah," White agreed.

She remembered from the transcript that the massacre was coming up. She didn't want to watch that. She raised the remote, her finger on the stop button.

Then Jessie saw what Joe must have seen that day.

White slipped the baseball cap off, wiped his hand over his spiky hair, then dabbed the sweat on his face with the sleeve on his shirt. Once. Twice. Almost delicately. And in the motion, the rhythm, and the hair, she saw the man with Carl Atherton at the farm.

A different face.

But the same motion. The same lines. The same hair.

The same man.

With a different face.

She pressed the reverse button and figures on the screen jerked and wiggled backwards in an odd parody. When White's face was on the screen again, Jessie nodded. She could see it now. Even though the face was different, the bone structure was the same.

She hit the stop button and sat in the darkness for a moment.

Then she got up and walked down the hall to Mac's office.

He looked up from his desk.

"You said Raymond White was killed in D.C.?"

He nodded. "Yeah."

"And you got confirmation by phone?"

"Yeah."

"Who called you?"

He shook his head and stood up. "Got the file right here . . . He opened the file drawer, found the folder, and pulled out a sheet of paper.

"Swann," he said. "Robert Swann."

Forty-eight

The rap of footfalls on the wooden floor jerked Cobb awake.

The knob rattled, the door opened, and a huge man filled it, paused for a moment, then walked toward him.

"Heads up," he said, and tossed the handcuff key to Cobb.

Cobb caught it, unlocked the cuffs, then awkwardly made his way to his feet.

"Now behind your back," the man said.

Cobb frowned. "Look, I can't run, and I'm—"

"Behind your back," the man said patiently.

Cobb put his hands behind his back, slipped the open cuff over his wrist, and closed it.

"Now show me."

Cobb turned and showed him, and the man walked toward him. He was amazingly light on his feet for someone that tall and carrying that much weight in his gut.

He checked the cuffs, then cocked his head toward the door.

Cobb limped, almost falling. The big man didn't help him. He was a pro.

They went through the door and into a vast barn, down the aisle, and outside and across the yard to the antebellum house.

The man took him in the rear door through a large but nearly empty kitchen, down the hall and through a sitting room, and into an office.

A man sat behind the desk. Tall, with spiky brown hair combed straight back and cold blue eyes, he wore a starched and crisply-pressed white shirt and a pair of pleated white pants. Early-morning light brushed his face and Cobb caught something as his head turned slightly, something about the skin around his jaw under his ears.

The big man placed Cobb in a wingback chair, then walked out.

The man behind the desk tented his fingers, staring at Cobb.

"Swann says you want to join the fold," he said. His voice was refined, careful, southern-cultured, but with a coloring of poor country in the shaping of the words.

"I can use the money."

"And the first consideration is a letter, I believe."

Okay, start the bluff. Cobb nodded. "That's right. Joe had figured a lot of it out. That's why he came back to the Athertons that night. But before he did, he wrote it down. I found the letter and mailed it to myself in Clear Creek."

"In your mailbox at home. That makes it easy."

"At the post office. I sent it return receipt. Only I can sign for it."

"Or someone with your I.D."

"You forget, it's my home town."

"Of course." He leaned back in the chair, turning his head slightly, and Cobb noticed again the skin under his ear. Smooth. A light scar. "I have a plane," he said. "We can fly to Clear Creek and get the letter

288

today. Now. I'll pay you in the post office and leave you there. A public place."

"It won't be there today. I mailed it yesterday. The soonest it would be there would be tomorrow."

Raymond's jaw tightened. "All right," he said. "Tomorrow. But it had better be there, Mr. Cobb." Leaning forward, he picked up a lighter from the desk. Sunlight glinted off it. "But first, I believe some kind of proof is in order — "

"You'll have it when we get to Clear Creek."

"Now."

Cobb nodded. "All right. He knew about the pipeline. That you were bringing aliens in to the Athertons and hiding them in the barn. That there were probably some in the barn the day he and the woman stopped there. Were there?"

The flicker in the man's eyes told him he was right. And something else was there. Fear. And more. Something that made it all make sense. A skittering darkness straight out of Danny Herbert's parallel universe . . . a nightmare gaining texture and breadth and depth . . .

Forty-nine

As she drove, Jessie put what she had together.

After White killed the people in the van, Joe had gone after him with all of his strength. Probably through Swann and Monroe, White had known about it and figured the only way to get him off his back and still run his pipeline was to set up a phony death. Swann and Monroe had helped him do that. Then he must have had plastic surgery. Changed the face—but not his gestures, his actions, the things that came naturally. Then that day at the farm Joe and White had met again and something had gone off in the back of Joe's mind—a gesture he couldn't quite put his finger on until he saw the newspaper. So he went back to the farm to make sure, and they had probably killed him there, then made it look like an accident.

But why her? The possibility she was a policewoman? Or that Joe had said something to her? Her mouth tightened. Most likely it was the simplest answer of all: she was a loose end. "No loose ends," White had said after killing the aliens, then his own partner. No loose ends. Her breath was like lead in her chest and she knew that was the answer. Just a loose end. A business decision.

Like Cobb would be.

Her hands gripped the steering wheel. She had all

of it but the piece she needed — where they had Cobb.

She drove back to the motel. In the room, she sat down with the White file again and looked through it. And the two photocopied receipts. She had asked Mac about photos of White, and he had shaken his head.

"None," he said.

"But you've got the video tape. Can't you get one from that?"

He shook his head again. "Quality was too poor. Light source was low, and because the camera is so small, it's not able to pick up a lot of detail."

"What about computer enhancement?"

Mac smiled at that. "Enhancement. That's an interesting word. It sounds like you can get something from nothing. But you can't. You're only as good as your source. And if your source is no good, what you come out with is no good."

So all she had were the receipts. She looked at them.

Ed's Quik Stop. On the receipt was the name, the address, phone number, time and date, then under that the amount and what it was for. 3:45 a.m. Oct 9. Gas. $17.50.

The other was a handwritten ticket from Billy's Bar-B-Q in Rappahannock. Nothing on it but the name and the order. Dble rbs. Slaw. $7.89

After getting directions to Ed's Quik Stop from the motel clerk, she drove to it. It was a small place a block off the main highway. She parked and went inside. She described White to the young Hispanic girl who was the clerk. She didn't remember him.

Jessie bought a 7-Up, went back to the Bronco, and drove to Rappahannock.

She got there a little after one. She stopped in another convenience store and asked for Billy's Bar-B-Q. The directions were complicated, and even knowing the way, finding the place was not easy.

She threaded her way through back roads, along woods and fields, and finally found it backed up on the river and surrounded by cars. The restaurant had been converted from an old filling station. The office was now the kitchen and the garage had become the dining room. There were huge smokers out back filling the air with an unbelievable aroma. Hickory smoke and slow-cooking pork ribs. She was instantly hungry. An anvil would have been hungry here.

She went into the dining room and taking a seat at the counter, she ordered the ribs and slaw and beer from a haggard, middle-aged waitress named Lolly. The ribs came and were delicious. There was no fat, the meat fell off the bones, and the sauce was hot, made of peppers and vinegar. The beer was cold and welcome.

As she was wiping off her hands with the fifth or sixth napkin, Lolly ambled back and started totaling her ticket. "Another beer, honey?"

Jessie shook her head. "No. I think those are the best ribs I've ever had."

Lolly nodded. "Yeah. Billy used to be a schoolteacher, but his ribs were so good he found out he could make more money this way." She finished with the ticket and placed it next to Jessie's plate.

Jessie glanced over the room. It was almost full. "Are you always this busy?"

"This busy? This is the slow time. You shoulda been here at noon. Or be here tonight. *That's* busy. People out the doors. They get take-out and eat in their cars or out back at the picnic tables."

"And this is not the best location. I almost didn't find it."

"You're not local."

"No."

"Most of these folks are local. Well—" she turned. "Come back—"

"Lolly," Jessie said. "Could you wait a minute?"

"Sure."

"I'm looking for a man—"

"Ain't we all—"

"His name is Martin Raymond White. About thirty or thirty-five. Good-looking, straight brown hair. Until about a year ago, he drove a van like a bread truck."

Lolly shook her head slowly. "Don't know any Whites. Sorry."

"Thanks anyway."

As Lolly ambled away, disappointment seemed to fuse with the beer, pressing darkly through her.

Another dead end.

Pushing the rest of the beer away, she finished cleaning her hands with the napkin, paid her bill, and went out to the Bronco. As she opened the door another car pulled into the parking lot. A lot of business for a place just known locally.

Jessie paused. *Locally.* If he knew about the place, the chances were he was local. Jessie walked back inside and saw Lolly behind the counter at the coffee machine filling two cups.

"Sorry to bother you again—" Jessie said.

Lolly smiled. "You ain't botherin' me, honey."

"You said most of your trade is local—"

"That's right."

"So if someone ate here, they would have to be local. I mean you don't get people off the highway, no tourists."

She shook her head. "No. Hardly ever no tourists. Except those that know the area."

"Would there be anybody here that would know most of the customers?"

She shrugged. "If anybody would, the owner would, I guess. Billy. Billy Riley," she said. "He's out by the smokers most likely. Go on out."

She had expected Billy to be huge and roly-poly; instead, one of the cooks directed her to a tall, angular, and trim man dressed neatly in khaki shorts and a pullover shirt. He sat on the top of a picnic table nibbling a rib.

"Looks like you'd get tired of them," Jessie said.

He smiled. "Never. What can I do for you?"

"I'm looking for a man named Martin Raymond White." She described him and the van.

"Don't know anybody by that name," he said. "Sorry."

"How about the description?"

Billy smiled. "That could fit a lot of people."

"Anyone come to mind?"

"Sorry, no. How come you're looking for him?"

"Child support. He hasn't paid in over two years."

"A bum."

"Yeah."

"Wish I could help you."

Jessie thanked him and turned toward the Bronco, then hesitated and looked back at him.

"The man I'm looking for is a snob. Puts on airs. Acts like he's an aristocrat."

Billy looked up, his eyes narrowing. Then he nodded. "Yeah," he said. "I do know a guy like that."

Fifty

"His name is Charles Hall. Charles, not Charlie or Chuck, but Charles," said Billy as Jessie sat down at the picnic table. "And that tells you a lot about him right there."

"How long have you known him?"

"About two or three years. Maybe that long. But a correction: I don't really know him. I'm not really sure anybody knows him."

"A loner."

"Yes, he really may be the definition of that word. After eating here, he came over to me one day, right here at this table, I think, and asked me if I wanted to go national with the ribs. I told him that the reason I quit teaching and started this place was because I didn't want the hassle any more. My being a teacher and taking off and doing what I wanted on my own appealed to him, I guess. He told me that he'd quit high school because he was smarter than the teachers, that they weren't really teaching him anything, and that after he'd quit, he'd really learned about the world. Started to read the best books. Fiction, biography, everything he could find on business and finance." Billy shifted his legs and leaned forward. "Now this is the hard part to explain. His attitude. He didn't come onto me like a bullshitter, but as if I were someone he was allowing into his realm of existence. And it was genuine."

"Snobbery?"

Billy shook his head. "No, it was even beyond that. Every time he came in, he would come out back to discuss things with me because he thought I was one of the few on the same plane with him. At first I wanted to call it a kind of racism, but it was even beyond that. Racism says all of that race are bad, all of my race are good. He didn't even like the people of his own race. It was as if there were only ten or eleven humans on the planet and he was one of them. The rest were cattle."

"The elite."

"Something like that, yes. But even more so. I remember one day after he left, another customer, Tom Ringgold, came over and said, 'I see you've met Charles.' Emphasis on the Charles. Tom had gone to high school with him in Port Royal. Turns out that Hall came from a poor backwoods family. But his mother was like Charles. Putting on airs. Saying that she was from an aristocratic background. The old noble southern family fallen on hard times. Shades of *Glass Menagerie*. She must have drilled it into Charles because he really believed it."

"Do you know where he lives?"

Billy shook his head. "No. Not around here, at least not any more."

"Why?"

"He used to come in a lot, three, four times a week. But I haven't seen him in . . . oh, six or seven months. Maybe longer."

"This Tom Ringgold, how can I get hold of him?"

"At work most likely. Has a video store right there as you go into town."

Jessie stood up. "Thank you, Billy, I — "

Billy stood down from the table. "There's something else."

"What?"

"Again, a little hard to put into words. Where most of the time these guys, elitists, are kind of a pain in the rear this guy is . . ." he shrugged. "Scary. That's the one word that comes to mind. Scary."

Fifty-one

Tom Ringgold's video store was between a fabric outlet and a frozen yogurt store. Tape boxes and posters covered every square inch of space in the medium-sized room, but strangely, it didn't seem cluttered or crowded. Jessie sensed an order to things.

The first poster was of Bogart and Bergman in *Casablanca*. Then Orson Welles's *Citizen Kane*. The classics came first here.

A blond-haired man in his late twenties sat in one of four contemporary metal and leather chairs around a heavy coffee table. On the table was a coffee machine and styrofoam cups. There were also movie and video magazines.

Sipping from a porcelain cup, the young man looked up and smiled. "Help you?"

"Are you Tom Ringgold?"

His smile widened. "My reputation has preceded me."

She glanced around the room. "I like your store," she said. "It's different."

He nodded. "It's meant to be. I love movies, especially the old ones. And I love talking about them. So—" His hand swept over the table and chairs as if it were a mini-kingdom. "What unheralded masterpiece can I interest you in? *Curse of the Cat People? Touch of Evil? Night of the Hunter?* . . ."

"Charles Hall."

He blinked, then smiled grimly. "Charles . . . ?"

"Yes, Billy Riley said you knew him. Went to high school with him."

Tom nodded. "That's right." He gestured to a chair. "Please sit down."

As she did, Tom drew her a cup of coffee and handed it to her. "Mind if I ask why you're looking for him?"

Taking the coffee, she smiled politely. "It's confidential."

"Trouble?"

"Not really."

His eyes leveled on her, and he smiled slowly. "I don't believe you, but it's okay."

"Why don't you believe me?"

"Because there was always something about Charles that was . . ." He shrugged, trying to find the word.

"Billy described him as scary."

Tom nodded. "Yeah. Scary. Disturbing." He glanced around the store. "I've always thought I've built *my* life around illusion. Movies. But Charles and his mother . . ." He shook his head. "They didn't know where the illusion left off and reality began."

"Did you know them well?"

"Well? No. We lived down the road from them, out in the county. We had to walk the same road together to get to the school bus stop. They moved there when I was eleven or twelve. My mother went over to meet them, and to be hospitable; she took a banana cream pie, and Edwina, the mother, told her that they didn't accept charity, especially from people of lower class." He smiled.

"Charles was the same way. He would barely speak to me. Both of us would be standing there at the bus stop, and he would sit and stare as if I didn't exist. And when he did say something, it would be about what a grand

299

family he came from, how they had been cheated out of an estate, and how someday he was going to buy back the estate and live there. And that little bit of information was rendered over about two years. After a while, his mother began driving him to school; then when he was about fifteen, she took him out of school and began educating him herself. When they threatened to arrest her, they moved. I didn't see Charles again until one day over at Billy's."

"What about the father? Was he the same way?"

"I don't really know. I don't think he was around much. There was gossip that he had deserted them."

"You said Charles was scary—"

"Yeah."

"Why?"

"Mostly it was the way he dealt with people—"

"Like they weren't there?"

"No. Like they were there, but didn't count. One day waiting at the bus stop, this other kid, Stew Patrick, was taunting him. Picking at him. Charles hit him, and Stew went down. Now I don't know if you've ever seen kids fight, but usually it's just pure anger. Elbows and fists and dust and rolling around." He drew himself more coffee. "But when Stew went down, Charles didn't dive in on him like most kids would do. He kicked him. Cold and precise. Right in the face. Then he stepped back, looked at him, then stepped in again and kicked him in the balls . . . sorry, in the—"

"It's okay, I've heard the term before."

Tom smiled and went on. "Anyway, he kicked him twice and his face never changed. He never screamed or got angry. Just kicked. Twice. Cold, perfect kicks. Then he left him there, and turned and waited for the bus. I've never seen anything like it before or since. I hope I never do."

"This family estate he talked about, did he ever say where it was?"

Tom leaned on the arm of his chair. "Well, you've got

to remember that we weren't having a conversation. I was being informed. And it was a long time ago." He sipped the coffee. "Along the Rappahannock someplace. Right on the river, because he said something about the view of the water."

"And it was the mother's family, not the father's?"

"Yeah."

"Do you remember the mother's maiden name?"

He shook his head. "No, if I ever did, I've forgotten it."

"Could it have been Raymond?"

He shrugged. "Sorry. Maybe. But it doesn't ring a bell."

"Can you think of anything or anyone that might help me find him?"

Tom sighed. "No. I saw him a couple of times at Billy's, but that was it."

Fifty-two

Jessie found a pay phone in the yogurt store and called Brian Tuck.

"This is Lynn Monroe," she said. "My partner and I visited you the other day—"

"I remember you, Miss Monroe. I never forget a beautiful woman."

"I need your help, Mr. Tuck."

"Please, make it Brian."

"Brian—"

"Now what can I do for you?"

"I'm looking for a Raymond family. They were rich at one time and owned a large estate somewhere along the Rappahannock."

"I've heard of the Raymonds. But there was more than one, I mean more than one Raymond, all the same family. Very well-to-do before World War Two. Then lost it all. Some kind of scandal. Which one did you want?"

She frowned. "I don't know. The name Raymond is all I have. No. Edwina Raymond. But she wouldn't have been the owner but the daughter. And the estate was somewhere on the river."

"That doesn't ring a bell. I can make some calls. How about calling me back tomorrow—"

She closed her eyes and fought against the panic rising

in her throat. "I don't have until tomorrow, Brian. I've got an emergency on my hands."

Suddenly the salesman bullshit was gone. "I'll make some calls. How about two hours?"

It sounded like a lifetime. "I'll call you then," she said. "If you get something before then, call me at my motel." She gave him the number.

Driving into Rappahannock, Jessie wanted something cold and she looked for Ed's Quik Stop, but missed it. She must have passed it without seeing it, she decided, and remembered it was a block off the highway.

She parked at the motel and walked to the convenience store next door, bought a 7-Up and ice and went back to the room. It was hot inside and she opened the windows and door to let some air through. Then she sat down and sipped the 7-Up. Looking at the files and papers strewn over the beds and desk and chairs, hopelessness pressed through her like a dark weight. She wanted to be doing something. Anything. But didn't know what.

The telephone rang, and she almost spilled the soda.

"I'm afraid I've got bad news," Brian Tuck said. "I called a friend of mine who does title searches. She knows everybody along the neck — "

"But — "

"But she's out of town until Thursday. I've got one of her associates working on it, but they're swamped. I'm afraid they're not going to be able to get on it, at least for a while."

Jessie put the soda down because she thought she would drop it. Suddenly, she had no strength. She felt like a defendant listening to a death sentence.

"I did get a little background if it'll help."

"Can't hurt."

"There were three Raymond families here in the county. W. W. Raymond came here around the turn of the century. He started with a small farm and ran it into a plantation-sized place. He had two sons, W. W. Junior and Theodore, called him Ned. They both had large spreads and at one time, they owned most of the county. Word is that during the thirties, the Raymonds saw the war coming and invested heavily in the aircraft and munitions industries. Very heavily. They bet everything on it. It all went pretty well until somewhere during the middle of the war, then they were caught sending out aircraft with defective parts. And what W. W. had built up over the years was lost almost overnight. They were not only crooked businessmen, which was bad enough, but they were also accused of being traitors. All three families lost everything. The reason I tell you this is that over the years, the Raymond property has been divided and divided again so tracing it down is going to be difficult. None of this is on the computer. It'll all have to be done by hand. It can be done, but it will take time. Maybe a lot of time."

"What about a house on the river?"

"You've got to remember this happened fifty years ago. I called a couple of old timers. Both remember the Raymonds, but the main house, W. W.'s place, was torn down. One man I talked to said all of them were torn down. Another said just W. W.'s place. And because they were thought of as traitors, if there are surviving houses, they would go by another name. One man I talked to, Farley Haskell, said it was almost like the county tried to wipe away any trace of them."

"And Edwina Raymond?"

"Sorry. Nothing there."

She sighed. "Thanks, Brian. Keep trying. I'll be in touch."

Hanging up the phone, Jessie lay her head down on the papers for a moment.

Time.

It would take time.

Time that Cobb didn't have. If he had any at all.

If he was alive.

She sat up, and stared down at the White file, and the telephone book beside it. Just for the hell of it, she opened it and looked up Charles Hall. Charles Raymond. Raymond Charles.

No listing.

Of course not. He wouldn't be listed.

She stared at the phone book and the file, then picked up the phone again and dialed the number for utilities, then asked for billing.

"Miss Crown."

Please, she thought. Please.

"Miss Crown. Hello —"

"Oh, sorry, Miss Crown. This is Mr. Raymond's bookkeeper, and I need to ask about the billing at his house, not his office. We haven't received a bill in over two months and I'm just wondering if there's a problem."

"What's the name on the account?"

"Charles Raymond."

Pause. The rattle of computer keys.

"Charles Raymond. I'm sorry, we have no account for —"

"Did I say Charles Raymond? I'm sorry. We've got a Raymond and a Charles and one is named Raymond Charles. Two first names, you know," she rattled on. "That's the second time that has happened. I mean with two first names. I do it with Douglas James. I mean James Douglas, you see —"

"What's the name you wanted?" came the weary reply.

"Raymond Charles."

Once again, Jessie heard the sound of computer keys.

"Yes. Raymond Charles. 227 River Road. Would you —"

Jessie didn't hear the rest of it — she dropped the receiver and was already running out the door.

Fifty-three

Jessie drove by the estate slowly. The property was surrounded by a five-foot-high wall, and the house was set well back from the road fifty yards or so. Live oaks and pines shaded the vast yard. Beyond the house were a barn and outbuildings.

She drove past the house and watched it in her rearview mirror until a stand of woods pushed up and blocked her view.

She eased to the side of the road and stopped. Carrying the binoculars, she left the Bronco and crossed the road into the woods.

Lacing quickly through the trees, she made her way to the wall and knelt, raised the binoculars, and glided them over the house. Front windows. A living room or parlor. Back along the side. French doors onto a small balcony. A library. The next windows were covered with curtains. And the next. The windows at the back of the house revealed the kitchen. A man stood there doing something. Looking down, probably at a counter. Then he raised a sandwich to his mouth. He was a big man with massive arms and neck. He turned away from the window and was gone.

Jessie lowered the glasses and hurried along the wall until she could see the back of the house.

Again, the kitchen. She could see the refrigerator, cabinets. The man's head. It looked like he was sitting at a table.

She moved the glasses. Back door. Hallway. Window. Beyond it a dresser and mirror. The next window looked into another sitting room.

She slipped the glasses back to the kitchen. The man ate the last of the sandwich and stood up, walked to the window, turned back to the counter, then turned to the hallway. As he passed the hall window, she could see he was carrying a plate and glass. He went into the bedroom. The big man placed the plate and glass on the dresser, then turned and drew a pistol from under his coat and with the other hand seemed to toss something. A moment passed, then he caught something. There was a flickering in the mirror over the dresser. Jessie concentrated on it.

Her breath hit her chest like a fist.

It was Cobb.

She almost dropped the glasses and, for a moment, lost sight of him.

Then forcing strength into her arms, she raised them again.

Now Cobb was in front of the window, and she could see him clearly. His hands were handcuffed in front of him, and he held a sandwich with them.

She lowered the glasses, and a long sigh of relief escaped her. He was alive. For a moment she was overwhelmed. Her heart pounded so hard she thought she was going to pass out. She wanted to cry. The problem was, she didn't have time. Instead, she pulled in a long, slow breath.

"Do something," she whispered to herself.

She looked back to the bedroom. Cobb bit into the sandwich and chewed.

She smiled. That's it, Cobb. Eat while I sit out here and worry.

Lowering the binoculars, she looked over the yard

and frowned. Too much open ground. It was fifty yards from the wall to the barn, and another fifty from there to the house. Fifty yards in the open. Leaning up against the wall, she started to put her hands on top of it when she saw the round metal object implanted in one of the wooden posts. She paused, then looked to the other wooden post. There was another one. Then she saw that it wasn't completely metal—there was a small glass center to it. She jerked back.

An alarm system.

She slipped away from the wall and into the woods. First, she had to get over the wall, then across the open ground. And there were probably other alarm systems. She leaned back against a pine. Okay, one thing at a time.

Smallest problem first. The open ground. She might be able to do that at night. She looked at her watch. Three o'clock. That left roughly five hours of light. Five hours was a long time. Next, the wall. How the hell was she going to get over the wall? Jump it. Maybe, but not likely. Her eyes moved to the posts. Go over at the post. Grip the post, pull herself up and—

She shook her head. The space was too narrow. With a ladder, she might be able to do it. Okay, go buy a ladder, go over the wall at night.

Then there would be the other alarms on the grounds.

"Shit," she growled. This was no good. It was all too complicated. Took too much time. What was the simplest thing to do? What would Cobb do?

Drive in. Go to the door. Ask directions. Get by whoever came to the door. To what? How many were there?

Drive in. That would get her to the house, but not in it. How could she—?

She paused.

Drive *in*.

It was the stupidest, wildest thought she had ever had. Absurd.

308

She started running back through the woods toward the Bronco. *Drive in*. She kept running. Moving. Because it kept her from thinking how really absurd it was, and she knew she was going to have to do it before she talked herself out of it.

Fifty-four

She ran to the Bronco.

"Shit," she whispered softly over and over again. "Oh, shit."

She worked it into a chant because she knew if she thought about what she was going to do too long she wouldn't do it. It was a really stupid plan, worse than the one she'd had for Swann. She shook her head. She had to stop thinking about it.

She turned the hubs on the front wheel to four-wheel drive; climbing into the Bronco, she opened the passenger-side door and began throwing out everything that was loose. Clothing. Shoes. Books. Fishing rod. Empty bottles.

Then she turned to the front and climbed into the driver's seat. She took the 9mm from her purse. And the clips. Two of them. Loaded. She slipped the clips into her rear pocket. Then she stuffed her purse into the console.

She checked the 9mm. Pulled the action back. Nosed a bullet into the chamber. Eased the hammer down. Reached around and slipped the pistol into the waistband of her jeans in the small of her back. It was secure.

"Oh, shit," she whispered and closed her eyes, then opened them again, drawing in a long breath.

She started the engine, and reaching up, she almost

put the seatbelt on. No. She let go of it, and reaching down, pulled the Bronco into four-wheel, then into gear.

Twisting the steering wheel, she angled out into the road and back the way she'd come.

Then she pressed down on the gas. Twenty. Thirty miles an hour.

The Bronco groaned, the four-wheel protesting the speed.

She pushed harder on the gas.

Forty miles an hour and climbing.

She sped along the road, paralleling the wall. Beyond it she could see the house.

She pushed down on the gas, gaining speed. Forty-five miles an hour.

Off to an angle and in front of her, the gate glided toward her. The gears of the Bronco screamed to a higher pitch.

As she came even with the drive, she swerved into it and blasted through the gate.

Sitting at his desk doing his books, Raymond heard the gate alarm go off.

The alarm kept beeping. Reaching into his desk, he took a Mac-10 machine gun pistol from the drawer, then stood up and walked into the hallway. Turning, he looked down it and through the glass doors. And saw the Bronco roaring down the drive.

Picking up speed as it came.

"What —" he whispered, then ran toward the front door.

"William!" he shouted.

In the back bedroom, lying on the bed, his hands cuffed behind him, Cobb heard Raymond shout.

The big man guarding him was sitting in a chair; he bolted up, turning to the door and rushing into the hallway, leaving Cobb alone.

Cobb rolled off the bed, got to his feet and

311

limped across the room to the door. Easing into the hallway, he saw the two men running for the door. Through the glass, he also saw the red blur of the Bronco.

His eyes widened in amazement. "Jessie," he whispered, "What the hell are you doing—"

Jessie pushed down on the gas and the gears and engine of the Bronco shrieked as she sped down the driveway.

The steering wheel shook in her hands. Gripping it hard, she centered the Bronco on the front steps and front door of the house.

Then an odd thing happened.

Everything around her was in motion—the Bronco, the live oaks streaking past, the house filling the windshield.

But where she was, it was quiet. Strangely calm.

She seemed to view it all with a cool detachment.

In front of her, she saw the men burst through the front door and raise their weapons. She never heard them. Only felt the thump of the bullets as they impacted the Bronco, then spider-webbed the windshield. She ducked down into the passenger seat, lying flat, keeping her hand on the steering wheel.

The Bronco hit the front steps and the four-wheel drive dug in, hauling it up the steps, straight up into the air, flying into the porch. It left the steps and the momentum kept it going up and forward. Across the porch. Plummeting through the door, ripping the frame and door away in a holocaust of glass and wood and splinters, then crashing to rest in the front hallway.

Cobb watched as the Bronco roared into the front of the house, then, incredibly, up the front steps.

"Oh, shit," he whispered.

Raymond and William kept firing as the Bronco started up the steps. It kept coming.

As it vaulted straight up over the porch, both men turned and ran.

It filled the doorway and seemed to hang there for a moment. Cobb could see the undercarriage. Then it tipped forward, inching through the air like a tape through a VCR, clicking frame by frame through the freeze mode. Across the porch. Into the doorway. The frame of the door split and huge shards of wood twisted inward. The Bronco followed. Glass glistened, then balleted through the air, catching the light. Still flying, all four tires in the air, the Bronco exploded into the hallway and inched down.

Reeling, Cobb tumbled back into the bedroom.

The Bronco slammed down, throwing Jessie forward into the floorboards on the passenger side.

Upside down, her feet above her, she shook her head.

Then the Bronco rolled forward, thumped into the wall, and stopped, the engine still running.

Jessie reached up and grasped the door handle, trying to open it. It wouldn't budge. Getting her feet under her, she tried again; using her legs as leverage, she put her shoulder into it. It was frozen, welded into place.

In the bedroom, Cobb sat up and listened. It was quiet.

Easing to the door, he peered cautiously into the hallway.

The Bronco sat there, bumper into the wall, engine chugging.

Using the wall, he eased himself up and limped down the hall toward the Bronco. He was almost to the side of it when William stepped out of the doorway of the sitting room. He staggered slightly, rubbing his head with his free hand. In the other was his pistol.

He took another step, still rubbing his head, and

Cobb charged him. Limping, propping himself up with his shoulder against the wall, Cobb ducked his head and rammed into the big man. Driving his shoulder into the hand carrying the gun, knocking it to the floor, he then slammed into the big man's rounded stomach, hoping for a soft spot.

He didn't find one. William's gut was like iron.

Cobb bounced back a little and William turned toward him.

Cobb lunged back into the big man, hitting him in the chest with the top of his head. William's arms flew out, and his head came down in reflex. Cobb snapped his own head back, catching William on the point of his chin. The big man stumbled backwards into the sitting room. Staggering, Cobb shouldered into him again, knocking the big man off his feet, tripping over shattered lumber, sprawling backwards into the debris.

Cobb sank to his knees and turned toward the pistol.

It lay in the hallway.

Pulling his good leg under him, he started to dive for the weapon, but caught a movement out of the corner of his eye as Raymond charged through the gaping hole where the door had been.

Twisting backwards, Cobb pushed himself up and vaulted backwards into the sitting room and the protection of the wall.

Screaming with rage, Raymond sprayed the doorway and wall with the Mac-10.

Hearing the shout, then the gunfire, Jessie sat up and looked through the back window. As she did, Raymond swung the machine pistol on the Bronco. She went down as the bullets raked through the windows and hammered the metal. She pulled the 9mm from her back and tried to sit up, but Raymond kept pumping shots into the Bronco. Instead, she twisted around, pushed in the clutch, and rammed the gear shift into reverse. Then, popping the clutch, she hit the gas with her hand.

The Bronco lurched backwards. Lying on the floorboard, she shoved the gas pedal all the way down. The Bronco roared, bolting in reverse.

"My house!" Raymond screamed and kept firing.

The Bronco sped backwards. The tires hit the debris and turned, sending the rear end into the doorway of the living room, through the frame and supporting beams. The walls and ceiling sagged. The Bronco dug in and kept going—bulling into the outer wall, splitting it.

In the sitting room, Cobb rolled up on his knees and saw the Bronco going through the wall and out onto the porch. The second floor sagged downward, and Raymond ducked through the front door.

Cobb pushed up and dove at the same time, hitting on his shoulder, rolling, and tumbling over onto the pistol William had dropped.

He got his fingers on it, gathering it into his hand. He slipped his fingers around the handle and through the trigger guard.

The Bronco rolled across the porch, then off it. The rear wheels dropped over the side as it tipped upward and crashed down to the ground, coming to rest on its rear door.

Above them, the ceiling cracked and opened, spilling lumber and furniture into the living room.

Raymond staggered across the porch and raised the Mac-10, sending a burst into the bottom of the Bronco.

Rolling up on his shoulder, and bringing the pistol up, Cobb angled the weapon in Raymond's direction and pulled the trigger until it was empty. The wave of shots caught Raymond in the back and blew him off the porch into the undercarriage of the Bronco; then he fell to the ground.

Dropping the pistol, Cobb crawled to William. The big man shook his head and tried to get up. Cobb kneed him in the face repeatedly and drove him into the floor.

William slumped and Cobb reached into the big

man's coat pocket, found the handcuff key, and freed himself.

He cuffed William, then crawled outside, across the porch and down to the Bronco's driver side.

"Jessie," he shouted. "Jessie, goddammit, answer me!"

The door swung up and Jessie fell out onto the ground.

He pulled her into his arms. They lay together in the dirt for a moment, then Jessie looked at the house.

"Wow," she whispered. "What a mess."

He nodded. "Yeah." Then he looked at her. "Why did you do it that way?"

"I tried to think of what you'd do, and this was the most macho thing I could think of."

His eyes roamed over the wrecked vehicle and he shook his head slowly. "My Bronco," he sighed.

"The county will get you a new one."

His eyes came around to her. "That's not a county car," he said. "It's mine."

Fifty-five

Sitting against the Bronco, they talked.

"After I saw the blankets it all fell together for me," Cobb explained. "And the size of the room, and the waste buckets. It was a holding area for people Raymond didn't want seen. The only illegal alien case connected to Rappahannock was the White."

"He was supposed to be dead."

Cobb nodded. "That stopped me for a while, until I got a good look at Raymond's face and the area under the ear. Plastic surgery. And the look in his eyes when I talked to him. Then when he started talking, I really knew . . . or as close as I'll ever come. He was a classic paranoid. Outwardly ordinary, but living in a world of his own. A world of conspiracies. An intricate labyrinth that held together—"

"The parallel universe."

"Yes. Exactly. His world crossed into yours that day at the farm. Do you remember a truck passing you earlier on one of the backroads?"

"I . . . don't know . . . maybe . . ."

"It did. He and Carl Atherton were in it, transporting aliens. They drove to the farm and into the barn; then you drove up. And out comes a cop. A cop that has

been after him. Again, remember he's paranoid. Perse-
cuted. Joe got out of the pickup asking questions . . .
Now remember, we're seeing this from Raymond's perspective, a warped perspective. The questions were bullshit questions, of course, because what he was there for
was Raymond and the truck. But Raymond was too
smart for him. Joe was fooled by the plastic surgery.
Raymond's plan was working. But all the time, Raymond was looking around, making sure he'd covered
everything, that he was playing the game better than Joe
. . . constructing a conspiracy against Joe's imagined
conspiracy. Everything at the farm looked ordinary.
Perfect. Except one thing, one piece of the plan — "

Jessie shook her head. "What — ?"

"There was only one vehicle there. The Athertons'
pickup. If Raymond was a visitor, how did he get there?
So he couldn't be a visitor. He had to belong there. He
introduced himself as Larry Atherton, thus putting the
final touch to a perfect plan, bettering Joe's plan . . .
Joe's imagined plan. Because in Raymond's world,
there were no coincidences . . ."

"Crazy," she whispered.

"To you. Not to him. He lived in a world of games
and conspiracies. It all made sense to him. Even the fact
that Joe lived here. That was just a ruse. He was undercover, here after Raymond. Then when Joe came back
that night, that was the confirmation Raymond needed.
Joe had to die, and since you were with him . . ."

"So did I. No loose ends."

"Exactly."

"And, of course, we came back here, just like we were
supposed to."

"And they were waiting for us. Probably at Joe's
house."

"And the Athertons?"

"This I'm guessing on, but from what you've said,
Larry was getting nervous. When you and Joe showed
up, he connected it to Larry somehow. Besides, they

were the only link to him. With them gone, and you and Joe, he would be in the clear. He could live in this house in the glory he thought he deserved."

"But why did he need you?"

"Because after we went to Joe's, we didn't go to the Athertons' like he thought we would."

"We went to see Brian Tuck, then back to Joe's—"

"Yeah. Then to the bait stand. Then to the Athertons. But why the detours? It didn't fit his scenario, it didn't make sense—"

"And he had to know why."

"Yeah, there had to have been a piece he hadn't seen . . . like a giant, sinister chess game . . . something he'd missed . . . and more than anything else, he had to know because knowing, keeping things arranged is what kept his universe in place. Without it, everything was chaos, and he was nothing, and that is the one thing he couldn't accept . . ."

"But all that convolution . . . folding back on itself . . ."

"That was his world . . . his universe."

"And ours," she whispered. "For a while. At least I hope it was just for a while." Her eyes met Cobb's. "And just how do we prove all this? It's so goddamn crazy . . . and now he's dead."

Cobb pointed to the machine gun pistol. "The Mac," he said. "It's probably the same one he used in the van. The ballistics will match. And we've got old William in there. Guys left out in the cold will do a lot to get off light."

She nodded. "I'll try and find a phone that works," she said and stood up, starting toward the house. She paused and looked back at him. "Then what?"

"You mean after we finally explain all this to the proper authorities?"

"Proper authorities. Interesting term. Especially now. But yes, after we explain to the proper authorities."

319

He smiled. "Do we go back to happy, normal lives? Just like that?"

She smiled slowly. "Something like that, yeah."

He smiled, too. "Deep philosophical question. What do you think?"

"I have absolutely no idea."

"Neither do I."

Her smile widened and she laughed softly. "Good," she said. "For a minute there, I was worried."

She walked into the house to find the telephone.